THE RAVEN BLEEDS

B.A. CHILDS

ACKNOWLEDGMENTS

If it weren't for a certain group of ladies, I'm sure I would have given up writing by now. Thank you to the bunch of *Cnuts* who constantly urge me on when I hesitate and lift me up when I'm down. I am glad beyond words at having been found and embraced by you all.
Thank you to my family who put up with my brand of crazy.
Thank you to my brilliant editor, you help me be a better author.
sarah@wordemporium.co.uk
And thank you to my awesome cover designer Darling Book Designs
bit.ly/3Zg7bGF

I was given one mission. Blow it, and I'll lose everything.

Katya

Father expects me to avenge him and my dead half-brother.
Failure to complete my mission is not an option.
Not only my freedom depends on it.
But what happens if I fall under the spell of my target?

Mikhail (The Raven) Korbicov

I know who she is, and I know why she's here.
She believes the lies her father tells her.
I have plans for the beautiful Katya.
But will she believe I'm not the monster here?

1

———

SWEAT DRIPS FROM ME AS I PUNCH AND KICK AT MY opponent. "Harder, Katya. You punch like a girl," my trainer taunts. It spurs me on, and I level up, hitting him with an uppercut before sweeping his legs out from under him with a kick behind his right knee.

Anatolé goes down to the mat with a yelp. As he rocks back and forth on the floor, holding onto his knee. I glance down, tilting my head to the side, while smirking. "Not bad for someone *who hits like a girl*, huh?"

Clapping from my left has me shifting my gaze from my opponent for a moment, which my trainer takes advantage of. He grabs my right ankle and pulls. Not expecting it, I slip, falling onto my left side, the air rushing from me.

The clapping stops and laughter ensues as my father approaches us. "For a moment, I thought you had him," Father chuckles.

"I had him, until you distracted me," I snap, rising to

my feet before offering my trainer a hand, and pulling him up off the floor. Without looking at him, I inquire, "Same time tomorrow?"

"Yes, Katya. Tomorrow," he answers before limping from the room.

"You can't afford distraction, Katya," Father frowns at me. "Distraction gets you killed."

"Yes, Father," I answer curtly. "You're constantly pointing it out." He's never happy with anything I do.

I don't flinch when he reaches out, gripping my shoulder tightly. It hurts like a bitch, but I can't show him that. He'll merely do it harder.

"Do not speak to me that way, young lady," he snaps. "I'm your father. You'll treat me with respect. You'd do well to remember it," he adds ominously.

Respect.

Father respects no one. The jovial, charming man others see when they meet my father is nothing but a façade. Behind the mask, he's a cold, calculating, monster.

Since we were young, we've been taught to obey him. His word is law. If anyone disobeys him, the punishments he doles out guarantees it doesn't happen again. I am well aware, having been the target at times.

Behind the tall, dark-haired, blue-eyed, handsome features, is a man who feels no love for anyone. Not his women, and certainly not his children. We're his statement to the world, showing he's capable of producing offspring. Tools to be used to his advantage. Father is a narcissist.

Nodding my head in defeat, I lower my eyes to the floor. "Yes, Father. I'm sorry. I'm a little tired from training. It's been a long day." I scramble for excuses, even though I know there's none as far as he's concerned.

You do as you're told, or there are consequences.

What would have happened if my half-brother had survived? Was my father this controlling with him? Tomas is the only person I've known Father speak of with any emotion. I can't help feeling some jealousy.

"You'll be ready by the end of the week, Katya. Plans have already been set in motion." Father's voice breaks into my thoughts. "The timing has had to be moved up."

My head jolts in surprise. "But, Father..." I'm not ready yet, is on the tip of my tongue, but Father's cold glare chokes the words in my throat. Instead, I nod. "Yes, Father, I'll be ready." There's no point arguing with him. I won't win.

"Good," he answers curtly. "Get cleaned up. My office, ten minutes." Turning away, he marches from the room.

Precisely ten minutes later, I'm standing in front of the large, carved desk my father sits behind. I don't miss his smirk as he checks his watch. "Good. Sit," he orders, and I slide onto the hard steel chair placed across from him.

Father may be seated in plush leather, but his *guests* aren't offered the same comfort. I believe it's so they know without doubt he's the important person in the room.

"You fly out Wednesday. Korbicov is attending his mother's charity auction on Friday. You will also attend." Father throws orders at me as if I'm one of his thugs.

He removes a black credit card from his pocket,

tossing it on the desk. "Your mother will go shopping with you. She has a list of what you need to purchase. Your passport will be ready this evening, and you are booked into the *Hilton Hotel*." My eyes light up at his announcement.

I allow myself a hint of excitement until he continues. "A man will meet you at the airport. He'll supply you with a weapon and act as your driver. When you arrive at the auction, find a way to get Korbicov to come to you." Father rattles off his plan. "Understand? I don't care how you do it. The moment you get close, kill him."

"But what if he doesn't, Father? What if I'm not his type? What then?" I know I'm pretty, but there are gorgeous women out there who can attract men like magnets. Why would the notorious Bratva Pakhan, *boss*, notice me?

It doesn't occur to me until much later that Father doesn't mention an escape plan for me.

"Because you'll ensure he does, won't you, Katya?" It's not a question. It's an order. Leaning forward, he places both hands on his desk. "Should I send your sister instead?" His eyebrows arch questioningly while his cold glare freezes me in place.

Gulping in a deep breath, I answer his question. "No, father. I'll do it. I'm the oldest in the family now. It's my responsibility," I babble, extending my hand to pick up the credit card. Before I can pull it back, Father clamps his hand over my wrist.

"Yes. You're the oldest now Tomas is gone. I should've had boys," he mutters, before locking eyes with mine. "But you must use what you have, don't you, Katya? The sullying of my name must be avenged, which means the perpetrator of these lies must die. Understood?" His grip is cutting off the circulation to my hand, but I dare not whimper.

"Yes, Father. I'll clear your name and avenge Tomas," I reply confidently. It's the one thing I'm sure of. Tomas' death will be paid for in blood. I don't mention Tomas might not be dead if Father hadn't sent him to do what he's now sending me to accomplish.

His grip loosens, and I pull my hand back, resisting the need to rub my tender wrist.

Father's phone rings and he pulls it from his pocket to check the caller ID. "Hello? Yes," he answers while making a shoo motion in my direction with his other hand, dismissing me.

When I reach the kitchen, Mother's sitting on a stool at the breakfast bar. "Are you ready to go shopping?" I murmur, leaning in to kiss her cheek, the smell of alcohol bleeding from her pores.

Mother is a shell of the person I remember from my childhood. Alcohol helps her cope, I suppose. Depression dulls the blue of her irises; eyes that were once bright and full of life. She appears older than she should, likely caused by her heavy drinking, and her once blonde hair is now flecked with grays. Father has this effect on people, especially women.

I don't know if Mother was ever in love with Father. But she accepts having had two children with him, there's no escaping him.

2

THE BLOOD ON MY HANDS CHANGES TO PINK AS I lather them with soap. It swirls in circles as it washes down the sink, draining away just like it did from my prisoner. I don't regret killing him.

The man was a thief. He stole from me. His death will serve as a lesson to others as the penalty for trying to cheat me.

Hearing footsteps, I glance back over my shoulder while toweling my hands dry. Henrí, my right-hand man and best friend, steps inside the bathroom. "We found it. It was right where he said it would be."

Instead of answering him, I nod in understanding before turning back to what I'm doing.

"I'll have someone dispose of his body," Henrí murmurs before leaving the room.

"Ready to go, boss?" Henrí murmurs. "Car's out front."

I blow out a slow breath before pressing my lips together in a firm line and rolling my shoulders before cracking my neck. "Why do we have to do this again?" I ask him, even though I already know the answer.

He chuckles half-heartedly at my question. Henrí knows it's rhetorical. Instead, he holds up my tux jacket while I do a second check in the mirror to ensure my bowtie is on straight. I slip both arms into the jacket he holds open for me before straightening my diamond and gold cufflinks.

I'm attending a banquet and auction tonight to raise funds for a children's charity my mother started before dementia took her memory away. It's called Beds For Babies. Having grown up in a privileged life, I've never felt unsafe or lacked a place to sleep, but Mama has.

She met my Otets, *Father*, under dubious circumstances. He was pretending to be someone else while doing a job for the Pakhan, his father.

As soon as Otets set eyes on my mother, he said he knew she was his.

When Mama found out who he truly was, she wanted nothing to do with him. Otets decided to kidnap her and make her understand his side of things. He had to do a lot of groveling and it took a long time for Mama to come around.

Mama tried to escape a few times, but eventually, she understood why he couldn't let her go. Not only was Otets in love with Mama, but if he did set her free, his enemies would make a point of hunting her down to get to him. They might not have killed her, but they would have made her life a misery, and would probably have done unspeakable things to her.

Not long after meeting, Grandfather died and Otets stepped up to take his place. Otets becoming a Bratva Pakhan was a huge hurdle for them to get over, but she did eventually. They married, and not long after, I was born.

Mikhail Nikolai Korbicov, nicknamed The Raven. It's an old myth in my culture that the raven is a trickster. The Raven knows things before anyone else. An ability that has served me well over the years. A raven tattoo covers my upper back and shoulders.

I grew up as an only child.

My father lies in a grave in our private cemetery, and my mother has practically no memory of me. She still lives in our three-story home, tended to by the best medical team money can buy. Placing her in a nursing home is not possible. It's not who I am. Family means everything to me.

If she were in a nursing home, someone would seek her out, to get to me. Mama will never be a target for anyone. I have, and will, kill anyone who tries to harm a hair on her sweet head.

Furthermore, I promised my Otets I would care for Mama should anything happen to him.

Despite my father being the Pakhan, he was always there for me and my mother. He ruled his men with an iron fist, but in the privacy of our rooms, he was always loving and soft. I remember how he made Mama laugh, and the games he'd play with me when I was young.

Before I grew old enough to learn the *business*.

After he died, Mama's health took a turn for the worse. It was like her mind couldn't take the pain of knowing Otets was dead, so she forgot.

"I'll be down in a minute," I inform Henrí. He knows

I won't leave without checking on Mama. Sometimes, if I visit her early enough in the afternoon, I can catch a glimmer of the Mama I remember.

The woman she was before Otets' death.

Tapping lightly on the door, I let the nurse know I'm entering. It may be my home, but I would not want Mama to be in an undignified position should I barge straight in. Her nurse calls out for me to enter, and I step inside. Approaching Mama slowly, my eyes scan her, my heart beating a little faster in the hope she's having a good day.

She sits in a large rocking chair at the window overlooking the garden, her now gray hair perfectly coiffed by the hairdresser who tends to her regularly. The once bright green eyes dulled by pain and heartbreak, brighten a little as she turns her head to gaze up at me.

"Hey, how are you today?" I croon gently, not making a move until she does.

"Oh, darling, you look handsome in your suit." Mama smiles up at me, at the same time reaching for my hand, which I gladly give her. Glancing over at her nurse, she giggles lightly, and my heart sings for a moment. "Doesn't my husband look handsome?"

I do my damndest to keep the smile on my face from dropping, but it's hard. My stomach lurches as my heart thumps with the disappointment of her not recognizing me. Maybe tomorrow, I tell myself.

The nurse's eyes sweep my face, sorrow evident in her gaze. I know she wants to correct my mother, but I shake my head slightly. Let her imagine I'm Otets for a moment. I'll have her remember me another day.

Maybe tomorrow, I tell myself as I take a fortifying deep breath.

"Are we going somewhere, Rinaldo? Should I be getting ready? Oh, where are my shoes?" Mama scans the room, worry evident in her voice.

"Shh, moy kotyonok, *my kitten*," I croon, using Otets' pet name for her. "There's a meeting I must attend. You stay in and relax tonight," I assure Mama, playing the role of my father for her. "It's late. Why don't you go to bed? I won't be long." My voice drops to a softer tone as I try to convince her there's no need to worry.

"Oh, okay." Disappointment's apparent in Mama's tone. "I'll be in bed waiting for you," she mumbles, tears forming in her eyes as she gazes into mine. "Be careful, Rinny. Be careful, okay? Promise me," she rasps hoarsely.

I promise, before kissing her gently on both cheeks and then both wrists, as I remember my father doing many times.

The nurse coaxes Mama out of her chair and over to her bed. I leave the room disappointed. Mama remembers me less and less. Someday she won't know me at all, and I'll be alone.

Before closing the door, I whisper, "I love you, Mama."

Standing alone on the top of the staircase, I take a few calming breaths before I head down to the foyer and out to the limo. Henrí glances over at me as I climb into the back seat with him. I give an almost imperceptible shake of my head. He knows what it means. He rides beside me in silence, leaving me alone with my thoughts.

The escort hired to attend the charity auction with me is exquisite in every way when the driver arrives at her address to pick her up. The dress I paid for is well worth the thousands of dollars I spent, as are the stilettos on her long legs. Her blonde hair is down and curled, the way I like it, and her makeup is minimal.

Makeup all over the bedsheets and pillows after sex is a huge turnoff for me.

She will get to keep all of it once the night is over, as well as a fat bonus.

Isla has been vetted, although it doesn't stop Henrí frisking her and checking her purse before she's allowed to enter the limo. Isla pouts a little when he takes possession of her phone for the duration of the time we're together, but she knows the rules.

Interpol would do anything to catch me and other men in my line of work in compromising positions. We must stay a step ahead of them at all times.

Isla may be one of my regular escorts, but it doesn't mean she doesn't have to follow procedures. *Trust no one.* My father's last words are instilled in my brain.

No one gets close to me without my right-hand man, Henrí, thoroughly checking their background. Henrí and I have been best friends since childhood. His mother, Kristina, is my mother's nurse. She's also Mama's best friend. Although my mother doesn't remember her most of the time, Kristina volunteered to care for her until the day this horrid disease takes her from me.

I shudder at the thought of someday losing Mama.

After the way my father died, it seems odd to others I would choose my best friend to be my right-hand man. But Henrí and I are different to my Otets and the man he thought was his friend, who met as teenagers, because we've been together since birth. We're practically twins in the way we think. I trust Henrí explicitly.

Isla irritates me tonight with her chatter. I'm beginning to wish I had come alone. It's bad enough I have to go entertain a bunch of rich buffoons, without having a woman nattering in my ear constantly.

My fingers twitch on my knee every time she opens her mouth. If she doesn't shut up soon, I'm going to reach over and hold her pouty lips closed. I'd forgotten how much she loves to talk.

Henrí senses my mood and places his hand on her thigh, gripping it slightly. Not enough to hurt, but enough for her to glance up at him in curiosity. He leans in, placing a hand behind her head, winking at me over Isla's shoulder before pulling her to him and taking her mouth with his.

Pulling away, Henrí releases his hold on her, allowing her to pull back a little for air. Isla steals a glance my way. There's excitement mixed with fear in her eyes when she locks eyes with mine.

"Have at it." I wink, letting her know I'm not jealous. If that's what it takes to close her pretty mouth, then so be it.

Henrí gathers her gown, pushing it up her long legs until it bunches at Isla's waist. I watch on, intrigued, as his fingers inch up under the material until he finds what he's searching for. The sound of tearing panties ensues. He loves exhibitionism, and this isn't the first time I've watched him.

She gasps, as if she's shocked, before breaking into a giggle. This isn't her first encounter with my highly sexual friend. As soon as she nods her head in consent, Henrí maneuvers her onto his lap, where she now has her back to his chest.

Isla's face is flushed with excitement as she throws another glance my way. She's enjoying what Henrí is doing to her and having me watching them appears to heighten her arousal.

Henrí unzips the back of her strapless gown, pulling it down so her natural perky breasts hang free. It's one of the reasons I chose Isla; she's all natural. Henrí smirks, and jerks his head slightly, silently offering for me to join them.

We've shared women before, though this is the first time in such tight quarters.

Removing my jacket, I fold it before lying it on the seat. Moving across to the seat facing Henrí, I slide my long legs in between theirs, forcing them wider, and begin kneading Isla's breasts. Rubbing and pinching her nipples, I'm intrigued as the once-soft skin puckers before forming hard pebbles.

With one hand around Isla's slim waist, holding her in place, Henrí teases her clit with the other, before rubbing her creamy juices up and down her soaked lips. She moans with pleasure, her eyes rolling back into her head before they spring wide again when I lean forward and bring a breast to my lips, biting her nipple lightly.

There is no resistance to our ministrations; moans, and gasps at each touch urging us on. Her breath hitches as Henrí slips one of his long fingers inside her and she begins to ride it as he undoes his belt with his other hand. He deftly slides a condom onto his thick cock before slipping his finger from her juicy hole.

She cries out in frustration at the loss. At a nod from Henrí, I bite Isla's nipple hard as my friend slams his cock into her from behind. Isla's left hand bangs on the privacy glass behind me as she pushes back hard on Henrí's intrusion. At the same time, her other hand lifts a breast, offering it up for more attention, the ecstasy of the two of us tending to her, evident on her face.

Isla groans with each thrust. Her breaths huff out as Henrí continues to pull her down hard on his cock. I twist her nipples hard while watching Henrí's cock slide in and out of her sopping wet pussy, the noise of her juices squelching each time he does. His finger reach for her clit again, which he rubs hard. Isla cries out as she orgasms while Henrí grunts through his own release, as I watch on.

I find women's faces fascinating when they cum, their features flushed, eyes rolling back into their heads, jaws slackened. Isla isn't faking hers, unlike some women.

Once her breathing settles, Isla appears to remember where she is. She tucks her breasts back into her dress, averting my eyes as if she's embarrassed at what just happened. I dig a pack of wet wipes out of a cupboard under the limo seats and hand them to her so she can clean herself up.

"Hey." I cup her cheeks gently, patiently waiting for her eyes to meet mine. When they do, I smile. "It's okay, there's nothing to be embarrassed about. Okay?"

"B-But I'm supposed to be with you tonight. I-I got lost in the moment…" Isla stammers. She glances down to my swollen crotch then back up to my face. "Do you want me to…" Her voice drifts off as I shake my head.

"I'm not angry with you, Isla. You did nothing wrong." My thumbs brush gently across her defined cheekbones before releasing her so I can shift my cock around in my pants to a more comfortable position. "I'll be fine," I assure her.

Henrí ties the condom he has removed, dropping it into the waste bin conveniently slotted into the limo door, before hugging Isla to his body. He murmurs in her ear for a few moments, and whatever he says to her has her giggling. He then sets about helping her clean up and straighten out her clothes. Once he's done with her, he cleans himself up, tucks himself back in, and buckles his belt.

By the time we reach the place where the charity auction is being held, my mindset has dissipated somewhat.

3

MOTHER AND I WENT ALL OUT PURCHASING MY clothes for the charity auction. The *Versace* fitted, pearl-colored, satin gown clings to me in all the right ways.

While the front of my dress gives a glimpse of my freed breasts side-on, it's not overtly sexual. The two separate pieces of satin are joined in the center as they rise from my slim waist, then crisscross each other from my mid-waist up over my breasts, before attaching to a collared section around my throat. There is practically no back in the dress. Instead, it dips slightly past the small indents in my spine before closing over my derriere. The lack of material on my back shows off the tattoo running down my spine.

The satin bodice is taut around my thin waist, showing off my flat stomach. At the rear, it outlines my ass, flattering its shape before dropping to the floor, where the material hangs in soft waves. A split in the front of the dress runs from the base of my hip to the floor so I can walk comfortably, while also allowing the men around me to catch glimpses of my long legs. It also allows men's imaginations to run wild, wondering whether or not I'm wearing panties.

My long, blonde hair has had highlights added and hangs below my shoulders in styled waves. The makeup I wear is minimal, except for the deep red lipstick covering my lips. Diamonds in the shape of teardrops on white gold grace my ears. Other jewelry I wear consists of a silver ring on my middle finger, linked by a silver chain to a bracelet containing smaller versions of my earrings which wraps around my forearm, from my wrist to my elbow. My nail polish matches the color of my dress.

The whole outfit is finished off with diamond-encrusted stilettos, made by *Jimmy Choo* and a handbag by *Mouawad*, who also styled my jewelry.

Father was unhappy at the amount Mother and I spent until I reminded him I had to look the part to appeal to my prey. If I arrived here looking anything but perfection, I would blend in with all the other pretty women. There will be enough single women falling over themselves to meet the Bratva Pakhan, Mikhail Korbicov, also known as The Raven.

Father informs me I'm not to damage any of the clothing or jewelry because I won't be keeping it. He enjoys reminding me I don't belong to this high-class world. I'm here to avenge him, so my sister and I can be free to live our lives.

Hopefully, when this is all done, he will disappear from our lives. He has promised Natalia and me enough money to keep us living a life of comfort without his shadow falling over us when this is all over.

Mother might have once loved the man who conveniently calls us *family* when he needs something from us, but I don't. Like my younger sister, Natalia, I fear him. No matter what I tell myself, though, I still feel the need for his approval, if not his affection. Not that I'm likely to ever get it.

Mikhail Korbicov is the reason my father has had to hide himself, and us, away in another country. The Korbicovs have spread their lies far and wide. If our family is ever to be able to live a life without fear of retribution, I have to end the Korbicov line forever.

Father's plan is simple. Get close to the last Korbicov male and kill him.

Father expressed his wish for Mikhail's mother to be done away with also, but I've decided his mother is of no consequence. From the intelligence I've gathered, Svetlana Korbicov is little more than a shell of the woman she once was. Disease has eaten away at her mind, erasing most of her memories of the life she once led. Death will take her soon enough.

The way Father speaks about Svetlana Korbicov, I believe he's jealous because she married Rinaldo Korbicov. He says Svetlana chose to marry the wrong man. According to him, he gave Svetlana the opportunity to walk away from the money and prestige of carrying the Korbicov name. One she didn't take. If she had, she might have spared herself so much grief.

We're outcasts, unwelcome amongst the tight-knit community run by the Korbicovs. They blame Father for the death of Svetlana's husband, and Mikhail's father, Rinaldo Korbicov. Mikhail has turned the other Pakhans against him.

My father is innocent. He was Rinaldo's best friend. He loved Rinaldo as if he were blood. The lies spread after Rinaldo's death are just that. Lies.

Although Father has money, he says it's nothing compared to what he should have. He states Rinaldo promised him the prestigious title of becoming the Pakhan someday.

Rinaldo was murdered before he could make the decree. Father is sure Mikhail organized the hit. He says Mikhail had the murderers make it appear as if my father did it, and he had to flee.

Now I've been charged with making things right.

From where I stand in a darkened corner of the room, champagne glass in my hand, I watch the arrival of my target with much interest.

Mikhail Korbicov is a man who commands attention. His six-foot-five frame towers above his pretty female companion. The black tuxedo is of the best materials and has been tailored to his body. Highly polished leather *Versace* shoes match the color of his suit. Mikhail's dark hair is cut short at the sides of his head, while the longer hair on top has been perfectly braided and hangs down between his broad shoulders. His handsome face sports a neatly trimmed mustache and goatee, his dark chocolate eyes missing nothing as they scan the room.

He reminds me a little of *Jason Momoa*, but with broader shoulders and more handsome.

Mikhail's bodyguard and childhood friend, Henrí, stays close by, his eyes continually scanning the room for threats.

I'm not afraid to be seen. I'm unknown here. My sister and I are secrets my father has kept and forgotten about until he could find a use for us. The time has come for me to seek retribution, to right the wrongs concerning my father.

From my advantageous position, I observe Korbicov's bodyguards enter, subtly surrounding the guest of honor. Unless one had studied the world of the Mikhail Korbicov, otherwise known as the Raven, it wouldn't be noticeable. Every move they make appears normal, but if someone were to get too close to Mikhail without permission, they wouldn't make it.

Infiltrating Mikhail's circle will be a challenge, one I'm sure I'm capable of. The plan is to catch Mikhail's eye without appearing as if I'm trying. I'm using the charity auction as a test run. Failure is not an option. My plan has to work. Father will send Natalia if I don't do this. I don't want this for my baby sister. Natalia doesn't deserve to be pulled into the dark world of vengeance. If Tomas hadn't failed, I wouldn't be here now.

But he did fail. Tomas died trying to exact revenge for Father. Mikhail's men killed my half-brother. They beat him to death, a photo of his bloodied body sent to my father.

I hadn't known of my half-brother and only saw pictures of him after his death. We never had the chance to meet. Our father kept his other family a secret from my mother, myself, and Natalia. Father says it was for our safety.

Now, as the oldest, I must take Tomas' place in seeking retribution for the wrongs against my father.

I cannot fail.

I *will* not fail.

The night wears on. A band begins to play and Henrí escorts the woman with Mikhail onto the dance floor. Henrí whispers in the woman's ear and she throws her head back in laughter. I can tell by her body language she's trying her best to attract Mikhail's attention, but he appears to be deep in conversation with the group of people he's standing with.

Once or twice during the evening, I've glanced over to find dark chocolate eyes watching me. I lock eyes with him for a moment or two again. He looks at me almost as if he knows what I'm thinking. My cheeks heat under the confident gaze of Mikhail Korbicov, the Bratva boss.

Good, my plan is working.

Each time he catches me looking, I'm overcome with an unnatural feeling. One I don't recognize. My face reddens while my body warms with emotions I don't understand. The desire to smile at him is overwhelming, but I can't appear too easy. He's not known to chase women; he doesn't need to. Women fall over each other to be noticed by him. I don't want to risk approaching him, to find myself rejected.

A man I don't know steps close to me, cutting off my line of sight to my target. He introduces himself and asks me to dance. I don't want to, but I don't want to appear obvious, so I accept.

We no sooner reach the dance floor, moving to the music, than my partner freezes in place. He looks over his shoulder at the same time as I glance up at Mikhail's tall frame. He glares down at my dance partner. No words are exchanged, but the man, whose name I've already forgotten, releases his hold on me and walks away.

Mikhail steps forward, pulling me gently into his arms, his right hand gliding around and down my exposed lower back. His strong fingers on my bare skin cause tingles everywhere on my body, goosebumps rising. He then catches my small hand in his. His large one almost covering mine as he pulls it close to his chest. My head falls back as we begin to dance, our eyes gazing into each other's as if we're lovers.

If I thought Mikhail was handsome from across the room, the man is truly breathtaking up close. His large, muscular body is rock-hard against me. I'm hypnotized, unable to break our stare until the song finishes. I hadn't realized we'd covered most of the dance floor, such was the magnitude of his hold over me.

Father warned me of his charm. I'll need to be careful.

The music ends and I take a much-needed step back from this powerful man. The loss of the heat of his body against me highly noted by mine. Disappearing into the crowd as soon as Mikhail releases me, I give myself a high-five. The plan is working.

A gong sounds, summoning all to the dining room, and I follow the crowd.

The tables are covered in white cloths, and large glass vases filled with brightly colored lilies and greenery decorate the centers. Fine china and silverware of the highest grade lie perfectly in position for each guest. Ushers greet each person as they enter, directing them where to sit.

I'm shocked when I find myself seated next to my target at the main table. As the waiter assists me to my seat, Mikhail himself appears beside me.

"It's okay, I've got this," he assures the young man, who immediately nods and backs away. Of course, he knows who Mikhail is and breaches no argument. "Your seat, malen'kiy olen'." His deep voice encourages, his head nodding at the chair he holds for me.

My eyes widen at his choice of words. *Little deer. Is this how he sees me? Do I look like a frightened deer to him?* Imagine his shock when he discovers too late, I'm more like the wolf, disguised as a deer.

I nod stiffly, sitting without protest. He pushes my chair closer to the table before sliding into the seat beside me. Forcing my eyes forward, I gaze around the table, noticing the woman Mikhail arrived with is seated on the other side of my attentive target's right-hand man, Henrí. She throws a scathing look my way, which I return with a sweet smile. This isn't a position I hoped to be in, however, it could work in my favor. Henrí clears his throat as he turns to me, and I glance at him in surprise.

"And who do we have here?" Henrí inquires, picking up my hand and raising it to his lips.

Before it reaches his mouth, Mikhail slides his arm over the back of my chair. I can't see what's exchanged in silence behind me, but Henrí releases my hand immediately with an apology. "Forgive my manners, madam." Before I can reply, he turns to the woman seated on the other side of him and starts up a conversation.

It doesn't go unnoticed how Mikhail's arm remains along the back of my chair. My cheeks burn when I peer up at him, finding his dark chocolate eyes locked on mine. His handsome face is blank as he gazes intently at me. I feel as if I'm sinking into his dark, unwavering pools.

My body tingles beneath his gaze, my nipples instantly hardening beneath the thin material of my dress. Mikhail's eyes drop to my chest for an instant, as if he can see straight through the satin material. A smirk appears on his lips and my body feels as if it's being drawn toward his with an invisible string. I hope I don't have to move too soon as I'm sure I'm going to leave a wet spot on my chair. I've not reacted to anyone like this before.

It's not as if I've been around a lot of men. Mama lived a secluded life, separate from Father's. He says it was to keep us safe, but all the while he had another family. My sister and I went virtually ignored until Father lost Tomas. Only then did he seek us out because he needed us to finish what Tomas failed to do.

Perhaps the glass of champagne has loosened me up a little. I shouldn't have had any alcohol at all. I'm here for a purpose, and it's not cozying up to the enemy.

Father would be furious if he could see me now.

Or maybe not. I might be able to use this to my advantage. It seems my target is interested in me, which is why I was sent here. I wasn't expecting anything to happen this quickly, but it could be a good thing.

It might not take as long as I thought to complete my mission. Father will be pleased. He'll be able to return to his precious country again. Without the threat of his impending death by the man sitting beside me, twirling strands of my hair between his fingers as he speaks to others at the table, Father can become what he always wanted. A Pakhan. We'll finally be free of him; able to move on with our lives.

But before he dies by my hand, I need to know why Mikhail is known as the Raven.

4

____

MIKHAIL

THE GROUP OF MEN I'M MAKING CONVERSATION WITH are loaded with money. They're boring me to tears, but Henrí says I should appear approachable if I'm to coerce them into pulling out their checkbooks.

What I suggested is we kidnap them all, threaten their wives and children with death, and have them hand over all their wealth. Henrí laughed, reminding me that's not how to *work the room*. He says Mama wouldn't be happy with doing things my way.

It's not as if I don't have enough money to support my mother's charity. I do, and more, but she wants it to remain a legal charity, relying on legal donations.

I'll do anything to make her happy. Even if she doesn't remember it.

There's also another reason I'm here tonight. Our intelligence informs me my arch-enemy has sent someone to assassinate me. Again. The damn coward hides while he forces others to do his dirty work.

It should be no surprise. He's the reason my father is dead. He can't hide forever. As soon as I get a lock on him, I'll go after him myself.

Pavel Ivanov. My Otets' best friend, also his murderer.

"Is a hundred thousand enough to get me a date with her?" One of the group, James something, nods toward the corner of the room.

Several of the men I'm speaking with look in the direction James indicates, including me.

In the corner is the most beautiful woman I've ever seen. She's tiny, with long blonde hair spilling down in soft waves over her bare shoulders. Her cream gown, sexy and at the same time demure, hugs her in all the right places, the slit down the side showing off one long shapely leg. When she glances up, her eyes momentarily catch mine, her bright blue eyes widening slightly. Her cheeks flush as if she's been caught doing something wrong.

My heart thuds heavily for a few beats until the beauty looks away.

"I'll raise you a hundred thousand," exclaims another man in our group, whose name I can't remember right now.

"She's taken," I grate out. "She's with me."

What the fuck?

The need to protect her is unfamiliar. All I know is, these leeches can't have her. The blood in my veins thickens as I visualize another man with her.

A man in a tux steps between the woman and my line of sight and I frown. He needs to move out of the way. What is he saying to her? Is she with him? Involuntarily, my hands curl into fists at the mere thought.

I want her.

When the stranger leads her out onto the dance floor, I follow them. Without excusing myself, I leave the group of men I was with, watching in puzzlement. The pair reach the dance floor and begin moving to the music, the unknown man holding her too close to him. I step up behind him, tapping him on the shoulder as I do. He twists his head, glancing up at me, a frown on his face until he recognizes me.

I say nothing as I glare down at him. He swallows deeply before nodding and stepping away from the young woman without any words exchanged. Smart man.

Stepping into her space, I place my right hand on her bare back while encasing one of her tiny hands in my left. I hold her hand to my chest as we dance, gazing into each other's eyes. Not a word is spoken. For once in my life, I don't know what to say.

Her skin feels like satin, while her hair, which brushes against my hand as we dance, is as soft as silk. A hum runs through my veins as I maneuver our bodies around the dance floor with ease. We move in sync with each other as if we've known each other for a lifetime.

The song ends and without speaking, the incredible creature steps back from me. She glances down at the floor and back to my face before biting her lush red lower lip before backing away and fleeing.

I instantly feel the loss of her body close to mine.

The gong sounds for dinner, which pisses me off as it thwarts my need to follow after her. To my surprise, though, when I reach my designated table in the dining hall, I find her waiting to be seated between Henrí and me at our table. Not wanting the usher touching the beauty about to join me, I take over her seating myself.

"You can thank me later." Henrí winks at me before lifting her hand to kiss it. Seeing the thunderous look on my face, Henrí chuckles, relinquishes the hold he has on her hand, and turns to Isla. I sit back, lying my arm across the back of my new dinner companion's seat in an act of ownership, flashing Isla a warning glance. She pales and looks away.

Mine.

The beautiful creature beside me hasn't made any objection to the change in seating arrangements. As for me, I'm ecstatic.

The meals arrive. Plates of delicious meats and vegetables are placed in front of each person. While this takes place, waiters serve champagnes and wines to those who wish to imbibe.

I wave the waiter away when he indicates my wine glass. I don't drink much, especially not in public. I'll have a sip or two of my *Macallan M* single malt Scotch whiskey when I get back to the house.

After I check on Mama.

"Are you enjoying yourself?" I ask the beautiful woman next to me, before inhaling her delectable scent. If I'm correct, her flushed cheeks and hardened nipples suggest her body is reacting to mine as much as mine is to her. Merely the accidental rub of my thigh against hers under the table has my cock harder than the silverware we're about to use to cut our steaks.

"I am," she murmurs so softly that I almost have to ask her to repeat herself. Instead, I lean into her, not missing her quick inhale as I do.

"So am I. Now," I wink at her, smiling broadly as the color in her cheeks rises. Do her cheeks flush the same color when she orgasms? I want to find out.

She takes another bite of her steak and as her lips close around the fork, I envision them around my cock, with that red lipstick on them. I find it hard not to moan at the image in my head.

I'm sure she feels the same. I can smell her arousal from here. How would she react if I slipped my hand under the slit of her gown and slid my fingers into her panties to check? I don't expect she'll agree to it, but I'm going to find out.

My cock twitches in agreement.

I allow my hand to drop to my thigh as I continue to use the other for eating. Little by little I edge it further up, the white tablecloth covering what I'm doing, until my entire hand sits on her bare leg. I lightly stroke the satin skin of her thigh with my thumb, allowing her to move away if she isn't in agreement with what I'm doing.

Glancing sideways, I wait for her to object. Her body stiffens slightly, her eyes flicking sideways at me, then around the table to see if anyone has noticed what I'm doing. Most of the people here are eating or chatting about the auctions happening after dinner.

Encouraged by her tacit assent, my hand slides higher up under her gown until I reach the seam of her bare pussy. It's then I realize she isn't wearing panties. I pour a glass of water with my free hand and take a sip to distract myself from letting out a moan of my own. My little finger rubs the junction of her legs and pussy gently. Inch by inch, I dip into the crevice until her legs fall open slightly, allowing me access.

One of the couples on the opposite side of the table enquires about Mama's health. They're one of the largest donors to her cause. As my fingers dip into the juices dripping from my delectable dinner partner, I answer their queries, my face belying the turmoil happening under the table.

It's all I can do to stop myself from standing and ordering everyone from the room so I can have my way with the woman next to me. The one who has now reached beneath the tablecloth herself, placing her hand over mine. She drags my hand to where she wants me, pulling her gown up a little, and widens her legs further.

I slam a finger inside her as she sips her wine, wondering if she's allowing me to do this so she can make a scene. I've been watching her on and off all night since I first arrived and I'm sure she hasn't had much alcohol. Leaning forward slightly, she pushes harder against me as I glide my finger in and out of her tight pussy. I accept her challenge and slip another finger inside her.

I side eye her cautiously. If it wasn't for me finger fucking her under the, I would never guess by her expression. Her face is blank as she grabs my hand and sets a rhythm, using her thumb to rub against her clit. Henrí asks me something and I answer. He glances down at my mystery guest and back up to me, a smirk on his lips. He probably knows what's going on down there, but I don't care.

With a wink at him, I curl my fingers inside her, hitting her in the perfect spot, and her whole body freezes. Other than her pussy pulsating around my fingers, the only outward sign of her cumming is a beautiful pink flush moving over her skin and a thin line of sweat above her top lip. She's practically sitting on my hand as she pushes harder and harder against it, taking all she can from her orgasm.

As her muscles begin to relax, I remove my fingers from her drenched pussy. I reach for my white serviette and wipe my hands. While no one is looking, I inhale deeply, before placing it in my suit pocket as a souvenir. The young woman watches my every move, her cheeks glowing when Henrí gallantly passes her his serviette under the table to clean up with.

I'm not sure how she feels about what we've done, because, for the rest of the meal, she avoids looking at or speaking to me. She doesn't appear to be bothered when I find myself toying with strands of her long hair, before dropping my hand back to her thigh. It's an almost intimate act as if we've been lovers, which we aren't. Yet. I'm confused at feeling the intense need to touch her. When this night is over, I'm going to fuck her.

I had intended taking Isla home with me tonight, but I'll be taking this woman instead. The woman I finger fucked under the table at my mother's charity auction, while people ate and drank around us, totally unaware. The woman who was sent here to kill me.

Katya Ivanov.

Finally, the dining part of the evening is over, and the auction begins.

There are boats, mansions, and holidays all up for auction tonight, alongside dinners for two and other menial items. There are also people auctioning themselves as dinner partners or companions for a day.

None of it interests me, but I have to stay until the end, for Mama's sake.

I was called away from our table to sign some contracts to do with the various legal sections of the charity. Afterward, I stand around, bored shitless, shaking hands with the successful bidders. It's not something I wish to do, but I do it anyway. I know I could pay some ditz to do it for me, but I promised Mama I would take care of her precious charity personally.

When I return to the table, Katya has disappeared. Henrí insists he only took his eyes off her for a second and when he looked back, she was gone. I'm more than pissed.

My men check the entire building, but she appears to have vanished on me.

5

KATYA

As soon as I know Mikhail's henchman isn't looking, I leave the table and dash to the bathroom.

Meeting my reflection in the mirror, I scold myself. "What the hell was that?" I ask myself. "You're a whore," I hiss, using the same words my father has used at times to describe me. Even if he hadn't thought it of me before, he would be convinced now. I imagine the look of disgust on his face if he knew what I allowed the man I'm here to kill to do to me under the dining table.

My throbbing pussy is fully aware of what Mikhail did to it, contracting sharply as I run my hand down the front of my dress and over my mound. When he inhaled the serviette he used to clean his fingers with afterward, I felt myself blush. I was horrified yet felt empowered at the same time as I watched him inhale my scent.

Placing the plug in the sink, I run water into it. Using paper towels, I reach up under my gown and clean the sticky mess up as best I can. Lucky for me, I've finished cleaning myself up when the bathroom door opens and the young woman who arrived tonight on Mikhail's arm enters.

She scowls at me momentarily before ignoring me as she reapplies her makeup in front of the mirror. Her skin is flawless, and her blonde hair, similar to my own is but not as long, is also fashioned in a similar style. The gown she has on is nowhere near as expensive as the one I wear, nor is her jewelry or shoes.

She appears to be a cheaper version of me.

She's probably an escort, paid to hang on Mikhail's arm for the night. *Is that what he thinks I am? Is that why he thought it was okay to do what he did?*

My throat tightens in disgust while my skin crawls.

Stomach churning, I make a beeline for the toilet cubicle. Once I've locked the door, I lean my hand against one wall and stand over the bowl, waiting. Although I don't vomit, I flush the toilet, before unlocking the door and exiting.

The woman remains standing at the sink. She turns and leans against it, her eyes narrowing at me as I step back into the restroom area. "Had a little too much to drink?" she snips. "Mikhail doesn't like women who drink too much. It turns him off."

"What business is it of yours what I do?" My surliness is obvious. She's not worth getting into a catfight with. I have one interest in Mikhail. As if I care what she has to say.

"I'll be going home with him tonight. Retract your claws, sweetheart," she sneers. "Mikhail is mine."

"Didn't seem that way when he had his fingers in my pussy under the table tonight." My words hit her like a slap to the face, her head jerking back and her eyes widening at my confession. I clap my hand over my mouth, shocked at having admitted what happened to a perfect stranger.

She lunges at me with a screech of indignation, but I sidestep her easily. Slipping up behind her, I wrap her hair around my hand and pull hard. When she slips a fraction, I take the opportunity to wrap my other arm around her neck, squeezing until she stops struggling, and her body goes limp in my arms.

I haven't killed her, merely put her to sleep for a while.

Lying her on the cold tile floor, my mind reels as I try to figure out my next move. Someone could enter at any moment and there would be questions.

I had intended to leave the auction. The first contact has been made with my target. But if I'm seen leaving the bathroom now, it may cause suspicions and my cover will be blown. As I try to work up a plan, the door to the bathroom opens.

Henrí stands there, his eyes immediately locked on the still form on the floor. He glances up at me suspiciously, his head cocked to one side, as his arm reaches up inside his jacket.

"Oh, I'm so glad you're here," I gasp, putting on an impromptu act. "I was in the cubicle when I heard someone come in. When I stepped out, I found her lying on the floor. Maybe she fainted or something," I babble breathlessly, acting as if I'm as shocked as he is at the unconscious woman. "I–Is she okay?" I stammer. "Should we call for an ambulance?"

I hope not, because it won't take a medic long to figure out what happened. Then I'll be in all sorts of trouble.

"No. I'll deal with it," Henrí replies swiftly, removing his phone from his jacket. I had been expecting a weapon of some kind to be in his hand. The resin, 3D printer-made pistol strapped to my leg has a single shot in it. Luckily, Mikhail didn't find it when he … did what he did.

"Get some men to the women's bathroom, quickly." Henrí's voice interrupts my thoughts.

Within seconds, four burly men are standing at the door. Henrí orders them to pick up the woman and take her home. He directs one man to stay with her to make sure she's okay. Two men step forward and pick her up, Henrí insisting they treat her with care or Mikhail will be angry.

I huff out a breath. If Mikhail likes her so much, then what the hell was he doing fingering *me* under the dining table? I'm not jealous of her, I tell myself. I'm angry at myself for allowing him to do such a thing in public. He doesn't even know my name. I silently huff in disgust.

Following the men out of the bathroom, I stand by as they take the unconscious woman down the hall and out a back door. A black limo waits for them and they slide her gently into the back seat, one of the men climbing in beside her. The door closes and the limo drives away.

I need to leave before she wakes up and tells Mikhail's man the truth about what took place.

Any escape plans I had are thwarted when I turn to retreat inside and walk into a wall of pure muscle. Surprised, I glance up to find Mikhail's dark eyes set on mine.

His arms encircle me as I attempt to step back, Mikhail's face appearing concerned as he continues gazing down at me. "Are you okay, malen'kiy olen'? Are you hurt?" he asks, his arms tightening around me, pulling me closer.

"I'm fine," I answer crisply, "Your girlfriend slipped in the bathroom and knocked herself unconscious," I add. "Shouldn't you go and be with her?" I want to say, *instead of standing here with your arms around me*, but I don't.

Mikhail's eyes narrow a little at my outburst, but it's the only outward sign he makes. "I don't have a girlfriend," he grunts.

Why does his statement make me feel better? It shouldn't matter to me. I'm here to kill the man, not make conversation with him.

An older woman appears behind the entourage now surrounding us in the hallway. "Mr. Korbicov," she addresses Mikhail respectfully. "We seem to be missing a young lady from the twenty-four-hour dates on the auction listing. A Miss Katya Ivanov. What do you wish me to do?"

Mikhail turns us, and tapping me lightly on my ass, he offers me to the woman. "Here she is." His deep voice echoing slightly in the darkened hallway. "I'll be along shortly, don't go anywhere," he leans down, murmuring in my ear before giving me a slight shove in the direction of the older woman.

What the hell is happening?

"What?" I attempt to twist out of the woman's grasp, my eyes wide in shock. "What do you mean, auction list? I'm not..." *Who put me on a list?*

I'm led to the stage by the other woman, still protesting, but my words fall on deaf ears. Who would place me on an auction list? I'm here to get close to my target, not be auctioned off like a slave. The woman places her hands on my shoulders as a spotlight shines brightly down upon me, practically blinding me. I shade my eyes with my hand, trying to see the crowd as a voice announces me as the next prize.

I should protest. I'm no one's prize. But everything's happening so fast, I don't get the chance.

The auctioneer starts the bidding at ten thousand dollars. My face must reflect the shock at the amount of money she begins the bid at. She places her hand over the microphone and leans in, whispering, "Smile and strike a pose, honey. It's all for a good cause."

Blowing out a slow breath, I bite my lip while deciding what to do. I could walk off the stage and tell them to go screw themselves, or I could have some fun. My time recently has been spent bending to my father's will, and I haven't had any time to myself.

Shrugging my shoulders, I tell myself what the heck, and smiling as broadly as I can, I slide my leg forward. The slit in my gown opens enough for all to see the sleek lines of my toned leg, but not enough for the gun strapped to my other leg to be seen. I always thought my legs to be one of my best assets. Throwing my shoulders back, I place my hands on my hips and beam out at a crowd I can barely see.

The auctioneer winks over at me as the auction gets into full swing. I don't know *who* is bidding, but the price quickly rises to two hundred thousand dollars. Strangely enough, I'm excited someone would believe I'm worth that kind of money. Until a nasty thought enters my head.

What will they expect from me?

My smile drops a little. *Am I being auctioned as if I'm a sure thing? Will my winning bidder expect sex? Hell, no. Not happening.*

I'm about to run off the stage when I realize the bid is at five hundred thousand dollars. *Who bids this kind of money for a date with someone?* Shading my eyes, I scan as many faces as I can make out. The man bidding is close by the stage. He wears a tux similar to everyone else. He's older, tall, with short graying hair. There's something about the way he looks at me I don't like.

I wish someone else would make a bid. He has countered everyone so far, adding a hundred thousand dollars at a time. The auctioneer is at the second call, while I pray for a miracle.

"One million dollars." A deep voice rises from the darkness.

There's an audible gasp from the audience.

"We have a bid for one million dollars from my right." The auctioneer's voice is filled with excitement. "Are there any more bids?" She allows time for more. "Okay then, going once, twice …"

"Two million," the man near the stage bids again.

Once again, there are gasps from the people watching, anticipation from the crowd evident as they wait to see if there's another bid. My smile drops as I gaze down at the man smiling coldly up at me.

Recognition hits me, along with memories I thought I had locked away in the past. Bile rises in my throat, sweat breaks out over my entire body, and I feel the need to throw up.

Tears fill my eyes as memory after memory flashes through my mind. Shame. Degradation. All the things I felt the last time I saw him come back to me full force, as he stands at the front of the crowd. His beady eyes are now glued to my bared leg. I wish I had an overcoat to cover myself up with. The need to flee is overwhelming.

I gulp visibly as the auctioneer once again counts down. "Last call," her voice even louder now over the speakers. The room falls silent.

Please no, my mind screams.

"Five million," the deep voice from beyond my range of sight calls loudly. The room turns as one as they seek out the second bidder.

"Good Lord," the woman next to me gasps before gathering herself. "Okay. You heard the man. Five million dollars for twenty-four hours with this beautiful young lady here. Are there any counter bids?" She waits for a moment to allow the man I can't take my eyes off to make another offer.

Please don't.

Everything seems to be moving in slow motion.

Why is Igor here? Could he be following me? A chill runs down my spine.

My legs tremble with each passing second, and I feel faint.

"Going once, twice, final call?" The loudspeaker crackles a little as the auctioneer checks with the audience. No one counters the offer. The man at the front of the stage scowls at me, his face reddened with embarrassment at being outbid. "Sold to... Oh," she gasps. "Sold to Mr. Korbicov himself. Congratulations, sir. You may claim your prize."

Mikhail strides forward confidently, the crowd parting to allow him through. His face is blank as he climbs the few steps to the stage, before stepping up next to me.

An arm slips under my elbow, before firmly gripping my hand. Thankfully, his hold is what's keeping me on my feet at the moment. It takes all my strength not to lean against him, my legs trembling. "You're mine for twenty-four hours, malen'kiy olen'." Mikhail's deep voice teases me, his breath against my neck cooling my heated skin like a breeze. Goosebumps rise all over my body as the audience applauds. He tugs my arm lightly. "Let's get out of here."

6

MIKHAIL

MY CHEST TIGHTENS AS I LISTEN TO MEN BIDDING ON Katya. I don't understand why it makes me angry, but it does.

My cock twitches in my pants at the thought of what Katya allowed me to do at the dinner table tonight. Never would I have dreamed of doing that to someone in public before. Yes, I joined Henrí and Isla in the back of the limo, but it was not a public place where we could have been discovered.

Henrí organized the new seating arrangements in the dining room as soon as the facial recognition camera confirmed it was her.

I knew Isla would be upset, but I pay her enough money to keep her mouth shut.

My man has rung through to let me know he has put Isla to bed and is waiting for her to wake. I hold no ill will for her and hope she's okay after Henrí discovered her in the bathroom where she supposedly fainted.

Lucky for me, he found Katya at the same time. After her disappearing act from the dining table, I was worried we had lost her. I doubt she would have made a fuss, being who she is and why she's here. All the same, it wouldn't do for her to be screaming sexual assault at Mama's charity, even though she appeared to enjoy it as much as I did.

I wouldn't forgive myself if such an indiscretion tarnished the charity's name.

Knowing what I do about her, I was confused at the pull I felt to her. When my hand crept onto her thigh under the table, I waited. There was no objection. She could have removed my hand at any time. The feel of her satin skin beneath the roughness of mine had my hand moving of its own volition, sliding closer and closer to the heat emanating from between her legs. Again, there was no objection.

Katya's legs had parted as if welcoming me to her mound, where I discovered she wore no panties. Her pussy was slick with want and if there had been no one else in the room, I would have gladly gone to my knees to taste the sweet scent rising from her arousal.

I reach down to subtly adjust myself in the tight containment of my suit pants. It wouldn't do for me to be walking around Mama's charity function with a hard-on tenting my pants like a teenager.

If she's going home with anyone tonight, it'll be me. After all, she came here for me, didn't she? It won't be for the same reason, though.

"Are you going to let Igor win her?" Henrí nudges me, bringing me out of my indulgent reverie.

"Hmm?" I frown at him confused.

"Igor is about to win the woman you had us all

searching for," my friend replies. "The bid is at half a million."

Like hell he is.

Igor Popov is not amongst my trusted people, but I do have dealings with him from time to time. He's known to treat women badly. He won't be getting his hands on Katya. Not now, not ever.

"A million dollars," I raise my voice to be heard from the rear of the crowd.

This might be a charity auction, but I can't let my guard down. From here I can keep a vigil for danger. My enemies don't care about the innocent. If they had the opportunity to take me out, they would.

When Katya first stepped up onto the stage, she seemed as puzzled as me at being on the auction list. The auctioneer said something to her, and Katya's face lit up in a glowing smile, brightening the room. She slid the slit open on her gown to show off one sexy leg. I let out a low growl, wanting to climb up onto the stage and carry her away.

Possessiveness has never been an issue before, but that's how I feel about the tiny blonde angel up there in the bright spotlight right now. It's a strange feeling to have. Especially about someone who's been sent to kill me.

Igor counters at the last second with two million dollars. He knows what will happen if he arouses my anger, yet he insists on pushing me. "Five million dollars," I counteroffer again. He will not win. Am I the only one who's noticed Katya's smile fall when she looks down at Igor?

Katya's face tells me she's about to run, but I won't let her. There's much to learn about this woman, so much

I want to know. It takes seconds for my long legs to reach the stage steps. Sliding up behind Katya, I slip my arm beneath hers, entangling our fingers. She's trembling. "Let's get out of here," I murmur as I pull her away and down the back stairs.

Henrí has already called for the cars to be brought around the front, and I head toward the exit, Katya in tow. Igor is waiting by the door for me when we get there. Henrí steps forward, placing his body between us, his hand on Igor's chest in silent warning. My bodyguards surround us, their hands on their weapons, waiting to see how this plays out.

Igor is an Avtoritet, *authority*, *gang leader*, which means he has some standing within the ranks of the Bratva. But for him to approach me, a Pakhan, unannounced and uninvited, is not the correct procedure.

There's no mistaking the hunger on his face as he rakes his eyes up and down Katya's body. The ignorant durak's, *idiot's*, gaze doesn't leave her until I force her behind me.

He's purposely pushing my buttons by ignoring me. I could kill him right here for his insolence, but he knows I wouldn't bring shame to Mama's charity. "What do you want, Igor?" Henrí snarls at the impudence of the man.

"Me?" Igor's eyebrows arch as he feigns innocence. He spreads his hands wide to show he means no harm, but like Henrí, I don't trust him. "My intention is merely to congratulate you on your prize, Mikhail. You must be expecting big things from such an angelic creature to be spending five million dollars on her," he smirks before thrusting out his hand. "It's a clever way to launder money through your sweet mama's charity. If you don't wish to be bothered with her, I'm quite happy to take her out of your hands. I'm sure I can find a use for her." The sleaze winks at Katya as she peeks out from behind me, the tremble in her hand as she grips the back of my tux tightly, evidence of true fear.

There is no love lost between this man and my five-million-dollar date.

My hands curl into fists at my side as my anger increases, but it belies the lack of emotion in my voice as I remind him flatly. "I'm standing right here, Igor. If you wish to remain an Avtoritet, you will mind your manners, understand?"

"I beg your forgiveness, Mikhail. I meant no harm. If you have a use for her, then by all means." He shrugs, throwing his arms wide as if Katya means nothing to him. It piques my interest even more. *Why is he determined to get hold of her?* "I'll wait until you're ready to toss her to the curb, yes?" Igor turns to leave, before halting and looking back over his shoulder. "Be careful, Mikhail. Danger comes from the unexpected," he croons, before leaving the building.

I make a note to investigate why Igor is here when he's supposed to be searching for my father's murderer. His use of my first name was meant to irritate me. He's not under my direct supervision. His Pakhan is my cousin, Anton, who is in charge of Bratva in the southern region. He was loaned to me by Anton, who will learn of Igor's breach of protocol when I arrive home.

I don't care what time it is over there.

"Um, sir? Mr Korbicov?" Rachael, the woman who ran the auction, calls out to me, wringing her hands together.

"Yes? What is it?" I snap, gripping the top of my

nose between my finger and my thumb before sighing in frustration.

"There are a few more items you're required to sign off on before you leave tonight, sir." Her voice is a little shaky when she observes the frown on my face. "There isn't much, but it's important. I'm sorry for bothering you, sir."

I bite my lower lip, and take a breath, before nodding my head. It isn't Rachael's fault my cousin's people don't show me the courtesy they should. It isn't Rachael's fault I have a case of blue balls, either.

Henrí, aware of my frustration, grins cheekily at me before patting me on the shoulder. "Come on, let's get it over with."

"The next person who stops me leaving this building had better be wearing a bullet-proof vest, because I'm going to shoot them," I hiss at him, as I stomp back into the room, dragging Katya behind me. I'm not letting go of her in case she disappears again.

My cock is still hard as steel and she's going to take care of it tonight.

Finally, every signature is signed, every T is crossed, and I is dotted.

"Come, Katya, it's time to go home," I declare to the woman who hasn't left my side since I bought her at the auction. Not that she could, with Henrí standing behind her while I sit at her side.

Her head rises from the table where she's been leaning on her folded arms. She must have dozed off, as for a moment, she appears confused. "Home?" she murmurs, before her eyes widen, her eyebrows knitting together in a cute frown. "You're taking me… home?" she repeats.

"Yes, of course, I'm taking you home. You're mine for twenty-four hours, remember, malen'kiy olen'?" I remind her, before looking at my watch and correcting myself. "No … twenty-two hours, now." *Dammit, I need to get out of here.*

Katya eyes me suspiciously, as if she's going to deny me my prize. "I paid five million dollars for your company. Would you deny me? Or would you rather spend time with Igor?" I arch my eyebrows questioningly at her.

I know I'm goading her.

The way her big blue eyes narrow delights me. She's fiery, this one. Still, the way her face paled when she saw Igor bidding on her; her fear of him was palpable. I'll uncover what's going on there later. "Just because you paid a lot of money to spend time with me, it doesn't guarantee I'll land in your bed, Mr. Korbicov," she baits me back.

I lean forward, my lips close to her ear as I inquire, "Are you challenging me, Katya? There are not many people with that kind of courage. Or stupidity," I shrug as her eyes blaze even more with her anger, soaking up her fire, "to go against a Pakhan. The way you responded to my fingers in your cunt at the table, I don't believe I'll have any problems persuading you to climb into my bed."

Fuck, she has me hard with her rosy cheeks and her fiery gaze burning holes into mine.

I lean forward again. "Would you rather I find my dinner date and take her to bed instead?" I counter, before standing. "Let's get the fuck out of here." I crack the tension from my neck as I call her bluff. If this little witch thinks I would force her, or any other woman, to climb into my bed, she's wrong.

I take two steps away. "Wait." Katya's hand on my arm stops me. "My purse and coat are in the cloakroom."

"Henrí will ensure they're collected, malen'kiy olen'." I smile down at her as my hand closes over hers, holding it in place as we head to the front door of the banquet room.

7

─────

KATYA

I can't believe I allowed Mikhail to goad me into accepting his *offer* to go home with him. I berate myself silently, my hands twisting themselves into the material of my gown in frustration. *What was I thinking?*

Mikhail Korbicov paid five million dollars to have *me* for twenty-four hours. *Who am I to deny him?* It won't matter if I take some enjoyment for myself before I kill him.

What Father doesn't know won't hurt me.

Mikhail guides me toward the front entrance of the banquet hall, his bodyguards surrounding us. The remaining guests line up to say their goodbyes to him. He's gracious as he shakes hands with the men, air kisses the women's cheeks, and thanks them for coming and making his mother's charity a success once again.

They treat him like royalty, which, in a way, I suppose he is.

The jealous glares of some of the women as they spy

Mikhail holding my hand to his arm spurs me on. The fake smile plastered on my face as I stand beside the Bratva Pakhan others aspire to be is beginning to hurt. So are my feet in these shoes.

Mikhail's men walk ahead of us, scanning the surroundings, as we exit the banquet hall and walk down the steps to where several cars await us. A black chauffeur-driven limousine awaits Mikhail. *Of course, he wouldn't drive himself here.* There are four blacked-out sedans, two in front and two behind as Mikhail helps me into the backseat of the limo, before climbing in beside me.

The back door on the other side of the limo opens and Henrí climbs in, effectively sandwiching me between himself and my target. *Doesn't Mikhail go anywhere without him?* I glance over at Henrí as he clips his seat belt on without so much as a glance my way.

Henrí hasn't looked at me since Mikhail warned him off at the dinner table.

I fake a yawn as the car begins to move away from the banquet hall. Perhaps if I pretend to be sleepy, Mikhail won't try anything with me. Then again, if he doesn't, I may not get the chance to be alone with him.

"Tired, malen'kiy olen'?" Mikhail doesn't use my name often, instead, he insists on calling me *little deer.* Is he doing it as an endearment, or does he call all women this? Images of Mikhail calling the escort he came to the dinner with, little deer, flash through my mind, causing me to clench my teeth in envy.

"In case you've forgotten my name, it's Katya," I answer curtly, before remembering who I was snapping at. I sigh deeply before apologizing. "I'm sorry. Yes, I am tired. I get a little snappy when I am."

I yelp in surprise as Mikhail reaches for me, pulling

me onto his lap sideways as if I weigh nothing. My legs are now on the seat, and I'm facing Henrí, who smirks over at us. "Perhaps I should have ridden with the men?" he chuckles.

Mikhail ignores him as he slips one arm around my waist, the other gently holding my head to his broad chest. "Sleep, Katya. I'll wake you when we get home," he murmurs as I gaze up into his dark eyes.

I tense at the word *home*, intending to correct him when I inhale all that is Mikhail. The aroma of woody spices slips inside my nostrils. A feeling of safety and serenity seeps into me, and I forget my protests. I wonder if I've been drugged when I find myself relaxing my head against Mikhail's chest. *It's too late now*, I think to myself as I close my eyes and allow myself to drift off to sleep.

Through the fog of slumber, I stir as I feel myself moving. The crunch of gravel under heavy feet wakens me fully. I'm being carried, bridal style, towards what I know is Mikhail's home, because I know everything there is to know about him.

One must study their prey in order to kill them.

I stiffen at the thought. "Put me down, Mikhail," I say, my voice a little croaky from sleep. "I can walk."

"Not on this gravel, with bare feet you can't," a voice answers, somewhat coolly.

My eyes shoot up to find it's not Mikhail, but Henrí carrying me.

Where's Mikhail? How did I end up in Henrí's arms?

Something happened while I was sleeping. What did I miss?

I struggle, attempting to escape his hold, but he shifts my body to where I'm hanging over his shoulder like a sack of potatoes. "What are you doing?" I shout as I pummel his back, to no avail.

Henrí doesn't answer, and I fight to breathe as he stomps up the steps leading to Mikhail's mansion, each step knocking the wind out of me.

Once we're inside, Henrí continues up a flight of stairs and down a long hall before he finally stops. He lifts me from his shoulder, dropping me to the floor abruptly. I would have slipped and fallen, except his arm shot out at the last second, grasping my forearm hard.

"Why are you treating me like this?" My eyes narrow at him as I ask.

Henrí doesn't answer. Instead, he reaches behind me, while still gripping my forearm, and opens a door. He strides inside the room, dragging me with him. I scowl up at him and he returns the look.

"She's awake." It's not a question, more of a statement.

"You'll remain here until someone comes for you," Henrí orders coldly, far from the jovial man I was seated near at the charity banquet. Releasing my arm, he drops my shoes to the floor before heading for the door.

He's not locking me in here.

While he has his back to me, I reach under my gown for the resin pistol I strapped there earlier. My fingers fail to find it. The holster's empty. Could it have fallen out somewhere?

"If you're looking for your gun, you won't find it. Mikhail removed it while you were sleeping. Katya Ivanov, daughter of Pavel Ivanov." Henrí stands in the doorway facing me, his face schooled.

I'm not fast enough to cover my shocked expression, at which Henrí chuckles coldly. "Mikhail is not called The Raven for nothing. He's known you were carrying since he finger fucked you under the table. Goodnight, Katya," Henrí steps outside the door to the room as it closes between us.

Rushing forward, I try the handle in desperation. Gripping it with both hands, I twist it from side to side. It's all in vain.

I'm trapped.

I've accomplished nothing, except to be caught in my own web.

Searching the room for a way out, my frustration grows as I find the windows all locked. Wrapping my elbow in curtain material, I attempt to smash one, yelping loudly when I almost break my elbow instead. The glass must be toughened laminate. The mirror joined to the dresser is also unbreakable I discover, when I punch it hoping to use a shard for a weapon. All the furniture is bolted tightly to the ground and is made of metal instead of wood. There are even metal slats welded to the frame, under the king-size mattress on the bed.

I sit on the edge of the dresser and blow out a slow breath, my cheeks rounded as I do. My elbow throbs and my knuckles are bruised.

Frustration mixed with fear for what will happen to me when Mikhail appears tightens my chest. It won't take much to kill me and dispose of my body. Mikhail will probably order one of his men to do it. A Pakhan doesn't usually get their hands dirty.

Will they torture me in the hopes I know where Father is? They wouldn't have to. I'd gladly give him up if I knew. He's made sure we don't know where he hides. Father always visits us. Even when I was taken from my home to be trained to kill the Raven, I was blindfolded so I couldn't give away Father's location if I were caught.

Like now.

I glance around the room in the hopes of finding a miracle exit I might have missed the first, second, and third time I did it. The room, or prison, has been well thought out. Frustrated, I throw my shoes at the wall, watching them bounce off and onto the floor.

I'm probably not the first person to find themselves locked in this room. *Was Tomas held here before they beat him to death?* The Bratva wouldn't hold him in such luxury. He was more likely held in chains in the basement.

Is that to be my fate too? Slouching over to the bed, I flop backward onto the large, soft mattress. Lying on my back, staring at the roof, I berate myself. I should've realized Mikhail knew who I was.

How could I be stupid enough to allow myself to be captured?

How could Father make me believe I could do this? I never had a chance to take down Mikhail Korbicov. I was doomed from the start.

Natalia and I will never be free of our father.

Natalia. Tears spill over my lower eyelids and lashes, down my face, dripping onto the gown I was so proud of mere hours ago, as my heart fills with dread for my baby sister. Father will use her next. She won't survive and it's all my fault.

I failed to kill Mikhail Korbicov.

Rolling onto all fours, I crawl up the bed, bury my face in a pillow, and sob loudly until there are no tears left inside of me.

It's still dark when I open my swollen eyes. I must've cried myself to exhaustion. The room is pitch black, except for the moonlight streaming through the windows, casting shadows everywhere. I roll away from the window side of the bed and search for a switch. The lamp is hardwired into the wall next to the bed. It's not bright but lights up the nightstand where I notice someone has placed a bottle of water and two Advil.

My head's thumping. Without thinking about who placed them there, I throw the pills down my throat, swallowing them and half the bottle of water. After screwing the lid back on the bottle, I place it back on the nightstand.

I need to use the bathroom.

My headache's forgotten momentarily, along with my full bladder, when I sense I'm not alone in the room. Scanning the shadows, I find the outline of a large figure near the door. As if it can protect me, I pull the quilt up to my chin.

When did I climb under the quilt? I was on top of the blankets when I fell asleep, wasn't I?

"Who's there?" I call out, doing my best to sound brave.

The shadow doesn't move.

"You know who I am." Mikhail's deep voice surrounds me in the dark as he speaks, causing goosebumps all over my body. "And I know who you are."

Checkmate.

"Then you also know why I'm here," I state the obvious flatly. "How long have you known?"

"Tomas told me you would come," Mikhail's deep voice rumbles again, the words hitting me like a sledgehammer.

"You *liar*," I shout, tears once again prickling my eyes. "Tomas couldn't tell you who I am. He's never met me. Besides, he's *dead*. You *killed* him. I saw the proof. He didn't even know about us..." I hesitate, dropping the quilt, my hands curling into fists, my chest heaving as I force myself to be quiet. Maybe he's testing me. He can't know Tomas is my half-brother. I didn't even know I had one until he was dead.

"Who told you that? Your father? Tomas is not dead, Katya." Mikhail's voice is calm and controlled as he lies to me. "I should have killed him in retribution for what your father did. Your brother—"

"*Half*-brother," I correct him. Even though I don't believe the story he's spinning, I allow him to continue.

"Your *half*-brother," Mikhail continues flatly, "had no wish to harm me, Katya. Instead, he faced me like a man." I tense as he approaches the bed in the darkness, my body coiled, ready to spring at him the first chance I get. "Unlike *his*... *your*, coward of a father, who shot *my* father in the back of the head and ran away, Tomas met me face to face." Hatred for my father drips from each word as he attempts to convince me he's telling the truth.

"You beat him to death for telling you who he was? Was it his payment for being honest with the Raven? The almighty Bratva Pakhan, Mikhail Korbicov?" I spew at Mikhail as his long legs appear at the end of the bed. The dull light of the lamp and my kidnapper's height leaves his face shadowed and hard to read.

I involuntarily jump when a pair of large, meaty fists land on the end of the bed, as Mikhail leans into the light, staring me down. His shirt sleeves are undone and rolled up to his elbows, showing off tattoos covering his thick forearms. He could snap me like a twig with them if he chose to. "I. Did. Not. Kill. Tomas," he reiterates, his teeth clenched, his dark eyes blazing in the dim light.

"Okay, you had your Avtoritets, *Authorities, gang leaders,* and their killers do it for you," I snap, unable to stop myself. "Same thing. His blood is still on your hands. Father told me how your men killed your father and framed him for it." I'm probably digging myself into an early grave, taunting him, but my anger has taken hold.

Mikhail's eyes narrow at my accusation, his teeth clenched tightly, grinding as he hisses angrily, "*I* did not murder my father." He exhales a frustrated sigh before continuing, "And no one, under my authorization or anyone else's, killed your half-brother, despite your father's transgressions. He's alive and well, living under another name. Tomas told me how your coward father tried to use him to kill me."

"He also told him, if he failed, he'd send you and your sister to get what he has convinced himself is rightfully his. Pavel told Tomas if he didn't manage to kill me, your father would have you sacrifice yourself. He knew you'd agree to take over for Tomas if he used your sister against you. He promised you and Natalia freedom, yes? More money than you'd ever need if you killed me, yes?" He fires question after question at me. "It's called manipulation, Katya."

I can't keep up. How does he know Natalia's name? How does he know what Father offered us? Could he be telling me the truth?

No. He's called the Raven, the trickster, for a reason. It has to be lies. Father promised.

"*Stop it. Stop lying,*" I shriek. "Father is going to set us free. Natalia and I will finally be able to live our own lives. When he becomes the Pakhan, he will let us be. He promised…" My words sound hollow. I'm not sure if I believe the things coming from my mouth anymore.

"Natalia won't ever be free, Katya. Neither will you. Even if you succeed, by some miracle in killing me, you won't live long enough to save her." Mikhail sounds tired, his voice merely a murmur now.

"What do you mean?" The tremble in my voice is evident as a chill works its way down my spine. "What. Do. You. Mean, Mikhail. Save Natalia from what?" I ask my captor, my voice rising with each syllable. Mikhail could still be lying I tell myself, as my heart thuds erratically in my chest, my breath coming in short bursts.

"Our Father has pledged her hand in marriage to his cousin, Igor Popov, sister," a shadow in the doorway answers.

8

———

MIKHAIL

My intel was correct when I was told Pavel Ivanov was sending another assassin. His daughter from one of the many women he held power over with his fists and his money. The man is desperate.

What is a surprise, however, is how captivated I am with Katya, from my first sighting of her.

As she stood in the corner of the banquet room, checking me out, I was doing the same to her. Her long blonde hair, blue doe-eyes, and pouty lips, down her sleek neck to her unbridled breasts, over the curves of her hips, and down the long sexy leg peeking through the slit on the expensive gown she wore. Katya seemed more like a deer caught in the headlights than a cold-blooded killer.

My first impression was right. She's no professional killer. I could tell from the beginning. *What was her father thinking, sending an angel to do the devil's work?*

Katya had ample opportunities tonight to use the gun strapped to her thigh, but she didn't.

When I danced with her, she could have attempted to shoot me.

When I had my fingers in her hot, wet pussy she could have tried to kill me.

Katya wouldn't have succeeded in killing me, even if she had tried. Several of my men were watching her from the moment she was identified. Facial recognition is a great tool. She was completely unaware my men watched her every move.

When she fell asleep on my lap in the back of the limo, I removed the resin pistol she had strapped to her thigh. Pavel deserves kudos for thinking of it, if it *was* his idea, which I doubt. Resin guns aren't common.

Everyone at the function was put through a metal detector tonight, myself and Henrí excluded. The resin pistol Katya carried didn't register.

I was too angry to deal with her, so I had Henrí take her up to the room Mama was held in when Otets kidnapped her many years ago. It's escape proof, and there's nothing in there she can harm herself or anyone else with.

Slamming the door to my office, I stomp to the mini-bar and pour three fingers of Macallans, before dropping heavily into my leather chair. The whiskey is meant to be sipped, but not tonight. I down the drink in two gulps, enjoying the burn as it slides down my throat, before pouring another.

My feelings for Katya, a woman I don't even know, fascinate me as much as it bothers me.

If anyone else at the charity function had been caught packing, they'd be bleeding out somewhere in the darkness by now. Not her. My darkest thought of punishment for Katya is putting her over my knee like a petulant child and spanking her shapely ass until she can't sit on it.

I can't remember the last time a woman had my attention like this. My Otets once told me, "When you know, you know. Even if they don't."

He knew as soon as he met Mama she was the woman he was meant to be with for all time. The reason he isn't here with her anymore is because of Ivanov.

But I'm not Otets, and she isn't Mama. I don't need the burden of having a woman to keep watch over. Katya doesn't belong in this world. I need to fuck her and get her out of my system, I tell myself.

The instant Katya was identified, I had Tomas sent for. I hoped he'd be able to get through to her if I couldn't. The last thing I want to do is get rid of her, but I will do what's necessary.

Anguish shrills her voice over the reported death of her half-brother but it could all be an act. It appears Pavel's convinced that he's innocent of my father's murder.

She wants to believe he'll let her and her sister live normal lives if she does as he wishes. As long as she kills *me*. Her innocence weakens my disposition.

I'm no saint, I know this.

But I'm honest about who I kill and have killed.

When Tomas approached me, I was more than tempted to kill him in place of his cowardly father, but his honesty had me rethinking my decision. He told me everything his father planned to do, including taking over as the Bratva Pakhan. A position he wouldn't get without murdering me, my mother, and Henrí, who is the next in line if I die before him.

Tomas informs me Pavel Ivanov will go to any lengths to become the Bratva boss. It includes sending one of his daughters to assassinate me while gifting his other to an Avtoritet, Pavel's cousin, Igor, to pave the way for him to take my place.

If I wasn't a Pakhan, I wouldn't care less who was killing whom, nor would I care about women being traded for favors. It's commonplace in our business.

But I am a Pakhan. I am the son of Rinaldo Korbicov, a man murdered by a coward. The same coward who has lied to and manipulated those he's supposed to protect. And now, he has manipulated them into killing for him.

My teeth grind together hard enough they could chip, as my hate for Pavel Ivanov grows even more, if that's possible.

It's time for him to die.

"W-Who are you?" Katya asks dubiously, her eyebrows knitted together as she peers into the semi-darkness.

"It's me, Tomas, Katya." A switch flicks on, flooding the room with light. Katya and I both blink as we become accustomed to it.

"How do I know you're not lying?" she asks, frowning in confusion as her half-brother steps closer.

Tomas removes a photograph from his jeans pocket and hands it to her. I watch Katya closely as she scans the picture of Tomas and her father standing together on a beach somewhere. Her eyes flick from the photo to the man in front of her and back as she looks for similarities. She's purposely ignoring me, which pisses me off.

Henrí enters the room and stands behind Tomas. Even though he's been a great informant, Henrí doesn't trust Tomas one hundred percent yet. After all, Pavel's blood runs in his veins.

"How can this be?" Katya contests. Her large blue doe-eyes widen further, if possible, her eyebrows now arched in shock. "I saw you lying dead. Father showed me a picture…" Katya's gaze switches from Tomas to me finally, her mouth moving, but no sound emitting. She seems lost for words.

"Henrí set up the photos, Katya." I move around to sit on the edge of the bed as I fill in the blanks. "We hoped his son dying might anger him enough to bring him out of hiding," I explain, before sighing heavily. "Instead, he sent you."

Katya's eyes narrow at my words as if I've offended her.

There's silence for several moments as her eyes, which are locked on mine, show numerous emotions.

Unexpectedly, her voice changes to panic. "Natalia." Katya's voice cracks. Pulling her to my side, I wrap an arm around her waist. She struggles for a moment before settling. "I have to find Natalia. Igor mustn't get his hands on her. Please," she pleads, her small fist gripping the front of my shirt tightly. "You have to let me go. Igor, he's a bad man, Mikhail." Tears stream down her face as she gazes up at me.

"When I was young, he…" Her voice trails off before she pulls herself together with a large inhale of air. "He used to visit from time to time. He'd take Mama into another room, and we'd hear her crying and begging. When he left, she had bruises, and she'd be in pain for days. One day he came…" Katya moves back from me a little. I don't like it, but she appears to need some space, so I allow it, removing my arm and resting my hands on my thighs. She sits back on her heels, her head lowered, avoiding everyone's eyes for a few moments. Her plump lower lip is sucked inside her mouth for a moment, and I watch in mesmerized silence. When she pops it out again, it glistens in the light.

"What is it? What did he do?" Tomas demands, his face pale, his voice hoarse, as if he's afraid to know. No wonder this man, no more than a boy, couldn't bring himself to kill me. He can't hide his soft side. I question how these two even came from Pavel Ivanov's seed.

Katya quietens for a moment, and she closes her eyes as if in prayer, her hands now clasped together beneath her chin. Blood thickens in my veins while my heart beats an unsteady rhythm as I brace myself for what I'm about to hear. "He-He…" Her head drops as her cheeks flame with embarrassment.

Pinching her chin lightly with my finger and thumb, I guide her face up to mine. "Look at me, Katya," I murmur gently. She does as I ask. "Tell me. There's no one going to hurt you," I add, keeping my voice as steady as possible, not wanting to startle her with the murderous anger boiling within my veins.

"He made me do awful things, Mikhail. He told me

he would do them to Natalia if I didn't agree. We were children." The pain in her hoarse voice hits me in the heart like nails. "I told father when he came, and he called me horrid names and beat me. He told me it was my fault for seducing him." Her eyes flick between mine as large rivers of tears flood from them. "I didn't seduce him, Mikhail." Katya's head shakes from side to side. She pleads with me as if I won't believe her, just as the man who should have protected her didn't. Her tiny fists curl tightly into my dress shirt as if she fears I'll walk away. "I didn't…" she repeats faintly, as I pull her onto my lap, much like I did in the back of the limo, folding her tightly in my arms.

Henrí watches me, a puzzled expression crossing his face. I shake my head at him lightly. *Not now.*

I hold her to me, kissing her head tenderly as her tiny body is wracked with heart-rending sobs. "He'll never hurt you or any woman again, Katya," I proclaim as she lets out the agony she's been holding inside.

Eventually, the sobs subside to hiccups, then to quiet snores as she exhausts herself. I lay her gently on the bed, wanting nothing more than to curl up beside her.

Not yet, I tell myself as I lead the other two men from her room.

"Tomas, you stay with your sister," I order. "If anything happens to her, I'll come for you. Understand?" If anything harms Katya, her brother will wish he was dead. Which he will be.

Tomas nods. He's not a stupid man, nor is he a coward. It took guts to face me with his father's ridiculous plan. Pavel Ivanov always thought he was better than my father. I tried to warn Otets, but he trusted his best friend. By the time he realized Pavel was conniving behind his back, it was too late.

One of my men is instructed to stand guard outside the door as a safeguard. Unlike my father, I don't trust easily.

Placing a call, I instructed Kristina to pick up Katya's suitcase from the hotel she was staying in. She won't be needing the room.

Normally I'd have my Avtoritets and their thugs do my dirty work, but this is personal. Pavel and his cousin Igor are going to die by my hand.

I've placed a call to my Avtoritets to spread the word to their street people. It's a matter of time before we know exactly where Igor Popov is.

Torturing him for what he's done to Katya will be an honor. He'll also tell me where to find his cousin before he dies. Henrí, always in sync with me, rubs his hands together in anticipation of what's to come.

It's been a while since either of us saw some action.

In the early hours of the morning, Henrí seeks me out. I'm in the gym, working out my anger and frustration on a punching bag. I've not slept more than a few hours since watching Katya's beautiful, pained face while hearing the distress in her voice as she told us what Igor did to her. Katya didn't need to go into details. I can read between the lines.

People have begged me for their lives, some for

death, and there is probably the blood of innocents on my hands. It's the dark underworld of the Bratva, which I accepted when I rose to be the Pakhan. What I *don't* understand is why Katya affects me like she does.

What would it be like to fuck her, to have her sweet pussy clamped around my cock like a vise, I wonder, as my cock swells uncomfortably in my sweats.

Stop it, I tell it silently as I palm my throbbing cock. I don't need the complications of a woman to interfere with my head.

As for Katya's cowardly father, her flesh and blood. To blame her for his cousin's actions shows him up as the weak bastard he is. As if I couldn't hate him enough for the death of my Otets. For the way he has treated his daughter, I'll pleasurably wipe him from this earth.

It's been two whole days since Katya admitted everything, and still, we don't have either Igor or Pavel. It appears someone has leaked to Igor that I'm looking for him. When I find out who, they'll be punished right alongside him.

Moles are common in the Bratva. Loyalty is hard to find.

Pavel showed his true colors when he shot my father from behind. Of course, he wouldn't stand up for his daughter after his cousin did those things to her. I slam the punching bag hard enough to break the chain holding it to the roof, sending the bag crashing to the floor several feet away from me.

9

———

MIKHAIL

"Whoa, I hope you don't ever get that angry with me, moy drug (droog), *my friend*," Henrí's eyebrows arch as he jokes with me, trying to lighten my dark mood. "I thought you might need this." He tosses me a bottle of water and I catch it in one hand, screw off the lid, and swallow half the bottle, before pouring the rest over my head. The coolness drips down onto my bare shoulders, back, and neck. "Igor has been located," Henrí informs me. "Do you want to do this yourself, or do you want me to do it?"

"Was he with his cousin?" I growl, ignoring the question for a moment.

"No, but intel says Pavel's been seen in town. Every available man is on the ground, Mikhail. We'll have him soon," my friend informs me. "Our people know what he looks like. He won't escape this time, brother." He claps me on the shoulder in reassurance.

"I've come up with an idea of how to bring him to the

surface," I state. I'm not happy about it, but the need to catch Pavel is overpowering and I'm willing to try anything.

"What's the plan?" Henrí's head jerks up, his eyes meeting mine. He knows by the tone of my voice it's something distasteful to me.

"We have bait, right here in this house. If we do it right, he'll come to us." I lay out my plan for Henrí. He's as unhappy with it as I am, but desperate times call for desperate measures.

Making my way upstairs to Mama's quarters, I acknowledge the guard at her door with a nod before entering her room. Stepping to the side of her bed, I gaze down at her frail figure. Asleep beneath her perfectly folded blankets, she looks peaceful. Her hair is down and neatly braided, while her face is soft with the calm of slumber.

The temptation to bend and kiss her on her forehead is strong, but I don't want to wake her. If she doesn't recognize me, the fear of having a stranger in her bedroom at night would be terrifying for her. For a few moments, I remain motionless, watching her breathe. The steady rise and fall of her chest calms the turmoil in my head.

I'm not sure how long I watch Mama sleep. Minutes? Hours?

Retreating from the bedroom, I vow, "I love you, Mama. I do this for you and Otets." Closing the door, I turn away and head down the stairs.

KATYA

Natalia's been promised to that animal, Igor. Tomas is alive and I'm locked in a bedroom in Mikhail Korbicov's home.

Mikhail hasn't been back since he left Tomas with me. I'm not sure what's going on, but I don't like it.

Food and beverages have been delivered to the room, but each time the person leaves, the door has been relocked. They brought Tomas a mattress, pillow and blanket. They also brought my suitcase. I don't know how they knew where to find it.

At least the room appears to be temperature controlled.

Although it's given Tomas and I time to get to know each other a little, over the past few days. He's told about the great times he had with his mother and our father. Tomas probably thought we led the happy rich life he did, but we didn't. He already knows some of the great times we had. It's not his fault I know, but I can't help but be somewhat jealous of him. Although we did both end up here.

I'm going stir crazy not knowing what's happening outside. I want out of this room.

I've failed Natalia. In a way, I failed everyone. I let my hormones rule my head. Now I'm a prisoner of the Raven.

Mikhail knew who I was all along. He knew when he first saw me at the charity banquet, when he danced with me, and when he had his fingers inside me. My cheeks burn at remembering how Mikhail made me feel then.

But now, I feel dirty. Used.

Not only by my father and Igor, but by Mikhail as well.

There has to be a way to get out of this room, this house. Natalia's out there somewhere. Perhaps she's already in Igor's filthy paws. I shudder at the thought. I don't want him to do to her what he did to me. I'm not my mother, I can't stand by and let that happen.

"Tomas," I plead with my half-brother. "I can't stay here. Natalia needs me. I have to go to her. I…"

"She needs *us*, Katya. I'm your blood too, remember? But how?" Tomas cuts me off, waving a hand at the door. "Even if we get out of this room, we won't get out of the house. There are cameras and sensors everywhere. How do you suggest we get past them?" he huffs, sounding as frustrated as I am. "Not to mention, Korbicov's goons."

My shoulders slump in despair. I don't want to admit it, but Tomas is right.

The conversation has dried up when the door opens and Mikhail strides in, flanked by several men I haven't seen before. One is carrying a leather bag; another carries what appears to be a folded wooden chair. Henrí enters moments later with two more men. My eyes flick to each individual before traveling back to the man in charge. Mikhail. He towers over everyone else, his large form commanding the attention of everyone in the room, including me.

The white button-up he wears is tight across his chest, clinging to the muscles beneath and untucked at the bottom. Both sleeves are rolled up, tattoos covering almost every piece of skin on his forearms, hands, and long, thick fingers. Fingers that know how to please a woman. The thought causes my thighs to clench. I'm curious to know if he has more tattoos beneath his shirt, but even though I strain my eyes studying his massive frame, I can't make any out. His long hair is down and damp, hanging in waves past his shoulders as if he has recently showered.

He has on a faded pair of black jeans and black work boots. It's not something I expect a Pakhan to wear, but the jeans hug him in all the right places. My abdomen squeezes in desire at the sight of him.

Henrí places the chair at the end of the bed. Without saying anything, he points at Tomas, clicks his fingers, and points to the chair. Tomas rises from the bed without protest and sits, his chest to the back of the chair. "Shirt off." Henrí finally speaks.

Tomas complies without question, but I have plenty.

"What's going on? What are you going to do to my brother?" My voice rises with each syllable, my fear for Tomas choking the words from my throat. *I've only just found him, please don't take him from me*, I plead inside my head, determined not to show them my fear.

Mikhail doesn't answer my question, he doesn't even glance my way. His face is void of any emotion as he states flatly, "*Half*-brother."

"Hold him still," one of the men states as he pulls something from his bag before approaching Tomas from behind. Henrí stands by holding his phone. He turns it on and begins videoing. First, he videos Tomas from the front, then moves behind him.

I can't see what's going on behind Tomas, but there's a buzzing noise coming from something in the hand of the man standing closest to him. Two men move forward, holding Tomas' arms. It's not forceful, but it does render him immobile. The man with the buzzing implement approaches Tomas, my brother flinching as the instrument touches his skin.

"A tattoo?" I glance over at Mikhail. "Why are you tattooing him? What are you tattooing on him?" I snap, my eyes narrowed on the man in charge.

"My ownership," Mikhail answers flatly, his face blank. "You're next."

His off-handedness offends me. "I belong to no one," I hiss. "What happens if I refuse?"

"Then you'll be held down and the tattoo will happen anyway." Mikhail's lack of emotion scares me more than the tone of his voice. "It's your choice, Katya. You can do it the easy way or the hard way." His cold stare cuts right through me.

"Why do we need to bear your brand?" I argue. "Tomas has been upfront with you," I remind him.

"You're both mine, now. I own you. You'll wear my brand to show this." *What happened to the caring man who was here when I confessed the awful things Igor did to me and my father's treatment when I tried to tell him? Why is he doing this?*

"You'll have to tie me to the chair. If I wanted your brand on me, I'd ask for it."

MIKHAIL

"As you wish, Katya," I reply off-handedly.

I hate that she's going to fight me on this, as much as it excites me. She's full of sass for such a tiny being.

Katya's dressed in a workout top, along with black gym leggings and runners. Precisely the type of clothing she may need if my plan works, and I've pushed her into escaping.

Everything she has on is tight and I can see every curve of her body, and the mound where her hot, little pussy awaits me.

Not yet, I tell myself.

Tearing my eyes away from Katya's tight body, I pull my phone from my pocket and place it to my ear, pretending I have a call. "Yes. You've seen him? And the girl? Okay, we're on the way." I signal Henrí. "They have Igor cornered with the girl. Let's go."

"What about them?" Henrí points to Tomas and Katya, playing his part excellently.

I point to Flav, my tattooist. "Finish before you leave this room, understand? Her too." I wave my hand carelessly at Katya, knowing I'm angering her.

Only the men closest to me wear the tattoo marking them as mine. Although my wish to mark Katya as mine is strong, it's an elaborate ruse to push Tomas and Katya into escaping. I'm sure someone would get word to their father they'd been seen. If he has an ounce of humanity in him, surely he'll reach out to them. If, or when he does, we'll take him prisoner.

I'd been called away on business. Someone has been messing with deliveries. Some of my men have been found dead. When I arrived back, Henrí and I decided we'd give Katya and her half-brother the push they needed to escape. That way they won't have to try to pretend to be evading us when they meet up with Pavel.

"We have to go. Now." I stride from the room as if I'm on a mission, Henrí and the other men following me, ensuring the door is unlocked as we leave.

"Do you think it'll work?" Henrí questions me quietly as we move.

"We won't know until it happens," I answer honestly.

I'm sure Katya will make a move as soon as she knows the door's unlocked. She loves her baby sister, I'm certain of it.

KATYA

Igor has Natalia. That's what Mikhail said, wasn't it? He had to be talking about Igor. I can't sit by and do nothing. If they go after him, Natalia could be caught in the crossfire. I must go to her, but first I have to find a way out of here.

"Have you done many tattoos?" I ask the man bent over my brother's back, concentration obvious on his face as he places the Raven's mark on Tomas' skin forever.

"Longer than you've been alive, probably," he mutters without looking up.

I climb off the mattress and walk around to the end of the bed, still feigning curiosity. "Exactly what are we being marked with?" I'm trying to lull him into a false sense of security.

"A Raven, of course," the tattooist quips, as he wipes at the blood rising from the needle digging into Tomas's skin. I take a few steps closer, my confidence building when the man doesn't recognize me as a threat.

I can see Tomas' back now. He has no other tattoos visible on him, unlike me. There's a vine tattooed down my spine with my mother's, Natalia and Tomas' names entwined in the leaves. I had Tomas added after Father told me he was dead; killed by Mikhail.

The tattooist is good. I guess I thought he'd be some half-assed street tattooist, not an actual artist. If he forgives me for what I'm about to do, perhaps he might have time one day to do a tattoo for me. One I want.

As soon as I'm in position, I make my move. Because I'm not a large person, surprise is the best way for me to take a man down. Stepping up directly behind the tattooist, I wrap one arm around his throat, grab my forearm with my free hand, and squeeze. The tattoo gun slips from his hand as he stands, and I grip him around the waist with my legs as tight as I can.

"Ouch, what the..." Tomas shouts as the needle scratches his skin. He bounds from the chair, his eyes wide. "Katya, what the fuck are you doing?" he yells as the man I'm trying to put to sleep twists and bucks, trying to throw me off him. I squeeze his neck harder.

No matter how fast it happens in the movies, knocking a man unconscious with a sleeper hold is not quick or easy. The tattooist bangs us into the wall, cracking the plaster, trying to knock me off him, but I stick to him like white on rice. I'm going to have some bruises tomorrow. The tattooist is losing pace, I can feel it. His hands reach up and behind him, as he tries to get a grip on my hair, but I've had it pulled many times. It doesn't loosen my hold on him.

Finally, he goes to his knees, then stops fighting as his body crumples to the floor, unconscious. I take the laces from my sneakers and tie his arms and legs. Patting his pockets, I search first for a weapon, which I don't find, then for his wallet. Removing a wad of cash, I tuck it in the band of my gym pants, Tomas watches wide-eyed as I move to the door.

"Katya, you'll get yourself killed out there." Tomas gasps as I move toward the door. I'm surprised when I turn the doorknob and it opens. Peeking out into the hallway, I expect to see someone standing guard, but there's no one.

I'm about to step outside the room I've been locked in for several days when Tomas grabs my wrist. "Where are you going?" he asks, confusion obvious on his face.

I glance at his hand before glaring up at him. "If you want to be Mikhail Korbicov's bitch, then stay here," I hiss. "But I'm going after Natalia. I promised myself she would never be involved in all the shit Father has caused."

For a few moments, we're frozen in a stare-off before Tomas grabs his t-shirt, slipping it over his head before picking up his jacket. "You're crazy if you think I'm letting you go alone. What sort of brother do you think I am?" he huffs as if he has a right to be angry.

I don't answer him. Truth is, I don't know what sort of brother he is, because I don't know him. This could all be some elaborate trap. I guess we'll find out soon enough.

10

____

MIKHAIL

"Tʜᴇʏ'ʀᴇ ᴏɴ ᴛʜᴇ ᴍᴏᴠᴇ." Hᴇɴʀí ᴀɴᴅ I'ᴠᴇ ʙᴇᴇɴ keeping an eye on the cameras since we left Katya and Tomas in the room with the tattooist. I have to give it to my girl. She's a fighter. It took guts to attack my man and bring him down.

I know she didn't kill him because you don't tie up dead men with shoelaces.

When she reached the door, I thought Tomas was going to get cold feet. I was hoping he didn't take after his old man by letting Katya tackle all this on her own. Not that she'll be alone. There's a tracking device in Tomas' pocket for good measure.

I'm surprised when instead of heading down, Tomas indicates they go upstairs instead. The hairs on the back of my neck prickle as I watch them move cautiously.

Mama is up there.

Henrí's hand grips my shoulder. "She's safe, my

friend," he murmurs gruffly. "There's Kristina and an armed guard in her room, in case."

I sigh loudly, pushing the air from my lungs in gratitude.

Katya and Tomas must be heading for the back stairs. I don't know how they know about them. Perhaps Pavel showed them a blueprint of my house. My fists clench in anger as I wonder who else he's given this information to.

Pavel knows this house like the back of his hand. Of course, he would have drawn a map of it in case Tomas or Katya found it necessary to attempt to kill me here. He probably gave them orders to kill Mama also.

I saw the way he used to watch her when she was with Otets. He wanted her. I didn't understand back then. At the time I still had some naivety, but Pavel took away any innocence I had. I know Mama loved my Otets. She would never have considered another man.

Henrí and I keep our eyes on the cameras as the pair of *fugitives* descend the back stairs cautiously. They have no weapons other than their hands, and I've ordered my men to remain out of sight and not to stop them.

I know I was the one who suggested we use Katya as bait, but I'm not happy about it. If anyone can flush Pavel out of hiding, it will be her. At least this way she'll have backup if anything goes wrong. I couldn't care less about her *half*-brother, but I'm sure Katya loves knowing she has more family.

Listening to the anguish in her voice when she thought I had Tomas killed practically brought me to my knees.

I know I'm no angel, but how can a father do what Pavel has done?

KATYA

We move as fast as possible to get out of Mikhail's compound before it's discovered we're gone. This has been all too easy I tell myself as I scale the fence surrounding the Korbicov compound. Tomas thuds down next to me. He had to lift me onto his shoulders so I could climb over the spiked metal bars without causing injury to myself.

The air outside has cooled around us and with each puff of breath we exhale, vapor clouds escape.

I hadn't given much thought to the weather, and I'm still dressed in a gym top, leggings, and joggers. Tomas has a t-shirt, leather jacket, jeans, and work boots on. I'm going to have to find a jacket, otherwise, I'll freeze my butt off.

"What now, Katya?" Tomas' voice invades my thoughts.

No sooner does he speak than the compound lights flick on high. Shouting ensues, along with dogs barking. *They've discovered we're gone. We have to move.*

"Come on." Tomas grabs my hand and we run. At least I'll warm up.

Car doors and engines pierce the stillness of the night. To evade Mikhail's men, we dive into the tree line beside the road. The compound is on the edge of the city. It'll take us a while to get there unless we catch a ride. We can't take the chance of it being one of Mikhail's men. They'll be everywhere. We have to proceed with caution, while at the same time, we need to find Natalia as soon as possible.

Spotlights flash through the trees and I pull Tomas to the ground. They skim over where we lie in the long grass and bushes before moving on. As soon as they disappear, we sprint further into the woods, not stopping until we reach a small house. Everything is dark within, and I'm guessing the occupants are sleeping. There's an SUV parked outside in the driveway.

Running my hands all around under the wheel hubs, while Tomas looks for something to break the glass with, I give myself a silent high-five when my hand locates what I've been searching for. "Found it," I whisper-yell to my brother as I discover the key for the SUV.

Unlocking the door, I climb inside, placing the gearshift in neutral so we can push it further away from the house before we start the motor. Once we have, I toss the keys to Tomas. "You want *me* to drive?" he sputters. His eyebrows arch in surprise at my answer.

"I would, but I don't know how to," I admit. Our family could never afford a car. Money was always tight, despite Father being impeccably dressed at all times. I guess it costs a lot of money to have more than one family. "I hope you do," I add. We'll have to do a heap of walking if he doesn't.

"Of course I do," Tomas huffs belligerently. "I used to drive Father's Porsche all the time."

"Well, lucky you," I snark sarcastically. *A Porsche?* He always came to our house by Uber. Ignoring Tomas' odd look, I climb into the passenger seat while my brother gets behind the wheel and turns the ignition on.

He doesn't turn on the headlights until we're a few miles away.

"Katya?" Tomas murmurs.

"What?" I blow out a breath.

"I'm sorry I didn't know about you or Natalia. I always wanted to have brothers and sisters. I hate him for not telling me about you both," he rambles.

I feel bad for believing he was spoiled, while Natalia and I missed out on everything.

Sighing loudly, I answer him. "I'm glad we have a brother, Tomas. It's not your fault Father treated us as he has. It's no one's fault but Father's. Now turn the darned heater on before I die of cold." I try to lighten the situation for a moment.

There's nothing we can do about the past, but we can undoubtedly make our own future.

As soon as we reach the city, our work begins. Igor was at the charity banquet. Hopefully he's staying in a hotel nearby and hasn't left town yet. If he is here, it would probably be somewhere nearby. And it would have to be swanky. Igor doesn't strike me as being the type to stay in a sleazy, bedbug-ridden place.

Tomas and I visited five top hotels, and I'm beginning to lose faith when we finally hit paydirt. The concierge was happy to inform us our cousin had stayed there, but he and his band of thugs had checked out not long before we arrived. He mentioned there was a young woman with them. She didn't seem happy about being with Igor, but when the desk clerk asked her if she was okay, she nodded.

I asked the concierge for a description of the young woman. He told me we looked similar, my knees growing weak when he described Natalia.

Where did Igor take her?

"The old guy with the blonde boasted about a wedding. She didn't seem happy about it," he shrugs, "but without her asking for help, there's nothing I could do for her."

Over my dead body is Igor marrying Natalia.

"My thoughts exactly," Tomas mutters. I hadn't realized I'd spoken out loud. *At least we're on the same page.*

"Where can you get married fast around here?" I demand of the concierge, who finally seems to realize this is an urgent situation.

He makes a list of a few places for us. This is no Las Vegas, but it does have a few available venues close by. Lucky for us, they're all in the same general area. Tomas pulls a roll of money out of his jeans pocket and pays our helpful friend. The concierge greedily takes the payment, stashing it in his pocket. Nodding to Tomas, he then dismisses us, turning his attention to people waiting at the desk to sign in.

Tomas and I don't have mobile phones since Mikhail's men confiscated them. Next door to the hotel is a phone store. Tomas purchases one with immediate startup. While he sets it up, I slip into a clothing store and buy a warm jacket and sweatpants. The air is freezing now, and my teeth are beginning to chatter.

Tomas meets me as I step out the door of the clothing store. "I punched in all the addresses the guy in the hotel gave us," he states, seemingly happy with himself. "Are you ready?"

I nod. "We don't have any weapons, but Igor and his men are bound to be carrying. We need something to protect ourselves with." We should've searched Mikhail's place for weapons before we left, but we couldn't take the chance of being caught.

"We'll deal with it when we get there. Let's go,"

Tomas urges. "If we wait any longer, we could be too late. Once Igor is married to Natalia, they'll be gone.

11

———

MIKHAIL

WE STAY BACK FAR ENOUGH TO KEEP AN EYE ON KATYA and Tomas as they move from hotel to hotel, searching for Igor Popov. Pride swells in my chest for the tenacity she has shown in her escape from my estate, even though it was set up for her. She must know Igor well to know what type of places he would hang out in.

"We should have allowed them a weapon," Henrí mutters.

"And where do you suggest we leave it for them? On the back stairwell? Under a neon sign saying, *we let you go on purpose so you could lead us to your father so I can kill him*?" I snark at him gruffly. I may want to fuck Katya, but I'm not stupid enough to trust her with a weapon. Watching her put down the tattooist shows me how cunning she can be.

The innocent act could merely be an act.

I haven't stayed on top this long believing everyone who feigns innocence around me.

"Do you trust her?" Henrí inquires, turning to face me in the close quarters of the black SUV we are sitting in.

I tap the top of the door panel in frustration, my brows knitting together in thought. *Do I trust her?* "Do I believe she loves her sister? Yes. Do I believe she was messed with by Igor? Yes. I also believe she mistrusts her father," I answer honestly. "But do I believe she will betray him? I'm not sure. Blood is thicker than water."

My friend nods silently.

"But you want her?" he adds after a few moments. Glancing over at him, I note the smirk on his face.

"Shut the fuck up or I'll shoot you in the foot," I growl. Henrí knows I don't mean it, and the fucker starts laughing and singing.

"You want to kiss her, you want to fuck her," he sings off-key. I pull my gun and sit it on my thigh. Henrí chuckles, but thankfully, he shuts up.

It would hurt me deeply to have to shoot him.

KATYA

Tomas and I haven't gone far when I sense someone watching us. I speed up my pace, Tomas walking alongside me faster as I do.

"What's got you spooked?" he mutters as we practically break into a jog.

"Someone's following us," I puff. "Next alleyway, we head into it, okay?" I'm not asking. Ever since we left the hotel, I've had this prickling sensation. It has served me well at times, so I'm going with it now.

As one, we break left at the next alleyway. A few seconds later, a man I remember seeing seated on a lounge chair in the foyer of the hotel where Igor had a room, steps warily into the shadowy alley. Tomas and I hide behind a dumpster, our ears on high alert. The man's footsteps edge steadily closer as I fumble around to find something to defend us with. There's nothing.

Tomas jumps out from our hiding place, seizing our stalker by the arm and taking him to the ground. He pounds his fists into the man's face, but the other guy gets the better of him. Pulling a gun from his holster, he aims it at Tomas' face, clicking the safety off. Tomas halts all movement.

The man stands and signals for Tomas to stand up and step back, before pointing the gun my way. He signals for me to step over to where my brother now stands, and I comply. I'm not stupid. I know he has the upper hand. Still covering us, he pulls out his phone with the other hand, speed-dialing someone with his thumb. "I got them. Bring the car."

MIKHAIL

Henrí and I both spot the goon following Tomas and Katya as they leave the hotel. I assume they're ignorant of him until the pair pick up their pace before ducking into an alley.

"Should we go help them?" Henrí rubs his chin with his finger and thumb as he asks.

My mind says yes, but something tells me they'll be okay. "Not yet," I answer. "We need to see what's going to play out. I'm sure Pavel knows Tomas is alive by now. It might bring him out of hiding." They better not hurt Katya, or I will tear them limb from limb.

We don't interfere when a dark sedan pulls up across from the alleyway and Katya and Tomas are frog-marched toward it before being forced into the back seat. The goon has a gun on them as he too climbs into the car, sitting beside them.

"I count six in the car counting your girl and the skinny one," Henrí murmurs as he puts the gearshift into drive. There is no love lost between him and Tomas. If he'd had his way, the boy would be dead now. He doesn't understand why I wouldn't sanction it.

Henrí was with me and Mama the day my Otets was murdered. He was also there when I swore my vengeance on Pavel Ivanov and his family. I meant every word of it until Tomas came to me and admitted what he was supposed to do.

Bratva isn't known for forgiveness. But it's not forgiveness Tomas sought. He asked for nothing when he told me everything he knew. He told me he expected me to shoot him. It was his bravery in facing me, knowing at any time he could expect a bullet as a thank you, that stayed my avenging hand.

Tomas strikes me as being too soft, to be of any threat. If my judgment of him is wrong, which I doubt, I'll kill him myself, regardless of my feelings for his half-sister.

I can't afford feelings. I can't show my enemies weakness. The Bratva is not a breed to become soft in. There are always people on the sidelines waiting for the chance to bring another down so they can step up.

It's similar to a hyena pack. As soon as one becomes weak, the others attack and kill it.

This is the life of a Pakhan. To continue, I must remain strong and fearless.

"They've spotted us." Henrí's voice breaks into my thoughts. "They're speeding up."

He punches the accelerator, and we weave in and out of the traffic, following our prey. The car in front unexpectedly takes a right turn from the left lane, causing several cars to collide, effectively ending our chase.

I jump from the car. "Get every man we have in this area, now. I'll try to keep up with them. You've got the tracker. It'll show you where to go."

Henrí doesn't like what I'm doing, but fuck him, I'm the boss. Slamming the car door, I take off on foot. They won't be expecting me.

Admittedly, it would be easier if I were wearing my joggers, but I'm not. I jog along the footpath, keeping my eyes glued to the car holding Katya. I can't let her down. I promised no more harm would come to her, and I meant it.

Visions of her being shot and bleeding keep me moving despite my leather shoes pinching my aching feet. For the amount of money they cost, you'd assume they'd be comfortable in all situations.

Lucky for me, I tower above most of the passers-by, which makes keeping sight of the car easier. The sedan turns into an alley on the right, two blocks away.

Once I reach it, I slow to a walk. No point rushing straight into an ambush.

Taking a deep breath, I steady myself before stepping into the alley, my eyes darting into the murky shadows.

Is there anyone waiting to shoot me? There's no noise, so I continue creeping along the wall toward the car. When I reach it, it's empty. The dark sedan is locked and parked near a closed door. Stepping closer to the door, I listen first, my ear up to the thick wood. Hearing nothing, I try turning the doorknob. It's locked as well.

Exiting the alley, I check what type of buildings are in the street. The one the locked door belongs to appears to be a chapel. The perfect place for a wedding.

My heart thumps in my chest with glee at the thought Pavel might be inside. After all, would he miss the wedding of his youngest daughter to his cousin? He believes it's his stepping stone to taking my place as Pakhan.

I know I should wait for Henrí and the rest of my men, but the anticipation of ending the life of my Otets' murderer is overwhelming.

The chapel is squashed in between a pizza shop and the alley. The bluestone exterior is a vast contrast to the brick and concrete buildings surrounding it. A sign at the door states, *'God forgives everyone."*

God's not going to forgive me for what I'm about to do.

Not wanting to put myself in danger of being shot as I enter, I take care as I sidle up the steps to the front doors, shaped as arches, open wide to the poor and the lost. I am neither.

Visions of my Otets still seated at his desk, his head half blown off, surprise etched on his dead face, haunt me as I enter the little chapel. My Mama sobbing, her head in his cold lap, fills my thoughts, along with visions of me, standing near frozen, watching on as Otets' men peel her from his dead body so they could take him away.

Mama remained sedated even on the day when we buried Otets. It was like she couldn't imagine life without him, and she was never the same. I lost two people the day Pavel killed my father.

Now it's time for payback.

12

TOMAS IS DRAGGED FROM THE CAR BY TWO GOONS who had been sat in the front seat. Meanwhile, the man with the gun pokes it hard into my ribs, letting me know he wants me to climb out of the car as well.

We're rushed inside an open door, which slams loudly behind us, the sound of a lock clicks once we're inside a darkened room. Blinking quickly, it's mere moments before my eyes become accustomed to the dimness.

"Well, well. What do we have here?" an all too familiar voice echoes. "How can this be?" Father feigns surprise as he cocks his head to one side. "My son, Tomas, has risen from the dead. It's truly a miracle, yes?" The sarcasm is obvious in his tone.

Tomas steps forward to say something when the sound of the doorknob turning behind us breaks the spell Father holds over everyone. A hand covers my mouth and I'm shoved forward into another room, more brightly lit than the last. Tomas arrives behind me in much the same manner. Another door closes behind us.

"Igor, look who has come to witness your wedding. Isn't it wonderful?" He claps Tomas on the back as if welcoming an old friend. "They've even risen from the dead to be at this momentous occasion. Eh, Tomas?"

Natalia sits on the end of a front pew. She doesn't glance our way at all. My gut clenches.

Narrowing my eyes on Father, I snarl, my anger palpable. "What have you done to my sister?" I have to save her. She doesn't deserve this.

He chuckles loudly as he steps closer to me, answering my question. "Your sister is fine. She's looking forward to being married, aren't you, Princess?"

Natalia echoes his words like a mimicking parrot. "Looking forward." Her lack of emotion scares me.

"See? Now we're all here. Let's get this done. Igor, where's the minister?" Father calls to his cousin, who appears from behind the altar with a small round man dressed all in black, wearing a white collar. He isn't held at gunpoint, but he does appear nervous.

Father claps his hands before rubbing them together in what appears to be glee.

"No," I screech, twisting and fighting to break free of the man holding me.

A familiar chuckle stills me for a moment as Igor Popov appears in front of me. "Ah, Katya. Are you jealous, little one? You could always be my mistress." The foul stench of his breath fills my nostrils, taking me back to a time I never want to remember. "We had such fun all those years ago, didn't we?" He turns to Father. "I could facilitate your rise to power a little quicker perhaps, if you are willing to do a two-for-one deal?" Igor's eyebrows arch questioningly.

"Like hell, you will," I snarl at him. "You've done enough damage to my family. You're not happy hurting me or Mother. Now you want to hurt my sister as well. You sick mother—" My head snaps sideways as Igor slaps my face hard.

"You will mind me, Katya. I will be your father's second in command when he becomes Pakhan. You will show me respect," Igor hisses at me.

"You deserve no respect." Tomas joins the conflict. I couldn't love him more if he were my full-blood brother right now. "What you've done to my sisters is disgusting. You won't touch Natalia—Oof." His argument is cut short when Father punches him hard in the stomach, winding him.

"You're all useless," Father snarls at Tomas and me. "I should've drowned you all at birth. I should've shot your mothers when they told me they were pregnant, fool that I am," he continues his rambling. "As soon as Igor is married to Natalia, I have no use for either of you. You're deadweights."

Tears form, but I won't let them fall; I refuse to cry in front of these assholes. Besides, this is not the time.

I wish I was back in Mikhail's compound, warm and safe, but I've burned that bridge. He won't forgive me for hurting his man and escaping his clutches. I've made a fool, perhaps an enemy, of him now. Tomas would be safe and well also if we had stayed put.

But we did escape. I can't allow my sweet baby sister to be subjected to the monster Igor Popov is. I will lay down my life to keep her safe.

Everyone has their eyes on what's happening at the

front of the church except myself and Tomas, who are off to the side. The goons' concentration on us lapses as the bogus ceremony begins when a reflection on one of the church walls catches my eye. Someone else is here.

Maybe they'll go for help.

Maybe they won't.

I check the tight group we're being held prisoner in to make sure no one else has seen what I did. *Was it my imagination?*

"Let's get this over with, Pavel. I'm tired of waiting," Igor growls, gripping Natalia's wrist tightly as he wrenches her off the church bench and onto her feet. She staggers a little as if she's drunk but makes no protests about her rough treatment. Wrapping an arm around her waist, Igor pulls her tightly to his side.

With all that's been going on, it hadn't clicked until now that Natalia is dressed in a familiar white gown.

"Ah, you recognize the dress, Katya, no?" Father sneers when he observes my eyes narrowing. He approaches me as more vile words pour from his mouth. "It was your mother's. She bought it in the hope someday I would marry her. It was never going to happen." He shrugs both shoulders as he cocks his head to one side. "Perhaps if she had given me boys, eh, who knows? She won't be wanting it now, anyway. The dead don't need wedding dresses. Stupid woman thought she had a say in what I do with my children."

Goosebumps rise on my skin at his last few comments "You killed Mama?" The shock of his words turns my voice raspy, the words spat out like rusty nails. Despite the fact she wasn't a great Mom, she was the only stability we had. A solitary tear escapes my eye, dripping from my lash onto my cheek before rolling down my face. "Did she know you're marrying my sister to a pedophile… to a rap—" The slap he delivers to my face is harder than the one before, if possible. My feet falter, my skin heating and burning from the force of it, but I stand steady.

I can't stop the tears this time though, and my father's eyes light up with glee.

"Ah, Katya, this is the problem." He dares to laugh, the sound hollow and eerie in the echo of the church. "Women believe they should have a say in how their life will be." I flinch when he cups my burning cheek and stares into my eyes. The crazed look in his tells me there is no winning here. "Preacher, get this service over with," he orders without looking away from me. "I have some *cleansing* to do." His wolfish smile tells me Tomas and I are not going to get out of this alive.

Mikhail should have killed Tomas. At least he wouldn't have to know how much of a monster our father is.

Tomas and I are held at gunpoint to witness the proceedings. The need to throw up is overwhelming, but I take deep, slow breaths in an attempt to control my nausea.

I turn my head away, not wanting to witness the travesty about to happen, but the goon next to me won't allow it. He transfers the hold he has on my wrists to one hand while he grips my face between his finger and thumb, turning it back to where Natalia stands. "Your father told you to watch. Do as you're told," the goon declares in my ear. "Before he disposes of you, your father might let me have you for a little while. He licks the side of my face from my jaw to my ear.

I grimace as my stomach rolls, acid rising in my

throat as I swallow hard. I will not give them the satisfaction of watching me throw up.

MIKHAIL

I'm too far away to make out whatever they're talking about at the front of the church, but the sound of a slap reverberates around the church. I'm holding position behind a large pillar near the front doors, waiting for the chance to slide behind one of the thick church benches for better cover.

Henrí and more of my men are on their way here, but they have to come on foot, due to the traffic being at a standstill. My second-in-command is communicating with me via a Bluetooth earpiece. I can't answer him, but I tap out texts on my watch.

Henrí tells me traffic lights have been hacked, causing collisions everywhere. This will be the work of Pavel. He always was good with electronics.

This is his way of keeping us from discovering where he is until he's ready to make his move. He's out of luck though, because I've found him and I'm not letting him get out of here alive.

All has gone quiet at the front of the church and when I poke my head out from behind the pillar for a second, I observe them all standing in front of the altar. At the back of the group is Katya, being held by an armed man. He grabs her face twisting it forward, appears to say something to her, and then licks the side of her face. The fucker will lose his tongue before he loses his life, I'll make sure of it.

If I thought I could do it without Katya being hurt, I'd charge the group and shoot them all. Instead, I wait for backup. For now, I'll compartmentalize my anger until I can unleash it. All hell will break loose then, church or no church. I tap out a message asking where the hell everyone is. Henrí doesn't answer.

I duck down and crawl on my elbows and stomach to the rear bench seat. When I'm sure they're all concentrating on what's happening at the altar, I slip under a few more seats until I'm about halfway to the front of the church. It's not easy for a man my size to move quietly, but I'm well-practiced at it.

Crackling sounds in my ear and Henrí's voice asks me where I am. He's at the front of the church with some of our men. More are in the alley near the side door. The car in the alley has been disabled in case anyone makes it outside and tries to use it to get away.

I message him to let him know my position, and before long, Henrí slides up beside me. We can see what's happening up the front from our position. Someone asks who gives Natalia's hand in marriage to Igor. My trigger finger itches when the pompous voice of Pavel answers the question.

We don't have much time.

13

———

MAYBE I'M HOPING FOR A MIRACLE, BUT I SWEAR I CAN feel Mikhail nearby. *Please let him come,* I beg the statue on the cross above the church altar.

He promised he wouldn't let anyone hurt me again. *Were they meaningless words? Is he angry we escaped, and he's leaving us to fend for ourselves?*

No, I tell myself. The escape was set up, I'm sure it was. It was too easy to get out of the compound. Mikhail is no fool.

Did he let us escape so he and his men could cut us all down? It would be easy to do. Mother is dead. All the family I have is here in the church. Mikhail could exact the revenge he claims he's owed for Father killing Rinaldo.

"Before this farce goes any further, I've got a question, Father" I cut the man in the black robes off in an attempt to stall, hoping someone is coming to stop what's happening. "Did you kill Rinaldo Korbicov?"

It works momentarily.

Father turns to me, his eyes blazing, his voice filled with anger. "Why are you asking me this? Would I kill my best friend?" Father makes out like I've offended him. He steps toward me, his eyes burning holes in mine as he halts in front of me. "Rinaldo Korbicov was never my friend, Katya. He was merely a means to rise through the ranks of the Bratva faster than I could on my own. Pretending to be his best friend was the hardest thing I've done, next to fathering cowardly children who cannot follow orders," he sneers.

His hands grip the front of his undone jacket as he leans closer to my face. "Yes. I killed Rinaldo Korbicov. I would've killed the entire family except one of his Avtoritets was watching. He saw me shoot Rinaldo and called in reinforcements immediately. I should've known there was a hidden camera in Rinaldo's office. My so-called best friend never mentioned it. Where was the trust?" he snaps as if he's offended that he wasn't informed about the camera.

Bile rises in my throat as Father brags openly about the killing. "It was after a large shipment Mikhail was in charge of, had arrived. Rinaldo sat in his chair behind his big fancy desk, smoking a cigar, excited his precious son was showing such promise as the next Pakhan. I was pouring us drinks at the bar when he commented on how Mikhail would be a good Pakhan, able to step straight into his father's shoes."

Father feigns shock as he focuses on the memory. "I asked Rinaldo why Mikhail, why not me? *I* had been his second for years. *I* deserved to be the next Pakhan." His clenched fist thumps on his chest with a hard thud, while his face turns red with rage at the memory of that day.

"Rinaldo told me he didn't believe I would make a good Pakhan. He said my pride would get in my way. Despite my challenging him, Rinaldo declared his word was final. He laughed it off, saying we were getting too old for this shit; we needed to retire and enjoy our lives while we still could."

Father huffs. "I spent a good part of my life positioning myself to be the next Pakhan. I decided to prove him wrong. Holding the coveted position of Pakhan takes cunning and the will to destroy anyone who gets in your way. So, I did the one thing to prove myself worthy."

He raises his finger as if it's a gun, pointing it at me as he relives the moment he murdered Mikhail's father. "Pop, pop." He mimics the sound of a gun. Twitching his thumb as if it were a trigger, an evil chuckle escapes. "And it was done. I don't know why I didn't do it earlier." Father cocks his head, smirking at me as he finishes his confession. "You could have been the daughter of a Pakhan, Katya. Unfortunately, you and your brother have shown your disloyalty to me. You'll be disposed of as soon as this..." he turns away from me, snarling at the man in the black robes, "*damn wedding* is over with."

Pointing at the priest, Father shouts, the noise louder in the near-empty church. "Get these vows over with. *Now,*" he yells. "I'm a busy man."

Tears tumble down my face as the horror of it all catches up with me. My father killed Mikhail's father. He's lied to us the whole time. I was sent to kill Mikhail. I could have taken my gun out of its holster and completed my task at any time. Then I would have been exactly like my father. I could've murdered Mikhail for nothing.

Now my baby sister is being married off to a monster, and my brother and I are probably going to die at the hands of our father. *Had he planned this all along?*

A click behind me halts my pity party. I dare not turn around or the goon holding my wrists will know something is up and warn everyone. Tomas is standing side-on to me, with a gun in his ribs. Glancing over at him, I catch his eye and I try to signal to him with my eyes that help is here. He frowns, unsure of the meaning at first, then nods slightly.

"It's over, Pavel. Lay down your weapons, you're surrounded." Mikhail's deep voice is distinctive above the priests as I make my move.

MIKHAIL

Listening to Pavel brag about how he murdered my Otets, and the plans he has to rid himself of Tomas and Katya is more than I can take.

We're going to have to get it right this time because there isn't going to be a do-over.

I could care less about Tomas, but Pavel will pay for what he did to Otets and everything else he has planned to do. Never in my life have I held this much hatred for one person.

Henrí has orders to take both Pavel and his cousin Igor alive, if possible. The men have been told not to harm Katya or her sister.

As soon as I show myself, Katya springs into action. She may be a tiny thing, but she's a fighter. Her body goes limp, and the goon holding her, reacting in shock, releases her hands, probably intending to catch her as she falls. Instead, she reaches for his gun, yanking it from his hand, and shoving it in his face, bringing him to an abrupt halt.

Tomas is now wrestling for the gun the guy holding him hostage had and they fall to the floor, curses from both soaring through the church.

Igor drags a young woman resembling Katya by the arm, toward a door behind the altar. My target, Pavel, has four of his men surrounding him as they shuffle him behind the church altar as well.

"Pavel," I yell as I fire my gun. It misses my mark but brings down one of his shields. I feel the burn of a bullet, but my adrenalin is pumping so hard I ignore it. Firing round after round, I continue to shoot at my father's murderer, the men shielding him dropping one by one. Pavel makes it to the door behind the altar and, using the thick wood of it as his shield while he fires back at me. A bullet grazes the side of my head and for a moment everything blurs, but my overpowering need to bring Pavel down spurs me on.

The door he hides behind is solid and my bullets aren't penetrating it. Pavel's, however, shatter pieces from the stone altar I'm crouched near, spraying them in my face. I can't get a solid shot at him. I spot Henrí sneaking around the other side of the altar, using a statue as cover. I'm reloading when I glance over to find Pavel aiming his gun away from me. Turning to see what his target is, I spot Katya standing over the guy who held her hostage, who is now on the floor.

Pavel's gun is aimed at Katya.

He's going to shoot his daughter.

"*Katya*," I shout, diving toward her. A gun goes off,

and something slams into me from behind with the force of a linebacker, right before everything goes black.

KATYA

Everything that happens next almost appears to be in slow motion.

Father uses the sacristy door as a shield from the bullets fired at him. When the shooting stops momentarily, he stands and aims his gun at me. It all happens as if in slow motion, when Mikhail, the man who had held me prisoner shouts my name at the same time he dives between my father and me. Instead of the burn of a bullet, I watch on, frozen in place, as Mikhail's body shudders before falling to the ground with an echoing thud.

It takes a moment for my mind to process what happened. Mikhail took the bullet my father meant for me. He saved my life. I stand frozen as I wait for Mikhail to move. He doesn't.

Raising the gun in my hand, I roar in anger mixed with a little fear, aiming at the door where my father had been standing moments before. I fire bullet after bullet until the gun is empty, and Henrí does the same. But the door has closed, and I don't know if we hit him or not. I want to kill my father for what he's done, but the need to find out if Mikhail is alive or dead is more important.

Tripping over my own feet, I reach Mikhail's prone body, lying on the altar steps. "Mikhail?" His name barely escapes my lips, my voice hoarse and trembling, my chest tight with dread, as I kneel at his side. Raising my face to the ceiling in an attempt to hold back tears, the face of a man on the cross peers silently down at me. I'm an omnist, and at this moment I pray Mikhail will have a pulse. Pressing my fingers to his throat, I feel for one.

It's there, but faint. I thank the statue above me. "Someone help me," I call out, my voice sounding foreign, even to me.

Mikhail's second in command, Henrí, has followed my father through the sacristy doors and shouts and thuds echo all around me. A man I recognize as one of Mikhail's men kneels beside me. He taps his ear, murmurs something unintelligible, and seconds later Henrí and several other men appear around us.

"He's alive," I croak as Henrí's eyes meet mine, calm but questioning.

Henrí steps into Mikhail's role, ordering the men around. They don't argue. It takes several more men than it did to carry Tomas. Mikhail is a large guy. Eventually, he's picked up and taken out of the same doors Tomas and I were dragged into the church through. I don't want to leave Mikhail's side, but I have to know what happened to Natalia and Tomas.

"Henrí, please take care of Mikhail. I have to go. I—" Henrí scowls in my direction, cutting me off.

"You stay with us," he growls before softening his voice. "Your brother and sister are outside. We got Igor, but your father escaped. He climbed up onto the roof and disappeared," he adds as if in answer to my unasked questions.

Although I breathe a sigh of relief Tomas and Natalia are safe, I cannot pretend the fact my father got away doesn't affect me. Father admitted to murdering Mikhail's father as well as killing my mother.

He tried to kill me too.

The car we were brought here in is still in the alleyway. The engine is running and the back door is open. Henri motions for me to climb in. After some difficult maneuvering, they get Mikhail through the exit door of the church, before gently loading him beside me. I rest his head on my knee, cupping his cheek as I will him to open his eyes, but he doesn't. Henri clambers into the front seat with the driver and tells him to take us to the compound.

"Mikhail needs a hospital. Take us there. *Now*," I demand. He could be dying, but I refuse to say the words out loud.

"We have everything we need at the compound," Henri replies calmly, locking eyes with mine in the rear vision mirror. "Hospitals ask too many questions.".

I remain quiet after my initial outburst. It's obvious Henri is now in charge, and he isn't going to listen to me.

I lean over Mikhail, whispering, "Thank you for saving me."

It might be the one chance I get to say it. Once we're at the compound, who knows what's going to happen to Tomas, Natalia, and me. I wouldn't be surprised if we're lined up and shot for our part in Mikhail being wounded. The Bratva are not known for their understanding.

After all, Tomas and I did escape, even though I'm sure it was a setup. But if we had stayed put, Mikhail wouldn't be lying here hurt right now.

But if we had stayed, Natalia would be married to Igor now. Who knows what he was going to do with her once she was his. His treatment of Mother and myself is enough for my imagination to send my stomach roiling, bile rising in my throat.

Mother.

Father boasted about killing her.

I allow a solitary tear to drip from my eye and roll down my cheek. Mother wasn't always present, and when she was, she was usually drunk. Though she was never mean to Natalia and me, she wasn't exactly loving either. I guess dealing with Father and Igor, she had become numb. We didn't understand our lives weren't normal until recently, when Father decided we would become pawns in his sick game of chess.

It seems like a lifetime ago that Natalia and I were living what we thought were normal lives. Natalia was at school, while I worked as a dressmaker in a local clothing repair store to help make ends meet and pay for Natalia to go to college. She was always the smart one of the two of us.

If Father ever gave Mother money, Natalia and I knew nothing about it. Mother held jobs here and there, but her drinking would eventually interfere. She was unemployed more often than she was employed. She wasn't the best of mothers, but she was the only parent I had growing up. Father was rarely around. Mother had her faults, I admit, but still, I'll miss her. I'm sure Natalia will too.

***

The drive back to Mikhail's compound is fuzzy. My mind picturing my father pointing his gun my way, replaying over and over in my head.

The cars line up out the front where a team of people

dressed in what appears to be medical scrubs are waiting with a hospital-type trolley bed. Mikhail is lifted from the car and placed on it. He hasn't opened his eyes or made a sound the entire ride here. His skin is pale, despite being well-tanned and there is blood all over his white shirt. *How can someone lose this much blood?*

I remain in a stupor in the back seat, not wanting to leave the sanctity of it. Mikhail had treated Tomas and me well, but I'm unsure of the reception we three will now receive from his second in charge and his men.

After all, I'm to blame for him being in the situation he's now in.

Henrí startles me when his head pops into the car, his green eyes somber. "Get out," he commands, his hand reaching for me. I slide across the seat toward him. There's nowhere for me to go, nowhere to run. Mikhail isn't able to save me now.

The jovial man who sat smiling cheekily at me at the charity banquet table has been replaced with a dark, formidable man. Henrí has transformed into the man he needs to be to control the situation in the absence of their Pakhan.

By clicking his fingers and pointing, Henrí signals two men over to where he has pulled me from the car. "Take them." He nods to where my brother and sister are stepping from another car. "Put them in the room for now."

I should voice my protest. Instead, my head bows in sadness. I want to be with Mikhail, but it isn't going to happen.

What happens next stuns me.

14

One of Mikhai's men grabs my bicep tight enough for me to cry out. Henrí steps forward and tears his hand off me. "She's not yours to touch. Understand?" he snarls in the man's face.

Turning to me, Henrí's face softens. "I'm sorry, Katya," he apologizes. His eyes drop from mine as he scans my body. It's not in a dirty way. Instead, he appears to be looking at something. "Are you hurt?"

I'm confused by his *Jekyll* and *Hyde* attitude. The guy grabbed my arm, and it hurt, yes, but the worry on his face is a mystery. Henrí places a finger under my chin, lifting my face toward his. "Are you hurt, Katya?" he asks again with purpose.

I frown at him. *What does he mean?*

"The blood. Is it yours?" Henrí waves his hand down the length of me. Glancing down, I realize my clothes are covered in it. Tears fill my eyes and before I can stop them, they tumble down my cheeks, dripping onto the stones under my feet.

"It's not mine." A sob tears from me. "It's Mikhail's." I tremble as the events of the day finally hit me. Unable to control myself, more sobs break free. My knees wobble, but before I hit the ground, Henrí scoops me up, and carrying me bridal style, he strides toward the house.

"Is Mikhail going to die, Henrí?" I whisper hoarsely, not bothering to hide my tears. "It's all my fault, I should not have—"

"You did what we allowed you to do, Katya. Your escape was enabled by Mikhail and me," Henrí mutters, cutting me off as he climbs the stairs. Despite my weight, he doesn't appear to be breathing heavily. "Your father shot Mikhail, not you."

He stops outside a closed door, gently placing me on the floor before punching a code into a panel on the wall, and the door swishes open. I don't know whose room this is and I'm unsure what to do, so I stand meekly by Henrí's side, brushing my tears away.

"Go shower, Katya. I'll have fresh clothes brought up for you," Henrí instructs smoothly. His hand on my back gently urges me inside, and I step into the room. The door swishes behind me and when I turn around, the door has closed, Henrí is gone, and I'm alone.

Despite my sadness at Mikhail's injuries, I'm in awe of the room I now stand in. My swollen red eyes widen as I check out my surroundings before heading to the shower. It's a colossal bedroom. The sheer size of it would probably take up the entire area of the home I lived in with my family.

Windows on the far side begin at floor level, taking

up the entire space of the wall before curving at the top to take the place of half of the ceiling. It would be a beautiful view on a clear, starry night.

A large king bed sits against the white-painted wall to my left and is positioned directly beneath the glass ceiling. The coverings match the color of the wall next to me, which is a denim blue. A pure white sheet is folded over the cover at the top of the bed. Everything is neatly tucked beneath the mattress and several matching pillows, are perfectly placed at the head of the bed.

There's not a wrinkle in sight.

The bedroom has all the markings of being decorated for a man. The furnishings are minimal, consisting of dark wood forming the frame of the bed and bedhead. Bedside tables are placed on either side of the bed and a dresser against the denim blue wall near the door matches the wood of the bed frame.

There are two dark wooden doors of the same color as the furniture to the right of me, and I'm guessing one of them is a bathroom.

I can't help myself when I open a door and find it's a walk-in robe.

My conscience tells me I shouldn't look, but I can't help myself. A gasp escapes me with the realization this is Mikhail's bedroom. If the size of the neatly folded clothes doesn't convince me, the size of the shoes does. Not even Henrí is as big as Mikhail. I discover several colognes lined up, and unable to resist, I open each bottle until I find his familiar scent. Not caring if it's frowned upon, I pick up a neatly folded black t-shirt, pour a few drops of Mikhail's cologne on it, and lay it out on the bed before heading for the other door.

The bathroom itself is larger than the bedroom Mother, Natalia and I shared back home. It's been decorated with a rainforest theme. The roof is glass similar to the bedroom, but the walls are what appears to be real stone, with real moss and ferns growing between them. On the floor are smooth pebbles and the shower itself is a waterfall. A half wall to the right of the room blocks the toilet area from view.

When I catch sight of myself in the full-length mirror on the wall, the day's events hit me with full force. My eyes, though still red and swollen, are not what takes my breath away. I'm covered in Mikhail's blood. Not a part of me, except my lower legs and sneakers, are exempt. I must've had blood on my hands when I brushed my tears away, as there are streaks of it on my face. Turning my palms up, I can now see the dark dried patches of blood on them that I hadn't spotted earlier amongst the turmoil.

Mikhail's blood is truly on my hands. I turn away from the mirror as memories of him assault me. Mikhail, holding me close as we danced at the charity. Mikhail, large and scary, standing at the end of my bed when I woke the other night, which then blends into him lying lifeless on the backseat of the car.

Tearing the clothes from my body as fast as I can, I turn the waterfall shower to as hot as I can bear before stepping under it. The products in the shower belong to Mikhail of course, which makes me cry harder as I use them to scrub the blood from my skin. I shampoo my hair as well, while huge sobs roll through me. After washing, I let my body crumble to the floor, the water still flowing over me.

I'm unsure how long I've been here when a soft voice calls my name. A woman I don't know reaches in, turning off the taps, before helping me to my feet. She clucks and murmurs soft words I don't understand, as she uses a large, soft towel to dry me off. Wrapping my long, wet hair in one, and my body in another, she leads me out of the bathroom into Mikhail's room.

The woman asks me to raise my hands and she slides Mikhail's t-shirt over my head; the one I poured drops of his cologne onto. I scrunch my hands in the material, bringing it up to my nose, filling my lungs with Mikhail's scent.

The woman smiles softly.

"Who are you? Do you know if—" I start, hesitating when she places a hand on my shoulder.

"I'm Kristina, Henri's mother," the woman answers with a beautiful French accent. "Mikhail is fine, Katya. He's awake and asking for you."

"He's awake? Are you sure?" I'm relieved he's alive, my heart thumping erratically in my chest as my throat tightens. At the same time, I'm surprised, with the amount of blood he lost. I don't say this out loud because I'm afraid it might still happen.

"Yes. He demands I bring you to him as soon as possible or he'll get out of bed to come and find you." Kristina laughs softly. The lines around her mouth and eyes give away her age. The light reflects off her shiny red hair, which is twisted into a perfect French roll and pinned with a large comb. Her light brown eyes are surrounded by thick, dark lashes and she wears a neutral tone lip gloss. Tiny freckles dance across her nose and cheeks, which are void of makeup.

Kristine directs me to follow her. As I do, I notice a long scar down the back of her right arm, but I don't say anything. It's another reminder the world of the Bratva is a dangerous one and that I need to always be on my guard here. These are not my friends. At the moment, the only people I can trust is my sister. Tomas has shown his disregard for my father, but I am yet to fully trust him. After all, he did turn his back on his own father.

If it came to it, would he do the same to me? I don't want to believe so.

My mind turns to what's ahead, as I walk behind the French woman on my way to Mikhail. Is he going to be glad to see me, or will he blame me for his wounds? There's no more time to reflect when Kristina stops at another door panel. As Henrí did, she taps in a code, and the door opens. Mikhail lies on what appears to be a large hospital bed. Machines are hooked up to him and beeps and bells are sounding from a large screen showing lines and numbers of red and green on it.

"You told me he was okay," I protest to Kristina.

"No, child. I said he was *awake*. Now go to him." She smiles gently as she steps aside.

I'm filled with dread as I walk with lead-laden feet to the side of Mikhail's bed. As soon as I sit in the chair provided, his eyes open, locking on mine. I reach for his hand and tangle our fingers together.

Mikhail's normally deep-tanned skin is pale. His right arm is in a sling and there's a large bandage wrapped across his wide, bare chest and up over his right shoulder. There's a deep gouge along the left side of his head, which has a sticky-looking, yellowish ointment on it, but no bandage. It runs from a fraction below his temple, along his head above his ear, stopping at his hairline where his hair grows longer. His long hair has been plaited, the bottom of the plait lying over his right shoulder.

How many times has he been shot? I allow my eyes to roam his body for a moment, to where the blankets have been folded mere inches above his abdomen. The beginning of a dark trail of hair starts at his navel before disappearing beneath the folds. An eight-pack has me catching my breath as I ogle it, before resting my eyes on his large pectoral muscles. His broad shoulders make the pillow behind his head appear smaller.

Not an inch of his upper body is void of tattoos except his neck.

When I reach his face, I ignore the smirk on his perfect, thick lips, scanning his strong, A-line nose before coming to rest on Mikhail's dark chocolate-colored eyes surrounded by thick, dark lashes. Butterflies flit around in my lower belly. If the man wasn't injured, I'd love to rake my fingernails down his thick body, listening as his breath hitches, while we have sex.

"Hey, where did you go, malen'kiy olen'?" his soft voice interrupts my dirty daydream.

If I thought all the tears I held inside were gone after my snotfest in the shower, I'm mistaken. Blinking fast, I try to stop more from falling, but one escapes, plopping onto my cheek before sliding down toward my chin. Mikhail untangles our fingers, lifts his hand to my cheek, and wipes it away with his thumb. Bringing it to his lips, he licks the salty fluid away. It's so damn sexy I want to jump him, and if he weren't wounded, I prob-ably would.

"Are you crying over me, Katya?" Mikhail croaks, his voice hoarse.

"You saved my life. No one has ever cared if I lived or died before. My father intended to kill me today. You took the bullet meant for me," I reply, my voice trembling. Picking up his large hand, I raise it to my mouth, kissing Mikhail's knuckles. "Thank you."

"I know how you can thank me properly, malen'kiy olen'." He smirks, two dimples indenting his cheeks.

"I will do anything you ask of me, Mikhail, but not until you're well enough. You've been shot." As if he needs reminding. "Once you're well, you can take what-ever payment you require from me," I inform him, my cheeks burning as I lower my eyes to the floor. If sleeping with him will pay my debt, then it's what I'll do. It's not as if it would be a hardship, the man is built like a god.

"Katya," Mikhail growls, his fingers tightening on mine, bringing my eyes back to his. He's no longer smil-ing. Instead, he seems angry. I frown at the swift change in his mood. "I thought you wanted me, too" he snaps. "It has nothing to do with… *payment*." He spits the word from his mouth as if it has a bad taste. He releases my hand and attempts to sit up, wincing with the effort.

The machine begins beeping faster as the numbers on the screen rise rapidly.

I've upset him. He shouldn't be upset in his condition.

Unsure of what's happening, I rise from my chair as people dressed in scrubs enter the room and rally around his bed. One checks Mikhail's pulse, while another presses buttons on the screen.

Someone in a white coat asks me to leave until they get things under control, and I rush to the door. I don't look back, even when Mikhail calls my name.

As I wander along the hall, I try to analyze what just happened. Although I've known Mikhail for a short time, it's as if I've known him forever.

I touch my cheek where he wiped the tear from my

face earlier as I contemplate his mood swing. When he's being gentle, Mikhail calls me malen'kiy olen', *little deer*, but when he's angry, as he was just now, he calls me Katya. He's hot and cold and I don't know which Mikhail I'll get from one moment to the next.

The men I've been with were jerks who took me on dates and then expected sex in return. When I refused, some took it anyway. Igor, Father's cousin, did the same when he came to Mother's house. None of them cared whether I was willing, so why should Mikhail? I owe him my life, so I guess if he wants to take payment from me that way, I won't fight him. For some reason it doesn't scare me as much as I thought it would.

Kristina appears from a doorway, pulling me from my thoughts. "Katya, is something wrong, child?" she inquires.

I confide in her regarding what had happened in Mikhail's medical room. "Perhaps I should leave," I sigh when I'm finished explaining.

"Is that what you want? Mikhail doesn't wish for you to leave," she informs me as she slips one of my hands in hers, giving it a light squeeze. I'm not used to people caring and I don't know how to react, so I remain silent. *How would she know what Mikhail wants? Has he said something?*

Kristina peers at me strangely before reaching out and placing her hand on my arm. "Come. I'd like you to meet someone." She steps back through the door, tugging me along with her.

The room we enter is spacious, as are all the other rooms I've been in. There's a king-size bed, neatly made up, against one wall, while on the other side of the room, there's a white leather set of armchairs and a two-seater couch. A thick rug is set on the floor, a small wooden coffee table sits in the center of it.

A fireplace with a fake fire glowing inside it gives the room a homely feeling. It has the same type of windows as Mikhail's room, rising from the floor and curving until it covers half of the ceiling.

Over by the window, Kristina and I stop beside a rocking chair. On it sits a frail-looking woman with perfectly coiffed gray hair. She glances up at us and I gasp.

"Lana, I've brought you a visitor." Turning to me, she introduces us. "This is Svetlana, Mikhail's mama," Kristina indicates to the woman in the chair, and then to me. "And this is Katya," she croons smoothly.

Svetlana turns her head to gaze up at me. "It's nice to have a visitor. How are you?" She smiles. "Come, sit. It will be nice to speak with someone other than my friend here." She giggles excitedly, indicating the seats near the faux fireplace. Kristina smiles, nodding her head in the direction Svetlana did.

Strolling over to the couch, I take a seat while Kristina assists Svetlana out of her chair and escorts her with one hand on her back, the other holding her hand as they walk over to where I'm sitting.

Once her ward is seated comfortably on an armchair, Kristina steps over to me and whispers in my ear, "She's having a good day today." After straightening up, she holds her hand out to me. "Here," she presses a pager into my hand. "There are some errands I must tend to. Press this button if you need me." With that said, Kristina leaves the room, but not before one of Mikhail's men enters and stands inside the now closed door.

I'm a little put out that Kristina felt the need to have

someone keep an eye on me. But then I remind myself not long ago, Father had convinced me to kill Mikhail and his mother.

Not anymore. I'm done bending to my father's will.

Intelligent green eyes land on mine. "How long have you been with my son?"

15

———

KATYA

I'M RELIEVED WHEN A MAID ENTERS WITH COFFEE, cream, and sugar on a tray. She pours our drinks, only speaking to ask how I'd like mine. As soon as she has finished her duties, she retreats without being told.

Svetlana takes a sip of her coffee before speaking. "So, you are Mikhail's girlfriend?" she proclaims, shocking me slightly.

"I–I, no… I'm…" I don't know what to say, or how to say it. Placing my coffee cup on the table, I search for the right words. "Mikhail saved my life. I'm indebted to him."

"Hmm," she hums. "He's not one to place himself in danger for someone he doesn't think highly of. Is that his shirt you're wearing?" Her eyes roam to my clothing and I gaze down, suddenly remembering all I'm wearing is underwear and Mikhail's t-shirt with his cologne on it. I glance up at Svetlana, finding a cheeky smirk on her lips, her eyes glittering with humor.

"Oh." My cheeks heat as I search for a way to defend what I'm wearing. I don't want to blurt out that I was sent to Mikhail's room instead of the one I had been locked in when I first arrived. "I–I," I stutter. I can't tell her Mikhail was shot saving me. "I needed a change of clothing and didn't have anything with me, so I borrowed Mikhail's shirt," I blurt, hoping she doesn't ask why I needed a change of clothing. I wouldn't lie to her, but I don't wish to purposely upset her.

"It's okay, darling. I used to wear Rinny's shirts when he was away, too." Svetlana reaches over, patting my hand soothingly. "I used to put a few drops of his cologne on my pillow at night, so I could surround myself in his smell while he was away on business. It comforted me when he wasn't home."

Oh my gosh, she's talking about her husband, Rinaldo.

"He's dead now, my Rinaldo. His best friend killed him. Shot him from behind." Sadness coats her voice, as her eyes well up with tears. She reaches for a tissue, wiping her eyes before the teardrops fall, then inhales a large breath. "It's all my fault, you know?" Svetlana confesses. "I should have told Rinaldo about the letters. If I had shown him instead of burning them, he might still be alive now," she mumbles, closing her eyes.

"What letters, Svetlana?" I prod her to continue.

"Please, my friends call me Lana," she replies, slowly opening her eyes, a soft smile on her lips. "The constant love letters. He was relentless. I was in love with Rinaldo, but Pavel wouldn't believe me. He kept telling me I had Stockholm Syndrome. You see…" Her voice lowers to a whisper, her eyes flicking over at the man at the door before resting back on mine. "Rinaldo was pretending to be someone he wasn't when we first met. Then his father was killed in a bomb blast, and he had to come home to become the Pakhan. He didn't want to leave me, so he brought me here and locked me up until I agreed to marry him." Svetlana unfolds her less than fairytale romance.

"I already loved Rinaldo, but when I found out he wasn't who he portrayed when he met me, I panicked. I was not brave enough to be the wife of a Pakhan. This life is not an easy one. Pavel kept telling me to leave Rinny. He offered to help me get away..." Her voice drifts away for a moment or two.

"Why didn't you take Fa... Pavel up on his offer?" I prompt, almost slipping and revealing who I am.

"Because I was in love with Rinaldo, despite his becoming the Pakhan. When I found out I was having Mikhail, I realized I could never leave him." Svetlana rubs her stomach, seemingly caught up in her memories. "A baby needs both parents, and I was not going to keep Rinaldo's child from him."

"Pavel bombarded me with letters, confessing his love for me. I read the first one, but each letter after that, I burned." Her voice rises sharply. "I thought Pavel had gotten past his feelings for me, but when he killed my Rinaldo. I began to doubt it. Pavel shot Rinny in cold blood."

Svetlana shivers, wrapping her arms around her body as if to comfort herself. Her sad eyes dip to watch the flames of the fire; I do the same. Silence falls over the room.

"You are not your father, Katya." Her words shock me.

I cock my head, the surprise on my face evident. Then she turns back to me, her dark eyes on mine. "Do you think I wouldn't know those eyes?" The frail woman declares softly, a smile tipping up the corners of her mouth. "I once debated who I wanted to live my life with," Svetlana admits. "Pavel was attentive and smart. But he always thought he deserved more than he got and was never good with rejection."

"Rinaldo exuded confidence and power, but at the same time he had a softer side I was privileged to see. He was like a magnet for my body, and soon my heart followed." The love for her husband is evident in her tone, mixed with the sadness in her eyes. "Your father wouldn't respect my decision. He thought Rinaldo would soon tire of me and toss me aside. It didn't happen. Then he tried to sway me into having an affair with him. When I refused, he told me someday I would be sorry."

"And now I am. I'm sorry I didn't go to Rinny with the letters. I'm sorry I didn't tell him the things Pavel said. I'm sorry my son has taken the place of his father as Pakhan." A tear escapes, dripping onto her pale cheek as she admits her woes. "Most of all, I'm sorry you've been pulled into this world."

I take Svetlana's hand in mine, and she returns it with a stronger grip than I expected. "You don't have to be sorry for me, Svetlana. I wasn't dragged into this world. I was born into it. Father is the reason I'm here. That's the truth. But I'd rather be here than with him," I admit honestly, deciding to leave out the part where I was supposed to murder her and her son.

Once Mikhail is well, I'll leave. I'll take Natalia, and Tomas too if he wants, and we'll start a new life somewhere out of Father's reach. I can't expect Mikhail to protect us after the trouble we've caused him.

The swish of the electronic door opening behind us interrupts my thoughts, and I turn my head toward it, seeing that Kristina has returned. She nods to the guard, who steps out of the room, and then she strides over to where we're sitting, a medicine cup in one hand. When she observes the two of us holding hands, her eyebrows raise in curiosity, but she doesn't question it.

"It's time for your medication, Lana," Kristina croons, as I release Svetlana's hand.

Kristina wanders over to the bed and pours water into a glass from a jug on the bedside table. Bringing it to where her friend sits, she hands it to her along with the pills. Svetlana breaches no argument, tossing the pills into her mouth and washing them down with the water.

"Come, darling. It's time to prepare for bed," Kristina coaxes Svetlana. "Katya can come and visit tomorrow if you like."

It's a polite dismissal, but I don't take offense. I'm feeling drained myself, but I still have to find Natalia and Tomas before I can rest. I say my goodbyes and Henrí's mother punches the code into the door panel to let me out of the room. I'm about to leave when Svetlana calls out, "Mikhail has that same soft side, Katya. You should trust in him."

Svetlana has given me so much to think about. Things about my father I had wondered about. Had he really loved her or was it just because she didn't want him. Did he kill Rinaldo out of jealousy over her? Could Svetlana's choosing Rinaldo over Pavel have been the catalyst for everything that's happened?

Perhaps when Rinaldo decided Mikhail would be his successor, it was the last straw for Pavel and that's why he did what he did. It's still no excuse, but I'm seeing things in a slightly different light now.

16

———————

KATYA

"Your sister and brother are down on the next level." The guard outside Svetlana's room breaks into my thoughts as if reading my mind. "I'll call someone to escort you there."

I freeze momentarily at his comment. Perhaps I'm not as free as I thought I was to roam Mikhail's hallways.

"Or you could point me in the right direction and I could find my own way there," I venture, testing her.

"Okay." His brows arch at the same time his lips press into an upside-down smile before answering me. "Take the lift at the end of the hall. Go down one level. The second door on the right is your sister's. Your brother's the third."

I recall my chat with Svetlana, and her love for her husband and son. This brings up thoughts of my own mother as I head in the direction the guard pointed.

I wish we had been closer. Her death by my father's hand is not what she deserved.

It's not that I didn't love her, of course I did, she was our mother. It probably stems from the way Natalia and I were often left to figure out life by ourselves while Mother drank her woes away. There were no hugs or storybooks read to us at night, and she was never sober long enough to teach us about cooking or boys.

Father added to the dysfunction of our family. His lack of emotion toward Mother and us, plus his manipulation of all of us, Tomas included, to try to *avenge* him. I hate the man who calls himself my father.

He admitted he had been filling our minds with lies this whole time. My father, Pavel Ivanov, killed Mikhail's father, and our mother. He confessed to it all in the church. I haven't forgotten he tried to kill me too.

When I reach the elevator, the doors are already open, and I step in, hitting the button for the next floor. It's easy from there to find Natalia's room.

The door opens automatically, and the moment I step inside, I hear her crying. Natalia lies on her stomach, her face buried in the pillows, which aren't doing much to muffle her sobs. Seating myself next to her on the bed, I rub her back gently.

Natalia raises her head, her blurry eyes locking on mine, before repositioning herself so her head's in my lap, much like she used to do when we were younger. Back when Father would leave the two of us, telling us he had to go away to work, while he was going home to another family. I run my fingers through her sand-colored hair, like I used to when we were children and she would cry herself to sleep. All she ever wanted was a real family. Like me.

"What will they do with us, Katya?" she cries. "Are they going to sell us? Father said Mikhail's people would sell us as sex workers or keep us for themselves to torture us until we begged for death." Her hand slaps over her mouth, and her green eyes widen as if in surprise at what she's saying.

"Mikhail and his men aren't going to torture us." *I hope.* "They know Father manipulated Tomas and me into trying to kill him. Father lied about everything, Nat." I brush some stray hairs away from her angelic face before asking, "How did you get here?"

"Father told me he was taking me on a holiday," Nat begins. "He said you were meeting us there. I was excited. Father has never taken us anywhere before." She frowns, her voice dulled with sadness. "It was my first plane trip. Then we met up with Igor at a hotel." Natalia pauses, a shudder running through her body, while mine tenses.

"Father gave me a drink at the hotel, and everything went fuzzy. I could understand what everyone around me said, but I couldn't get my words out," my sister cries, tears erupting again. "My head was screaming, yet my mouth agreed with Father and Igor." A shiver runs through her body. "Father was going to marry me off to him, to Igor. How could he do that?" Natalia wraps her arms around herself.

"Igor was muttering in my ear the entire ride to the church. The things he told me." She hiccups, her teary eyes widening as they meet mine. "He's an evil man. And Mama. Father said he disposed of her." Her shaky hand raises to her lips. "You don't think…"

My face must give away what Father had admitted in the church was true, which sets off more tears. I'm sad about what's happened, but there's too much going on right now.

There'll be time for mourning later, I hope.

Finally, my sister's tears slow to an occasional hiccup, and I try to brighten things by changing the subject. "Natalia, do you want to meet your brother?" I blurt. There's no reason to keep it from her.

"I have… I have a brother?" she stammers as she sits upright, interest brightening her puffy eyes while her eyebrows knit together in a frown.

"It appears we do. Well, a *half*-brother. It seems all those times Father went away to *'work'*." I do air quotes with my fingers. "He was going home to his other family." I reach for her hand as I stand. "Come." I give her a slight tug.

"He's here? Does he work for the Bratva?" Natalia's eyes flash with interest as she scrambles off the bed.

"No." I draw the word out. Catching my lip, I chew it for a moment before deciding to tell her the truth. After all the lies Father has told, I choose to be honest. "Tomas was sent to kill the Pakhan. When he failed, Father sent me to do it." I try to gauge her reaction. "Remember the guy with me at the church? He was in the car with you when we were brought back here to Mikhail's." Natalia nods slowly, still a little confused. "You were probably still suffering from the drug Father gave you. That was Tomas, our brother."

Natalia cocks her head, a frown on her face as she tries to find the missing pieces, while letting my words sink in.

With a sigh, I return to the bed. Pulling her down beside me, I explain everything. Natalia has a lot of questions, all of which I answer as best and as honestly as I can. When I finish, I wait for her to process it all.

Natalia rises and begins pacing in front of me, one

arm across her middle, one finger tapping her lips. I know it's a lot, but I know my sister is strong enough to deal with it, as long as Tomas and I are with her.

Her eyes slide my way, but she doesn't stop. "Are we prisoners here? Are they going to kill us?"

Sighing loudly, I admit, "I don't know what's going to happen to us. I don't believe Mikhail means us any harm. After all, I've been roaming the house freely," although I haven't attempted to leave, but I keep that to myself. "Mikhail—"

"You've been chatting with Mikhail? As in *the* Mikhail Korbicov, the Pakhan?" Natalia cuts me off as she halts in front of me, frowning. I squirm under her gaze, my face flushing.

A smirk tips up her lips. "Oh, my gosh." Natalia's eyes open wide as she stares down at me, pulling at her lower lip with her finger and thumb. "You've got feelings for him, yes? Are you sleeping with him?"

"No," I deny profusely, while remembering what happened beneath the table at the banquet. My face warms even more as my sister continues to stare at me, her eyes gleaming.

"But you want to," she snickers. "You've got the hots for the sexy Pakhan. Oh, Katya. Imagine if you married him," she giggles with glee. "You'd be the envy—"

"Whoa, Nat," I interrupt. "Not so fast. No one's talking marriage."

I don't want to bring her down, but allowing her to raise her hopes, and mine, of anything happening with Mikhail is a silly fantasy. Fantasies are for children. "Come," I stand and hold my hand out to her. "I'll take you to meet our brother."

MIKHAIL

It's late evening, judging by the sky outside my window.

These damned machines beeping are driving me nuts. I've been waiting, hoping Katya will return. She seemed genuinely worried about me when she came in earlier. The machines going crazy probably frightened her.

My parents and my best friend are the only people who've ever shown true affection for me, but I'm sure it's what I see in her eyes when she looks at me. The way her eyes scanned my body had me rock hard. Thankfully, my boxers contained my erection, otherwise, it would've been an embarrassing sight.

Whenever Katya is near, my body has a mind of its own. If she were anyone else, I probably would have had her restrained in the basement awaiting torture for her father's digressions.

Like Igor is right now.

Thankfully, Henrí put her in my bedroom. I wouldn't put it past one of my Avtoritets or their gang members, to attempt something as payback for my being shot. There are hotheads out there. Some in the Bratva are no better than animals bred with a bloodlust.

All of my men in the compound know Katya, her sister, and their brother are under my protection. However, there are bratoks, *lower-ranked thugs*, who wish to rise within the ranks and they could take it upon themselves to commit payback.

I'll have Henrí make a declaration that the three are untouchable. Anyone who ignores it will die by my hand.

The thought of someone hurting Katya again is unbearable.

I'm unsure whether I'm dreaming, or if it's the effects of the painkillers, when the door opens to my room and a shadow enters. I don't have the glass ceiling in this room so it's quite dark. I open my eyes slightly, scanning the shadowy corners without moving or changing my breathing. Perhaps it's an enemy here to finish me off. Perhaps Pavel has worked up the courage to kill me face to face.

My hand slides under the blankets, where I wrap my fingers around the butt of my gun. Luckily, Henrí brought it to me when I asked. You never know who Pavel has paid off.

The slightest sound of bare feet on marble floors reaches my ears. Whoever it is, approaches with hesitation, probably for fear of waking me. I can't let on I'm awake, so I remain still. The machines will give me away if I tense or change my breathing. I'm at a disadvantage because of my wounds and having lost a lot of blood.

If I could have walked when I attempted to get out of bed to follow Katya earlier when she left the room, I would have. But my knees buckled and Henrí and several nurses put me back in bed, Henrí threatening to handcuff me to it if I tried it again.

I told him I'd rip his head off if he tried, but he laughed at me. He knows I don't mean it… mostly.

The shadow is close now; I smell their cologne. It's familiar, but I can't place it. A hand reaches out and I make my move, grabbing a small wrist and gripping it tightly.

"Ow," a female voice yelps. "Mikhail, it's me. Katya. Ow," she yelps again as I pull her closer to the bed. I release her wrist before wrapping my hand tightly in her long, blonde hair. Is it really her? Or have these painkillers addled my brain.

"How did you get in here?" I'm confused; this room is coded. "I–I couldn't sleep." Katya gasps, my grip on her hair still tight. "I needed to… I had to make sure you're alright," she babbles. "Mikhail, please. You're hurting me," she whimpers.

She's really here, I tell myself as I loosen my hold. *She came back.*

"Why are you wandering around in the dead of night? How did you get into my room?" I demand. Henrí, Kristine, and the doctor are the only people with the code.

"That's two favors you owe me," Henrí mutters from the doorway. "I'm off to bed," he adds as the door closes behind him.

My eyes have adjusted to the darkness now as I turn back to where Katya remains standing beside my bed. She's dressed in what appears to be a T-shirt and nothing else, her long legs peeking out of the bottom, her feet bare. Wafts of cologne pierce my nose again and I realize why it's familiar.

"Why are you dressed in my T-shirt, wearing my cologne?" I frown at Katya, puzzled when I remember she was wearing one earlier when she came to see me as well. I like my shirt on her.

"I–I didn't have anything to wear after my shower.

There was blood," she stammers awkwardly. "Your blood was all over me."

I remain silent, not knowing what to say when she blurts out "I didn't know if you were okay. I needed to…" Her words fade.

"What did you need, malen'kiy olen'?" I ask softly, not wanting her to scurry away again. "Tell me. What do you need?" My mind tells me not to trust her, but everything I've seen so far tells me different. The innate need to touch her whenever she's close is confusing to me. I'm used to being in charge of everything. Having everything go to plan. But when Katya is near my heart and head are all about her.

I've never felt like this around anyone before. If it turns out she's playing me, I have to admit, it's something I really hope isn't true. I slide my finger down the control panel, hitting the on switch for the lamp above us. It lights up the top area of the bed, so I can see her angelic face.

"I know we've just met." The words fall softly from her lips. "And you know what I was sent to do." I nod, remaining silent. "But when I saw you dive in front of that bullet today…" Her voice drifts off momentarily. "My heart exploded with the bullet you took for me. I thought Father killed you. Don't judge me, but I needed to feel you again, and this was my way of doing it." Her words are hushed as she blushes profusely while pulling at the front of her, *my*, shirt. "I can't explain it, it just is," she adds, her voice so quiet I almost miss it.

A tear glistens on her cheek as she admits to her feelings for me. Katya deserves better than a man like me. A man of violence, a man involved in the filthy underbelly of the Bratva, but I'll be damned if I can let her walk away after her admission.

If this is an illusion caused by the drugs, they've been feeding me, then I don't want to wake from it.

"Come, Katya. Lie with me a while," I command gently, patting the bed.

Gingerly, she climbs up, careful not to pull the cannula from my opposite arm. It hurts wriggling over to the edge of the bed, but I don't let on. It's hard to fit her in here with my large frame, but we succeed. Katya rolls onto her side, her hand on my stomach, as I slide my good arm around her, pulling her close.

My hand slides up under the T-shirt, gliding over the thin scrap of underwear she has on, my fingers spreading over her ass cheek. My cock decides it's a good time to wake up, and I groan a little with the discomfort. I only have one good hand to adjust it with and it's currently curled around the young woman beside me.

"Are you okay?" Katya lifts her head from its resting place on my chest, her hand splayed on my stomach.

'I'm fine malen'kiy olen'," I try to convince her. "Your body this close to mine has woken my cock. He hasn't received the memo to behave himself." I chuckle, trying to lighten the situation.

I don't mistake her quiet gasp, her body stiffening at my bad joke. I probably shouldn't have put it like that, but I'm not a man of etiquette.

"I might be able to help with that, but…" She breathes, her hand tracing my tattoos as it works its way down my abs to the trail of hair disappearing under the blanket. I frown when she stops there.

17

———————

MIKHAIL

"But what?" I question her, intrigued. She tips her head back to look at me.

"I don't want to hurt you," Katya murmurs.

"You won't," I assure her as I hit the painkiller button connected to my IV. Her circling fingers continue down to where my cock is anticipating her touch with eagerness. I writhe beneath the blanket, attempting to move my erection into a more comfortable position. With both my arms out of action at the moment, it's not easy; a grunt of annoyance escapes me.

"Are you okay? Should I go?" Katya mutters, her body tensing.

She thinks she's hurting me. "Don't you dare," I growl, gripping her tighter, while wishing my other arm wasn't in a sling so I could move her hand to where I need it to be.

There's silence for a few moments before Katya leans up on her elbow, her beautiful face so close to mine that her breath warms my cheek. "Okay, I'll stay. But on one condition." Her voice takes on a stern tone. "You let me do all the work. If those monitors start beeping, I'm putting the brakes on immediately. Understood?"

I chuckle at her demands before answering. "Yes, malen'kiy olen', I understand." I'll agree to anything as long as she doesn't stop. Removing my hand from around her body, I tuck it up under my head. "Have at it," I tease.

Katya sits up, her blue eyes now dark, her gaze so intense it almost burns my skin.. I don't know this young woman intimately yet, but it appears the thought of having control over me excites her. Once I'm off this damned machine, I'll show her who's in charge. In all places, especially the bedroom. I can feel my cock getting even harder at the thought, as precum leaks out, dripping down my shaft.

Climbing over my body as gently as she can, she positions her knees on either side of me, seating her firm ass inches below my cock. She leans forward, careful of the wires, her mouth closing on mine. The kiss is gentle and sweet. Running my tongue along her lips, I find them opening, inviting me to explore inside her mouth with my tongue.

I groan in protest when she pulls away before lowering her head, her warm tongue licking my uncovered nipple before biting it. The pleasure-pain of it prompts a hiss from me and again when she repeats her movement. "Stay still," Katya orders softly before kissing and nipping her way down my large frame, her nails scraping along my abs as she does.

It's a foreign feeling for me to submit to anyone. I've always been the one in charge. It's usually me dominating the woman, but I feel Katya needs this. She revealed Igor did things to her, but I've yet to hear the worst of it, I feel. It makes me want to go and hunt him down, and I will, but right now isn't the time.

This is Katya's time.

Katya moves back until she can pull the blanket off my lower body, leaving nothing but my boxers covering my needy cock. She remains still for a moment before closing her hand around my length. "Is this for me?" she smirks, my cock pulsing as she traces her fingers gently over the satin of my underwear. "Will it hurt you if I remove these?" Katya murmurs.

"Take them off," I insist. I hurt all over, but at this moment, I don't give a shit. All I can focus on is the desire to be touched by the angel straddling my body.

Katya moves back towards the end of the bed, grips both sides of my boxers, and drags them slowly down my legs. My cock springs up in relief. When I glance up, Katya is chewing on her lower lip, her eyes glued to it. I wish the lamp was stronger so I could read her face better as I remove my hand from behind my head to give my throbbing cock a pump or two, attempting to find some relief.

"Hands off, Mikhail," my little dominatrix orders me. "Put it back behind your head."

I do as I'm told, a chuckle rumbling through me as I do. This is painful yet fun. It would be a lot better if I weren't lying here, marginally incapacitated.

Her cool hand closes over my bare cock, bringing my thoughts back to the present. Her fingers don't meet as she wraps her small hand around my girth gently. She's trying not to hurt me. "Harder," I grunt, and she does, right before leaning forward to lick the seam at the top where precum is leaking, her tongue delving into the crease. My cock twitches as I hiss at the intrusion.

She continues exploring my cock with her tongue, almost causing me to convulse when she runs it along the tender area beneath the head. Meanwhile, the fingers on her other hand stroke the inside of my thighs and my balls. I've not taken things this slow before. Sex has merely been a way to release tension with women hoping to claim me, but here, with Katya, I'm enjoying every sensation.

My free hand grips the pillow behind my head as she returns her warm mouth to the tip, gradually sliding deeper. The urge to grab her head and slam my throbbing cock down her throat is tremendous, but I agreed to let her do all the work. Katya won't be able to take my entire length, I tell myself, as she hums. "Fuck, Katya," I gulp, attempting to lift my head to watch her.

Her large doe eyes are on mine as she swallows me little by little. The head of my cock hits the back of her throat and I wait for her to gag, but she doesn't. Her throat convulses as she swallows, tightening around me.

"Fuck," slips from my mouth. Katya has taken my entire length and is now sliding up and down over me. When she groans, it vibrates throughout my rigid cock, down to my balls, and I can't contain the moan of pleasure.

"Fuck, Katya," I grunt over and over, my vocabulary shortened to those two words as pleasure steals my ability to speak. My greedy girl sucks and licks harder, her hand squeezing and tugging my balls when she works the tip until they draw up tight. The desire to hold her head in place and watch her choke on my cum as it spurts from my body, is strong, but I can't. She's been forced by others, and I want this to be a good memory. One of her choice. I'm so close, but I don't warn her, although I'm sure she knows when her mouth speeds up.

I don't remember any woman making me feel the way my malen'kiy olen' does right now. She's a mixture of frightened deer and sexy vixen. Mine, I tell myself as stars explode behind my eyelids, my heart beating in time to my release. As my cum spurts down Katya's throat, my free hand tangles itself in her hair, so I can see her face. Raising my head, I watch as drops of my cum spills out at the corners of her mouth when she can't swallow it all. Spasms rack my body, my eyes blur, and the machines beep loudly in protest. Katya pops my cock from her mouth, checking the lines on the machine next to me before she continues licking me clean.

Smiling like a Cheshire cat, Katya rolls to the edge of the bed, sliding down until her feet hit the floor. She picks up my boxers, slipping my feet into them and sliding them back up my legs. Despite just cumming, my cock twitches in eagerness. "Down boy." She winks, as she pulls the blankets up over me.

Katya climbs back onto the bed as the doctor and nurses arrive in the room to check the machines., lying beside me, feigning innocence. Her arm is casually draped over me, while my good arm is wrapped around her. My chest still heaves a little, but the beeping is calming down.

The nurses check my vitals while the doctor looks on unimpressed. He has probably formed an idea of what went on to cause the fluctuations on the machines, but he knows better than to incur my wrath by raising the subject. The nurses agree nothing is out of place. They tell him I'm stronger than earlier tests stated I was.

"You weren't supposed to do that," Katya hisses as they leave, gently smacking my stomach. "I told you if the machines beeped, I was stopping."

I kiss her forehead. "Haven't you heard, *malysh*, *baby?*" I chuckle before continuing, "What doesn't kill you makes you stronger."

Otets told me once that he knew the moment he saw Mama that she was meant for him, and now I know what he meant. Now, I've found my missing piece. Katya is mine, whether she knows it yet, or not.

***

MIKHAIL

I've had enough of lying in bed. After another argument with the doctor, I removed the cannula from my arm and insisted they let me be. If they don't, I'll shoot them all.

Henrí laughs at me, but he knows if I get angry enough, I might do exactly that.

It's been several days since Katya came to my room. Henrí says she's spending quality time with her sister and new-found brother.

I believe she's avoiding me.

Tossing aside my blankets, I swing my feet over the side of the hospital bed.

"Where do you think you're going?" Henrí asks. His brows crease together in a frown, but his eyes sparkle in mischief. He knows Katya's absence is pissing me off.

"For a walk," I grunt as my bare feet hit the floor. Pain jolts through my body, but I keep my face blank. "I'm not staying in this room any longer. Tonight I sleep in my bed," I snarl at the doctor. I know he's trying to do what's right, but I'm done with being weak.

"Would you like me to get your clothes, Mr. Korbicov?" The nurse with the big breasts, who keeps shoving them in my face every chance she gets, asks sweetly.

"No," I answer her sternly. "I know where my clothes are. I'll get them myself," I add, not looking her way, refusing to encourage her.

I let go of the bed, finding my balance before I take a step. The big-breasted nurse reaches out her hand as if to help. "Don't," I growl. *I can do this on my own*, I try to tell myself. Her hand pulls back as if she's been burned. *What do I care?* "Everyone, out," I order.

The doctor and nurses look at me, confused.

"You heard the boss," Henrí backs me up, even though I don't need it. "Out. Now." He knows I don't want anyone here in case I stumble and make a fool of myself. If anyone saw, they could tell the wrong people. It wouldn't take much to try a coup. They wouldn't succeed, but my men need to see me upright in case anyone other than Pavel Ivanov feels it's their time to rise to the position of Pakhan.

"Okay, my friend, what is going on in that head of yours? You are supposed to be healing. You know I can run things until you're back on your feet—"

"I *am* back on my feet," I interrupt him.

"Fuck, Mikhail. What don't you understand about the fact you almost died the other day?" Henrí explodes. He doesn't often raise his voice, and for him to yell at me, he has to be extremely angry.

My head jerks up from where I'd been concentrating on taking a step without staggering, to lock eyes with my best friend. "You think I don't know that? I hurt like a bitch every time I move, but you know I can't be out of sight for long. The wolves will circle quickly, Henrí. You know this," I hurl back at him.

"This," he waves his hand at me, "has nothing to do with the Bratva, Mikhail, and you know it. It's all over a pixie of a woman named Katya. A woman sent to kill you, and she almost did, even if it wasn't by her hand. She's the daughter of your father's murderer, Mikhail. Have you forgotten?" Henrí doesn't back down from me, ever. It's why we make such a great team. "I nearly lost my best friend, my brother, just days ago. Do you have any idea how that felt? How would I have told your mother…" His voice fades.

I hadn't thought about how my getting shot affected him. While worrying about Katya, I had forgotten about my friend. We might be seen as unfeeling and tough, but we also love and are loved. To show our feelings in public can mean a death sentence. Henrí's been holding in his pent-up anger and fear until now.

Sighing, I lean against the bed. I concede, lowering my eyes to my feet before looking back up at him.

"I'm sorry, brat, *brother*," I begin. It's foreign for me to apologize, but Henrí deserves it. "I allowed my cock to control my head for a while. But I'm back now." Straightening to my full height, I refuse to give in to the pain. "Let's finish this." I take an unsteady step before forcing my legs to keep moving, the strength returning as I do.

"That's more like it," my friend mutters as he follows me out the door.

The basement below my house is unlike most. It's a place designed to deal with *personal* business.

When Henrí and I enter, a naked Igor is chained, hands and feet, to four posts. He's elevated to around seven feet off the ground, face down. The room smells of urine and feces. Igor's face is red and contorted with pain. His arm and leg muscles are bulging as he tries to gain even the slightest relief.

I reach up, grab a chain, and tug, Igor emitting a grunt of pain when I do. "Wake up, Igor, I have questions for you," I croon.

Igor's eyes pop open as if he's surprised I'm here.

"What, you thought I was dead?" I chuckle. "You're not that lucky. Pavel isn't a good shot unless his target is up close with their back to him," I snark.

"What do you want with me? You know Anton will be mad when he hears about this." Igor thinks I care about my cousin's feelings. He'll be told what happened to one of his Avtoritets of course, but for now, Igor is mine to deal with. He caused trouble in my territory, which makes him my problem to deal with.

"Anton doesn't give a shit about you," I taunt him. "You are a replaceable commodity," I continue. "He's probably already found someone. Once he knows what you've been involved in, he'll have no sympathy for you. Besides," I draw out my last words for effect, "you'll be long dead by that time."

If possible, Igor's ashen face pales a fraction more.

"You–You can't kill an Avtoritet," he stutters.

I stroll over to him, wrapping my hand around his throat and squeezing as I tell him, "You are so wrong, Igor. I can and will kill anyone who interferes with what is mine." I continue to squeeze his throat, cutting off his air supply until he's bucking and writhing, trying to get away from me. When I release him, he coughs and splutters, wheezing as he draws in much-needed oxygen.

"Where is Pavel is hiding out?" I demand once Igor stops coughing. "Your answers, Igor, will decide whether you die a quick death, or a long, slow, painful one." I yank his hair back, so his face is level with mine. "Be assured, Igor. Either way, you *are* going to die. I cannot let you go after the shit you pulled. But it's your choice how fast it happens," I inform him flatly. "I will be back soon for your answers."

Releasing his hair, I exit the room, Henrí close on my heels.

As we walk away, I call to Igor's guard. "Get a hose in here and hose away the stench. It smells like shit." Chuckling at my own sick joke, I head upstairs again.

My body hates me right now, but the need to see Katya is stronger than the pain. She has been avoiding me and I want to know why.

18

———————

KATYA

Natalia and Tomas are at the rear of Mikhail's home, seated on the edge of a teardrop-shaped swimming pool, dangling their feet in the water.

Tomas has a pair of multi-colored swim shorts on, while Natalia wears a deep blue full-piece bathing suit. They appear to be deep in conversation when I step up beside them.

"Hey," I greet my siblings. "Where did you get those?" I point at their attire.

"The lady. Kristina?" Natalia appears unsure of the right name. "Well, whatever her name is. Anyway, she showed us a room where there were all sorts of swimwear and towels. Tomas and I found some to fit us, and here we are."

"Why aren't you swimming?" I ask nonchalantly. "It's a beautiful day for it."

"We were waiting for you," Tomas replies, smiling.

"I don't have any swimwear," I tease back, enjoying a

conversation not based on death and destruction for once.

"I found you a pair," Natalia replies. Pulling her feet from the water, she runs over to where some deck chairs sit under the shade of a large palm tree. "These would look great on you, Kat," she calls.

In her hands is a skimpy sky-blue bikini, similar to the color of my eyes. My face reddens simply thinking about how little of my body they would hide. "Here," Natalia is in front of me now, smirking at me. "As soon as I saw them, I knew they'd be perfect on you."

"There's nothing to them," I huff, glancing at her. She's still smirking at me. "Why don't you wear them?"

Nat's eyes drop for a moment, before lifting to mine again. "You have the body for them, Kat. You should show it off. They wouldn't suit me as well as they would on you." She looks away again as if she's uncomfortable with the conversation.

Not wanting to darken an otherwise good day, I say nothing. Taking the barely-there pieces of material from my sister, I walk back into the house looking for a bath-room. Once there, I change into the skimpy swimwear. The bottom is a G-string, while the top barely contains my breasts. Thankfully, no one but Natalia and Tomas will see me in the pool. Wrapping a towel around me, I head back outside to my siblings.

"See?" Natalia's hand sweeps my body as I drop the towel by the pool. "I told you they would look great on you. There's no way it would look that good on me."

Without answering, I dive into the pool to hide my embarrassment. Warm water washes over me, cocooning my body. I wonder about Natalia's statement as I remain underwater until I reach the other side of the pool.

Natalia appears to lack confidence in her appearance at times. She's stunning and has a great body. She's taller than me, standing at five foot seven inches, has the same large blue eyes and long blonde hair I do, and a gorgeous curvy figure. I hope someone hasn't made her feel uncomfortable about her body.

Natalia has been fighting off the boys since long before I was even noticed. I was constantly having to play the role of big sister, fobbing off unwelcome advances to my younger sibling. I've never been jealous of her. I was more her protector.

My sister is naïve when it comes to the male species. If I had my way, she'd stay that way, but I know sooner or later she'll catch someone's eye. I can't be her protector forever, and she can't remain innocent. But I can be her big sister, here for her to answer all her questions when she needs me.

Especially if Father was telling the truth about Mother. I don't doubt that he has killed her, but there's a tiny spark of hope still in my heart, until I see her body.

I push up from the bottom of the pool, breaking the surface. As I sweep the water from my face, I detect one of Mikhail's guards watching Natalia's every move. He isn't what I want for my sister. Bratva is not the life for her. She deserves better, and I'll do whatever I can to get her out.

The guard's eyes flick to mine as if he senses he's being watched. I scowl back at him, but he dares to wink at me before turning and walking away.

I wonder if I should mention him to Mikhail, before chiding myself. He has more important things on his mind and doesn't need me annoying him with trivial things. I'll keep an eye on this guy myself.

After splashing and playing in the pool for hours, we wrap our towels around us and head inside to find food. Swimming always makes me hungry.

Mikhail's cook is in the kitchen and whips up plates of delicious sandwiches for us. We learn her name is Anya. She's a short, stout woman, with graying hair cropped close to her head, and a stern face. As we eat, we introduce ourselves to her and include her in our conversation. The sternness leaves her face and by the time we finish our lunch, Anya is smiling.

We decide to head upstairs for showers and to change our clothes after we've eaten. Tomas has found a large library on the first floor. He and Natalia appear to be bonding over their love of literature. I'm not much on reading, not having had a good education, but I'm glad they are finding some common ground.

Most of my childhood was stripped away by Mother's drinking and Father's absence. I had to grow up fast and left school early to take care of Natalia. Her life was more important than mine. I found a job to support us and to make sure Natalia had everything I didn't. Clothes, education, protection.

I step into Mikhail's bedroom, noticing right away everything has been tidied. The maid has been. Not that the room was a mess, but I've been sleeping here since everything happened at the church. If I'd asked for another room, it probably would've been granted, but I love sleeping in Mikhail's bed. I enjoy gazing up at the sky and fantasizing about him being here with me.

I can't recall how many times I've dreamed of him being here with me, holding me tight in his strong arms.

How many wet dreams have I had in this bed since I climbed onto his hospital bed that night? How many times have I gotten myself off, while pretending Mikhail's strong, thick fingers are inside me, instead of my own?

Since the night I gave him head on his hospital bed, I've not been to the hospital room. I'm embarrassed at my forwardness. Mikhail was a man in obvious pain, and I took advantage of it. He was on so many heavy drugs he probably thought it was a drug-induced dream.

My actions that night were not that of a rational being. I was more like a sexual predator, preying on the weak. And it's exactly what Mikhail was at that moment. Weak. He would never admit to it, though.

A Pakhan must be seen to be in control at all times.

When he remembers what I did, he'll probably be angry with me for emasculating him at his weakest moment. *I'm no better than Igor*, I scold myself. The difference is what I did was not for my gratification; it was for Mikhail's. *Wasn't it?*

I finish my shower, still in my head about what happened in Mikhail's hospital room. Wrapping a towel around my hair and one around my body, I wander back into the bedroom. My suitcase isn't on the floor where I left it. The walk-in closet door is ajar, and I enter it hoping to find my elusive suitcase. I'm shocked to find my clothes hung up, some neatly folded next to Mikhail's on the shelves.

The maid must have mistaken me for one of Mikhail's many women he surely has. Do they all have their clothes placed next to Mikhail's when they're here? Curling my fists at the thought, I endeavor to find the maid and let her know Mikhail and I are not in a relationship.

I'm in this room because this is where Henrí put me when Mikhail was shot. I'll repack my case later and move it to Natalia's room. We've shared a bed before. I'm sure we can do it again.

As I rummage through the small amount of clothing I brought with me, I realize I'm running out of things to wear.

The thought brings me back to the reality of how we all ended up here. Tomas was sent to assassinate Mickail. He failed, so I was sent to do the job. Instead, the man saved my life. If not for him, I might be dead now. He was shot because of me. His wounds are my fault. I might as well have shot him myself.

Mikhail may be in a weak state right now, but he won't be for long. What will he have in store for me when he's well enough to exact punishment? Will he take his pound of flesh? Or will he simply have us all disposed of?

Who will he punish for his being shot? It's my fault. Tomas has made his peace with Mikhail. Natalia is an innocent party to all of this. But me? I am the guilty one. I wore a resin gun beneath my dress to kill Mikhail Korbicov, the Bratva Pakhan.

***

MIKHAIL

The doctor isn't pleased when I order him to remove my bandages. He mumbles such things as sepsis and other infections I might get. The graze on the side of my head is healing, even though it still stings like a bitch, while my shoulder wound hurts like hell. The Dr. says I'm lucky to be alive. Pavel's bullet could have hit my heart, but luckily, it deflected off a rib and landed in my shoulder instead.

I'm determined to show my men I'm fine, which will help them be strong as well.

The cook informs Henrí that Katya and her siblings are out by the pool, but when I arrive there, they've gone. My house is spacious, something I used to like, but right now, every step I take is like walking while my body is on fire.

"Go and sit," Henrí orders. "I'll find them and bring them to you." He doesn't wait for an answer, turning and heading up the stairs. As I reach the bottom step, Henrí turns back to me. "Do not even think about it. Go." He points in the direction of my office. "Sit."

I glare at my friend, while he glares right back at me. I want to ignore him, but I do need to sit. My body hurts like hell, and the world keeps tilting. The doctor was probably right. I shouldn't be out of bed yet, but there is work to do. Without any more argument, I turn and head for my office.

While I wait, I make phone calls to my men asking why Pavel hasn't been found yet. It's excuse after excuse, and by the time Tomas enters my office, Henrí close behind, I'm angrier than a bear after not eating all winter.

I glance behind the two for the women. "Where are Katya and Natalia?" I snap while rubbing my temples.

"They've gone shopping," Tomas answers nonchalantly, shrugging his shoulders.

"What the fuck do you mean, they've gone shopping?" I snarl as I rise from my chair. The room spins, but I'm too angry to let it matter. Henrí was set the task of telling them they weren't to leave the compound. I can't keep them safe out there. There are too many variables outside my gates. Katya could've been killed when I let her escape earlier, even though I was tracking their movements. I can't let any harm come to her again. She's mine, even if she doesn't understand what it means yet.

Moving around the desk, Henrí places his hand on my shoulder placatingly, but it's not going to work this time. "Where did they go? Who did they go with?" I shrug his hand off, the movement causing my wounds to throb. Taking a deep breath, I attempt to steady myself. "You were supposed to keep her safe," I accuse Tomas as he steps back from my wrath. At least he has some smarts. If I could reach him right now, I'd break his neck.

"I didn't get the chance to tell the men the women weren't to leave the compound, Mikhail. I didn't think I needed to. This is on me." Henrí tries to cool the situation down.

Turning on my best friend, I unload again. "You promised you would keep her safe. You're supposed to be my second, yet you can't stop two women from leaving the house," I yell. I can tell he's trying his best to stay cool in front of Tomas. Although his face is blank, his cheeks are tinged with pink, belying his embarrassment. I don't give a fuck right now. My woman is out there in the city *shopping*, while her father, who recently tried to kill her, and almost succeeded in killing me, is out there too.

"We'll find them, drug (*droog*), *friend*. You need to calm down. You're not even supposed to be out of bed," he states quietly. He's a brave man standing this close to me. He's my best friend, but I want to slit his throat at this point. Lucky for him, I'm not armed.

"Find out who took them shopping," I demand with a glare, letting him know he's on thin ice right now. "And you." I turn my anger to the brother of this wandering pair. "Why didn't you go with them?"

"I–I don't like shopping," Tomas stutters weakly, his face paling under my glare.

"For fuck's sake," I yell again, my pain forgotten for a moment. "Do I have to do everything myself?" Flinging my uninjured arm at him, I state sharply, "You didn't consider informing me or Henrí about this until now, because?"

Tomas shakes his head. "Shit, I'm sorry. Katya said she was running short of clothes, and Natalia suggested going shopping. One of your men offered to take them." He runs his hand through his untidy hair before cuffing his neck. "I told them to let someone know. They told me they had," he continues as he points to himself. "Me."

"Who are they with?" I'm sick of excuses. Time is of the essence. Pavel found Katya before. He can do it again. He probably has someone watching the gates. "How long have they been gone?" I fire the questions at both of them, while my chest tightens with worry. Pain fires in all directions through me, but I'll be damned if I'm lying down while Katya is in danger.

Again.

19

MIKHAIL

Henrí picks up the phone on my desk and hits several buttons. I know he's calling the front gates to find out who was with the women. When he lowers the device slowly, I already know something is wrong.

"What?" I snap. "What is it?"

"No one's answering," Henrí states as he pulls his gun from its holster, checking he has a full magazine.

"Alert the men," I instruct as I press a button under my desk, which opens a wall panel to the left of me. It's my weapons room.

Stepping inside, I find holsters and pistols, along with racks of heavier weapons. I strap a double holster on and fill them with my handguns of choice, along with two daggers, which I slip into scabbards on either side of my waist.

"Kevlar, boss," Henrí's tone offers no choice as he tosses a bulletproof vest at me. He waits to ensure I remove my shirt and put mine on before he grabs one for himself and Tomas as they do the same.

"Give me a gun," Tomas states. When neither of us looks at him, his voice rises. "They're *my* sisters," he states firmly. "They're *my* responsibility. I shouldn't have let them go." He voices the obvious. I give him a glare that would have the boldest of my men withering, but he stands strong against it, repeating, "Give me a gun, please."

If anything, his voice is stronger than before. It reminds me of the young man who stood before me and bravely filled me in on his father's plans. I nod to Henrí to let him have a weapon.

"How good is your aim?" my best friend asks Tomas. "I don't want anyone getting shot accidentally."

"I'm better with a machine gun than I am with a pistol," the young man admits.

Henrí tosses Tomas an Uzi, along with a couple of magazines.

The men line up in the foyer as Henrí hands out extra weapons, while yelling orders. They all carry pistols around the compound, but if the gate guards have been compromised, we'll need better weapons and more ammunition. It's all hands on deck. Everyone has their earpieces turned on, to keep in contact with each other.

As soon as everyone has their orders, I head for the monitors to check the CCTV cameras. We rewind to the time Tomas says the women left, which was over an hour ago. The car they're in is visible as they pull up at the gate. It soundlessly shows a guard moving toward the car. He must've suspected something. As he approaches, a hand holding a gun, extends from the driver's side window. The guard dances like a puppet on strings before falling to the ground. A second guard steps up to the doorway, gun in hand, but before he can get a shot off, he jerks and falls down as well.

Before continuing, the front passenger door opens and the body of a man is pushed out onto the ground, unmoving. The car door closes again, and the vehicle speeds away.

"Who's driving the car?" The sun reflecting off the windscreen has thrown the camera off, and we don't have a face or name yet.

"Nikolai. He told everyone you okayed their shopping trip." Henrí taps his ear. "He must have shot the Uri before they got to the gates. Maybe the guards heard something through their earpieces and were curious about what was happening in the car. He must've forgotten he still had it turned on. Or maybe Uri became suspicious. He was in the car with him."

Not anymore, he's not. It was Uri who was pushed from the vehicle before it disappeared off down the road.

It appears there's only one man left with the women, for now. He must know he's a dead man when I catch up to him. His death will be slow and excruciating. *No one touches what's mine.* Nikolai hasn't been with us long. I had reservations about him, but Uri vouched for his cousin. I guess Uri isn't a good judge of character. Unfortunately, he found this out too late.

"He's ditched his earpiece now, the asshole. Maybe Uri became suspicious somehow, and tried to let us in on what was going on. Goes to show blood isn't thicker than water sometimes," Henrí states sarcastically. I'm about to say something when Henrí puts a finger up in the air. "But what our little friend doesn't know is, every car has our trackers on it." That little tidbit is on a *need to know* basis, and he doesn't need to know. "This should work to our advantage."

He pulls his phone from his pocket and taps it a few times. "He's right there," he points the red flashing dot out. "Tell the men to change channels. I don't want Nikolai to know when we're coming for him." Henrí calls some men over and tells them to pass the word to the rest of the men.

After they've all gone to get vehicles, Henrí turns to me. "We can handle this, Mikhail. I promise I'll bring our women home. Your injuries…" His voice fades at the odd expression I must have on my face. "What? You know you can't move fast enough —"

"*Our* women?" I interrupt, teasing him. Arching an eyebrow at him, I don't pretend to hide my smirk. "Since when were they *our* women?"

"Stop changing the subject, Mikhail. You need to stay here. You can coordinate everything from here. Your injuries—"

"I'm fine," I interrupt him again, my smirk now a scowl. "Get the men to check the compound perimeter. Warn your mother. Tell her to get Mama ready to go into the panic room and make sure she's armed." If ever Pavel was going to make a move on the compound, it would be now. "Get some men up there as well. Someone we trust."

The gate guards and Uri were killed an hour ago. Pavel could already have men in the compound.

"If Pavel touches a hair on my mother's head, or Katya's, he will die a long, slow, death," I grate.

Everything is set and the cars are ready out the front of the house. The doctor treating my wounds tells me I shouldn't be moving around so much. Ignoring his orders, I threaten him into giving me something to keep me going until we get both women back.

An injection will take the edge off the pain. Enough so I can move without feeling like I'm tearing apart but still have clarity.

The doctor's unhappy with me, but he gives me an injection anyway. He also hands me some pills in case the injection wears off. After stating to me he takes no responsibility for my actions, he stomps away.

He gets paid enough to do as I ask. He'll get over it.

Henrí and I lead Mama and Kristina to the panic room Otets had built years ago. Once they're securely locked away, I order several of the men to stand guard at Mama's bedroom door to make it appear as if they're still in there. I don't believe Pavel would have the guts to make a move on the house, but then, he's getting more desperate.

Tomas is waiting inside one of the cars when Henrí and I reach it. "Why are you behind the wheel?" I ask him as we slide inside.

"I might not be much of a fighter, but I've been driving fast cars since I was a kid," he offers, pride evident in his voice. "I can out drive any one of your men, and my father's. This is my strong point. All I need are directions. Strap yourselves in and hold tight to the *'oh shit'* handles."

Without waiting for a response, Tomas hits the accelerator and we're off, our wheels spinning in the loose gravel of the driveway. Henrí, with his phone on his lap showing the tracking app, directs the cars. We're weaving a net and as we gain intelligence, we will close it on Pavel. He will have no way out of the city.

Meanwhile, I contemplate how Katya is feeling right now. Natalia will be terrified, but Katya is resourceful. I'm sure she'll be working on a plan of her own. I hope she doesn't do something stupid and get herself hurt or killed.

My knee jerks up and down with impatience, even with Tomas driving like a speed demon.

"She'll be fine, brat, *brother*." Henrí's words cut into my thoughts. "Katya is resourceful. You know she thought of the resin gun by herself, yes?"

"How do you know that?" I hadn't, but it makes sense. Katya's a resourceful woman.

"She told me herself. You don't think Pavel would have the brains to think of it, do you? I'm sure she's plotting something already," my friend adds, trying to reassure me.

That's what I'm afraid of.

I'm not one for praying, but I tip my face to the heavens and ask whoever might be listening to keep Katya safe.

KATYA

I wish I hadn't mentioned to Natalia about needing more clothes. How had I forgotten how much Natalia loves to shop? She's excited immediately, asking one of Mikhail's men, Nikolai, if he knows of places to go nearby. Nikolai is the man who was watching Natalia in the pool. He states he knows of some great places nearby. I thought he came across as a creep by the pool, but he offered to take us, so maybe I'm wrong.

I still have the credit card Father handed me when I left to carry out his terrible plan. If he hasn't blocked it already.

Nikolai says he has to run our plans by Mikhail first, which, on one hand, I understand, but on the other, I am a bit pissy about. I'm a grown-ass woman. I don't need anyone's permission to do anything.

It's not long though before Nikolai arrives to tell us our shopping trip has been okayed. He brings another man with him, who he introduces as his cousin, Uri. I've seen Uri around the house in the time I've been here. They're Mikhail's men, so I see no reason to mistrust them.

As soon as we pull up at the gates, Nikolai shoots Uri in cold blood, before doing the same to the guards.

Nikolai killed those men in cold blood. It leaves no doubt in my mind he won't hesitate to kill us. *He's a monster.*

It's so unbelievable, I don't react at first. Instead, I tell myself this isn't happening. Natalia's screaming pulls me out of my head, prompting me to react, but it's too late. The distinct click of the door lock sounds before the separation shield between us, and the front of the car rises.

Natalia is shaking and crying beside me. She hasn't really seen violence up close before. She was under the influence of drugs at the church and was shielded from the shooting. The shock of what she has just witnessed, can never be undone. I never wanted her to see the violence this world brings with it, but I've failed her badly.

Pressing the intercom button located on the panel in the car door, I query our kidnapper, forcing my voice to appear calm. "What are you doing?" Nikolai doesn't answer. Instead, he lowers the shield. I watch as he removes something from his ear that looks like an Air pod and tosses it out the window. "Mikhail will kill you for this," I yell, though surely, he already knows.

"We'll be gone before they find us," Nikolai sneers, looking in the rearview mirror at me.

"Where are you taking us?" I demand, ignoring his insinuation.

Who is we? Does he mean the three of us?

"I'm taking you to your father," he replies with a shrug. "But cutie, there, she belongs to me now. She's part of my payment."

Natalia lets out a loud sob as my mind races.

Why did I agree to this shopping spree?

I know why. To please Natalia. Now I've allowed us to walk straight into Father's hands. The man has no morals. He's still offering Natalia up as compensation to anyone who will do his bidding.

I know why he's not offering me.

I'm not a virgin.

Father. No. I refuse to consider him my father any

longer. *Pavel* probably wants to punish me for failing to do his bidding. I'm of no other use to him. If he thinks holding me hostage will weaken Mikhail, he's mistaken. Mikhail's in a hospital bed, recovering from the wounds Pavel himself inflicted. He probably doesn't even know we're gone.

And if he does know, why would he care? Natalia and I are collateral damage. We're disposable. We mean nothing to him. He'll probably be glad we're out of his hair.

Tomas might try to find us, but he won't have much of a trail to follow.

If Natalia and I are going to get out of this, I'm going to have to do something desperate. But what? I don't have a weapon. Or do I? This is a car belonging to the Bratva. Surely they keep a weapon on hand in here somewhere in case of emergencies.

Trying not to raise the driver's suspicions, I remain still, allowing my eyes to roam the car. I click each button within reach, but out of sight of Nikolai. Just when I'm beginning to believe it was a stupid idea, I find a switch under the drinks console. Pushing it with my thumb, I pray this is what I'm looking for.

The console slides sideways, bumping into Natalia as it does. She stops crying, peering at me in surprise, her eyes red and swollen. I glance down at the two hand guns encased in foam. Taking one, I lay it on my lap where Nikolai can't see while I check whether it's loaded or not.

"Keep crying, Nat," I whisper out the side of my mouth as I slide the clip out of the gun. "We need to cover the noise in case he's listening."

My baby sister hams up her crying while watching every movement I make. Her lack of acting skills would be funny if this weren't such a serious situation. The driver can't see her unless he turns around, so it doesn't matter.

Removing the second weapon, I check it as well. It has a full magazine the same as the first one. Sliding it across the seat, I advised Natalia to put it in the pocket of her dress. Her eyes go wide in shock, but she does what I ask.

I know she doesn't know how to fire a gun, but this is the time for her to learn. It's not something I ever wished for my baby sister, but I guess she has to grow up sometime. This is the life Pavel forced on us, and if we don't defend ourselves, we'll be thrown to the wolves.

"Point and shoot," I whisper to her. "The safety is off. Be careful." I don't want her accidentally shooting me or herself. "Only use it if you have to, okay?"

I don't want to tell her she might have to defend herself if they get me first. It's hard to think about it, but I have to. As far as we know, there's no help coming. Mikhail, if not, Henrí knew we were going shopping with Nikolai and Uri because someone okayed it— Nikolia told us so.

Besides, Mikhail is in the hospital room, recovering. The guards and Uri are dead, so no one has been informed of Nikolai's treason.

I know the only way out is to shoot Nikolai, but he's in control of the vehicle. It might crash and we could be injured or worse, dead. The car slows as it turns up an alleyway. This is the one chance we might have of escaping without being killed.

"Close your eyes and block your ears, Nat." Glancing sideways, I check to make sure she heeds me, which she does. Bringing the gun up, I point it the back of his head and fire. The noise is loud in the confined space. Blood spatters on the windscreen in front of Nikolai. His body is thrown forward with the power of being shot at point-blank range and his head hits the steering wheel, setting off the car horn.

My ears are ringing, but thankfully the headrest behind Nikolai stopped most of the blood and brain spatter hitting my face. I wipe it away as best I can, while my stomach does somersaults. I don't have time to dwell on it though, so I take a few calming breaths.

We need to get out of here fast. Someone might call the police. The last thing we need, is to get arrested. Trying to explain our current predicament would only raise more questions, and I know the Bratva only tell law enforcement as minimal as possible.

Unfortunately, Nikolai's foot presses on the gas pedal, and the car lurches forward. It bumps and scrapes against the alley walls until it crashes into a large dumpster. Steam and, or, smoke pours from the engine, which sputters and then dies. Thankfully, the doors unlock.

Grabbing Natalia by the hand, I pull her out of the car with me.

20

———

MIKHAIL

HENRÍ AND I ARE RECEIVING INFORMATION FROM MY Avtoritets and their men constantly. The net is closing. Pavel is surrounded in the city with no way out. This is my territory, and he's about to find out what that means.

Tomas was right about his driving skills, and when this is done, I'm offering him the position of my driver. We've made it into the city in no time. Admittedly, every bump in the road is painful for me, but thanks to the injection the doctor gave me it's not as bad as it could be. Hopefully, the effects will last long enough to destroy Pavel Ivanov for good.

"Next left," Henrí directs Tomas, who turns quickly into a narrow alley.

The moment we turn, we find the car we're looking for. It's at an odd angle halfway down the alley, facing away from us. "Wait here, I'll be right back," Henrí murmurs, a frown on his face.

Exiting the vehicle, Tomas follows Henrí's lead. Their

guns are drawn as they approach the other car warily. When they reach the side of it, Tomas glances back at me. The fear on his face is obvious, and I scramble from the car.

As I do, I observe crimson coating the windscreen and I pick up my pace. My mouth runs dry at the thought it could be Katya's blood.

I've seen dead bodies before, but the thought it could be her hits me harder than anything I've ever felt. Each heavy footstep brings me closer, my heart thudding violently while my throat tightens.

"It's not them, Mikhail," Henrí informs me as I reach them.

Heaving a sigh of relief, I stick my head inside the car. Nikolai lies across the front seats, the back of his head almost completely gone. He died quicker than I would have allowed him to, had I caught him first.

Opening the back door of the car, Katya and Natalia are gone, and the console is open where I keep extra weapons. Both guns are missing, and the extra magazines are gone too.

Did Katya do this? I can't imagine Natalia shooting anyone. She's little more than a kid. I step back and straighten up, my eyes flicking to each shadow in the alley. There's no sign of the women.

Was Pavel here? Did he kill Nikolai? Has he taken Katya and Natalia again? He attempted to kill her at the church, and he would've succeeded, except I saw him aim his gun at her. I took the bullet meant for her. The man has no feelings for anyone else but himself. He's a narcissist.

He's also a dead man walking.

Henrí taps his earpiece, and I tap mine to listen in on the conversation. My men have Pavel cornered. I ask about the women, but Boris, one of my Avtoritets is unsure. It's a relief when they don't appear to be with him, *but if he doesn't have them, where the fuck are they?*

Neither Katya nor Natalia knows this city well, or this country for that matter. They don't have any way to communicate with us either; that's on me. I didn't see a reason for them to have phones because they were all together, and safe in my home.

"Fuck," I yell, letting out the frustration I feel, while at the same time punching the car window. It shatters with the force of my anger, the pain in my knuckles helping me to focus.

I'm torn between finding Katya and catching Pavel.

I pace for a few moments before coming to a decision. The thrill of hunting Pavel is only dulled by the pain wracking my body.

"Tomas." Katya's brother turns to look at me. "We're going to capture your father. You know what this means, so you need to decide once and for all which side you're on." Pavel is kin to him. If he chooses the wrong side, I'll have to kill him. I don't have a problem with it, even though it would put a wedge between Katya and me.

Damn it, when did I care what anyone thinks of me?

"Pavel stopped being my father as soon as he involved us all in his stupid plans to become the Pakhan," Tomas states solemnly. "He has no love for anyone but himself. I know that now. He tried to sell off my youngest sister, and he tried to kill Katya." Rubbing the back of his neck, he stares down at his feet in thought as his voice fades.

It doesn't go unnoticed that Tomas refers to Pavel by his first name. Still, my fingers strum the butt of one of my pistols, in case.

"Pavel has brought nothing but fear and pain to us all. Yes, my childhood was better than my sisters', but that's just another reason to disown him. I stand with my sisters," the young man finishes quietly.

Good. He's made the right decision. I side eye Henrí, knowing by his relieved expression, he was having the same thoughts I was.

Pursing my lips, I come to a decision. "Let's go. We'll pick up Pavel, then head back to the compound."

Leaving the other car where it is, I send orders for a cleanup crew to the location. Most of the police force is in my pocket, but I can't chance an honest cop finding the body and asking questions. Returning to our car, the concern in Tomas' voice is obvious as he climbs into the driver's seat. "What about Katya and Natalia?"

"Your sister is a resourceful young woman. I'm sure she'll be fine. They're probably on their way back to the compound as we speak," I assure him.

I hope I'm right.

Tomas pulls up around the corner from the building Pavel's reportedly holed up in. It would have been easy to wait in the car for my men to take my enemy, but this is personal.

Dimitri and several of my men have the building surrounded. They want to go in guns blazing, but I'd rather take Pavel alive. He has a lot to answer for. My father's death is one of many. But if he gives us no choice, it will be by my hand. It's my right.

Henrí and I step inside the back door of the building. It's dark inside, which gives us an advantage. Pavel isn't likely to try an escape out the front of the building. Treading carefully, sticking to the darkest parts of the hallway we're in. Signaling to Henrí to go left, I go right, continually sweeping my eyes back and forth as they become accustomed to the murky shadows.

A creaking floorboard to my left alerts me. It's not Pavel, I can tell by the shadows' size, and it isn't Henrí either. Flattening myself out to make a smaller target, I fire, satisfied when the body drops with a heavy thud. The silencers we fitted to our guns as we climbed out of the car have worked in my favor.

Moving to the next room, I find two more men. One gets a shot off at me, but it's wide and hits the wall. Diving behind an armchair, I grunt in pain as I fire off two more rounds, both hitting their targets and the men fall, their guns clattering on the floorboards. Inhaling some slow, deep breaths, I prepare to leave the shelter of the armchair.

I no sooner move from my cover than several bullets pierce the wall where I had been mere moments ago. I immediately return fire, plaster erupting from it as the bullets penetrate, followed by a grunt and a thud. Another man down. Reaching the next doorway, I glance around the open frame, attempting to get a glimpse of the enemy before they see me.

The area appears clear, so I step into the room, scanning every nook and cranny. Finding nothing, I move on. Henrí meets me at the next doorway, and without speaking, I signal to the stairs ahead of us. He nods and leads the way, creeping upwards to the next floor. The steps occasionally creak under my large frame. There are more rooms at the next level, and Henrí and I separate again.

My pain level is increasing with each step, and I hesitate long enough to tip some of the painkillers the doctor gave me out of the bottle and into the palm of my hand. I swallow them dry, wincing at the acidic taste they leave behind. We need to find Pavel, fast.

As if he read my mind, Pavel's voice reaches me from the darkened room Henrí had crept into mere moments before.

"Well, well. Your Pakhan sent you to find me, eh? He should have come himself. Now it will be your blood on his hands." There are muffled noises I can't make out before the thud of a punch connecting with flesh reaches me. It's a sound I know well, having delivered them to enemies myself over the years.

"Where is your precious Pakhan, now? Probably hiding behind my useless son and daughters. So much for blood being thicker than water, eh?" Pavel's evil chuckle echoes slightly in the darkness before another thud and grunt of what I realize is an injured Henrí reaches my ears. I can't lose Henrí. He's my best friend, my brother. My chest tightens, while anger trickles down my spine.

I can't leave him in Pavel's hands. He's liable to shoot Henrí at any moment.

"On your knees." My enemy's command sends chills through my body. There's another thud as I move along the hallway wall until I reach the doorway where I believe Pavel is about to murder my closest friend, my brat, *brother*.

I'm not an innocent man; I've killed many men and ordered the deaths of many more. But Henrí is as close to me as my mother. He's family. I can't remain in hiding while Pavel murders him.

"Pavel," I call loudly. "You might as well let Henrí go.

Even if you kill him and manage to kill me, you won't get out of here alive. The place is surrounded."

I'm trying to turn their attention to me for a moment, giving Henrí a chance to make a move. Slipping across the doorway to the opposite side, I allow them a glimpse of me. Several guns fire my way, and I move farther down the hall as the wall is churned into powder as bullet after bullet explodes through it, while Pavel shouts at his men to *get me*.

There are yelling and muffled sounds coming from inside the room now, and I take the chance to dive inside, coming to rest behind a large chair. Knowing Henrí's on the floor, I fire at the shadowy men I glimpsed as I entered. The chair I'm using is made from thick wood which I hope will take the brunt of the bullets. Henrí is struggling with one man while another lies prone on the ground. Neither one of those is my target. Scanning the room, I realize Pavel's no longer here.

Pushing to my feet, I race to Henrí's side. Leaning down, I place the gun to the head of the man he's struggling with and pull the trigger, his head exploding like a watermelon. Henrí tosses his attacker off him. Blood spatter coats his face and clothes, but it doesn't affect him.

"What took you so long?" My friend grumbles as he takes his weapon back from the dead man's holster. He pushes himself up from the floor, brushing himself off.

"Next time you need me to babysit your ass, tell me and I'll be here sooner," I tease, not letting on how relieved I am he's not seriously hurt. "C'mon. Pavel can't be far."

KATYA

"Y—You killed him," Nat splutters as I drag her from the car.

She's never seen anyone killed before. Matter of fact, neither have I.

I've never killed anyone before either, despite Father training me to assassinate Mikhail and his mother. My stomach roils and vomit rises up my throat, but I swallow it down. I'll compartmentalize my feelings for now and deal with it later. Right now, I need to get us both to safety.

The safest place I know of is with Mikhail. *Does he know we've been kidnapped yet? Is he looking for us?*

Or does he believe I've double-crossed him and gone back to my father?

"It was him or us," I answer her, trying to sound confident. "Come on, Nat," I urge her on. We need to find a cab and try to persuade the driver to take us back to Mikhail's compound. Hopefully, someone will pay the fare when we get there.

It doesn't take long to flag one down. Before pushing Nat into the back seat, I make sure our guns aren't visible. The other pistol is still in Nat's pocket, and I tuck mine in the back of my pants before I slide in beside her. We don't want him to think we're going to carjack him. Yet. If he won't take us where we need to go, I might have to use my gun to persuade him.

"We need to get to the Korbicov compound. Do you know it?" I ask the driver. His narrowed eyes lock on mine in the rearview mirror. He's suspicious. Forcing myself to relax, I smile as widely as I can as I lie. "I'm his fiancée. Our car broke down, and we need to get back home. There's a bonus in it for you if you get us there as quickly as possible."

I know I'm no such thing. At the same time, I hope this man isn't an enemy of Mikhail's. The silence inside the cab is thick, as the driver looks from me to Natalia and back. I'm sweating, and probably look a mess, while my sister looks like she's about to throw up. For a few moments, I wonder if I'll have to flash my gun at him, but then the man shrugs his shoulders and pulls away from the curb.

On reaching the compound gates, my instincts tell me something's wrong. There are no guards at the gates. *Why haven't they been replaced?*

Mikhail should know of Nikolai's treason by now. *Where is he? Was our kidnapping a ruse to lure him out? Has Father captured him? Is Svetlana safe?*

All these questions race through my mind.

"Wait here," I order both the driver and Natalia as I slip out the back door of the cab. Continually scanning the area, I creep to the guardhouse. Inside, I pull the gun from the back of my pants as I scan the small building. I find the cold bodies of the men who had been shot earlier, along with two more. Someone has dragged them all in here and left them. They guards were on the ground outside when we left. I don't remember the faces of the other two.

Trying hard not to ponder about what I'm doing, I search the pockets of the dead. As I do, I hear the sound of shots being fired in the distance. My heart rate jumps at the sounds. They aren't nearby, which is good, but I'm almost certain they're coming from the direction of the house.

Relief momentarily washes over me as I find a wallet with a large wad of money inside. Removing it, I toss the wallet back on the ground and exit the guardhouse.

Stepping outside, I return to where the cab is waiting, the engine still running and hand the money over to the driver as I thank him. Natalia climbs out of the cab, and it leaves. I guess I wouldn't want to stick around either.

Another volley of shots reaches us.

"Nat." I grab both her hands to ensure her complete attention. "You need to stay here. I have to get to the house." Mikhail's in trouble. I don't say this aloud. I'm sure he can defend himself, and if not, Henrí and his men should be by his side. "I'm worried about Mikhail's mom." It's partly the truth. "We don't know what's happening—"

"I'm coming, Kat," Natalia interrupts me. "I've got a gun. I can help." She gulps, pulling the gun from her pocket and pointing it at me. My eyes widen as I grab the nozzle, moving it in a different direction.

"You don't even know how to fire one," I snip. "And you only point it at something you intend to shoot," I add. I don't have time to argue with her. "You stay put. I'll be back for you." This time I'm stern with her, using my *don't push me* tone. "I have to go, but I'll be back as soon as I can."

21

KATYA

Staying close to the trees, I make my way as quickly as I can to the house, without being seen. When I arrive, I observe a dead body near the front door, just as gunfire rings out from inside. Slipping behind the hedges nearby, I make my way to the side of the house, then around to the back. Gunshots ring out from near the garage where Nikolai got the vehicles he drove us away from the compound in, so I veer away from the area. I'll have to find another way in.

Sneaking around the side of the house, I find a ladder, probably used by the maintenance crew. I slide it up until it's level with the first balcony, then check whether anyone has seen me. As soon as I believe it's clear, I shimmy up the ladder as fast as I can without slipping and breaking my neck. Thankfully, I'm wearing joggers and not high heels.

Once up there, I push the ladder away in case someone decides to try the same thing.

The balcony door isn't locked, and I breathe a sigh of relief. Holding my weapon in both hands, I step inside. I wait for my eyes to adjust to the difference in light before continuing. I listen for footsteps, but I can't hear anything other than the sound of bullets flying and the grunts of what sounds like men fighting.

Svetlana is on the third floor, which means there's no way to get to her other than using the stairs. I can't take a chance on the lift in case someone is waiting when I open it. I'd be a sitting duck. I'm sure Kristina, Henrí's mother will be with her, but she must be terrified. Her dementia-riddled mind wouldn't understand what was happening around her.

I try the light switch near the door, but it appears the power is out again. It's been flickering on and off since I got here. Sighing, I open the door to the room and am about to step out into the hallway, when someone runs past. Remaining as still as possible so I don't attract attention, I spy through the small gap in the door, as a man turns back and fires at someone behind him. There's return fire and the man's body crumples before tumbling down the stairs.

Waiting a few moments, I quickly glance around the doorframe in the direction the shots came from. Seeing no one, I slip out of the room, and remaining close to the wall, I head for the stairs to the second landing. I'm almost to the top when a bullet ricochets close enough to my face for splinters from the stair railing to sting my skin. Stifling a yell, I bob down, the gun trembling in one hand, the other on my chest making sure my heart doesn't fall out of my chest it's beating so fast. I wait for another, but it doesn't come. Releasing the breath I'm holding, I continue upwards.

A grunt to my right freezes me in my tracks. Peering around the banister newel, I recognize the guard Mikhail posted at his mother's door the night I met her. He's wounded, blood pooling on the floor at his side. As I scoot closer to him, he brings up his weapon. *Does he believe I'm here to kill him?*

Perhaps he thinks I'm the enemy. After all, he knows I'm Pavel Ivanov's daughter. His blood loss has made him too weak to lift his arm, and I crawl closer to him. "It's alright, I'm here to help," I assure him. "Where's Mikhail? Is he safe? Is Henrí with him?" I fire my questions at him rapidly.

A shot fires not far from where we are, and I know if we don't move, we'll be prime targets. "Come," I order him, "You'll have to help me. We need to get you somewhere safer." I place his injured arm around my neck and with my assistance, he stands. He struggles to walk, but we finally make it to a door, which when opened, presents us with an elegant guest room. As soon as we're inside, I close and lock it. "What's your name?" I ask as we limp into the room.

"Denis," the wounded man grunts.

I help Denis sit on the edge of the bed, before removing his jacket. His white button-down is stained with blood. I pray Mikhail will forgive me for tearing up the beautiful soft sheets. I need to bandage Denis's wounds before he bleeds out.

"Thank you," Denis grunts through gritted teeth, as I clean him as fast and efficiently as possible before bandaging his wounds. There's a through and through in his forearm and I think his wrist has been shattered. He has two flesh wounds on his side and a bullet in his thigh, which looks like it's still in there. I'm amazed he's still able to function.

"You didn't answer my questions." I ignore his gratitude. Any human would do the same for a wounded man, wouldn't they? I'm shocked when Denis informs me Mikhail, Henrí, and some of his men, left the compound looking for Natalia and me. "Do they know what's happening here?" I check.

I silently berate myself for allowing Natalia's enthusiasm for shopping to compromise the compound's safety. My feelings about Nikolai were right, when I first noticed him ogling Natalia at the pool. He didn't have the authority to take us off the grounds, and now everyone's lives are at stake. We've played right into Father's hands again. Why do I keep doing stupid things?

Denis shakes his head. I don't think he's far from unconsciousness, but I need answers. Pacing the floor in front of him, I pinch my bottom lip in thought. "Where are Svetlana and Kristina?" When I receive no answer, I glance sideways at the wounded man. "Denis," I speak his name loudly and he jolts up straight. "Where is Svetlana? Is she still upstairs?" I try again. After what Svetlana told me, I don't want Pavel anywhere near her.

Slurring his words, Denis manages to tell me they're in a panic room. I sigh in relief, knowing they're safe. After making sure Denis is lying flat on the bed, I close the heavy curtains before I leave the room. Hopefully, no one will find him there until this is all over.

Heading for the next flight of stairs, the lights flicker off again, and I detect the smell of smoke. My pace quickens. If they've set fire to the house, it might force Kristine and Svetlana from the panic room. I don't know much about them. It could be fireproof, but I don't know for sure.

I wish Mikhail were here.

Why hasn't anyone told Mikhail the house is being attacked? I'm sure he would come directly home if he did. Surely, he doesn't consider saving Nat and me to be more important than protecting his mother and his home.

I can't tell him we're here either because I don't have a phone. Nor do I know his number. Ahead of me are two more dead bodies, one I recognize as Mikhail's man, although I don't know his name. The position of his body exposes the earpiece he wears. I crawl to the bodies and check their pockets for anything I can use. Removing the earpiece. I check whether it works. Whispering into it, I wait for an answer, but none comes. It must be broken.

Breathing a sigh of relief when I find a cell phone in his pocket, I hold it in front of his face to unlock it and look for Mikhail's number. Disappointment floods me when I don't find it. Of course, I realize. Mikhail wouldn't be on these thugs' phones. He doesn't personally order these guys around, Henrí and the Avtoritets do. I find Henrí's number and dial it. It doesn't ring. Instead, a robotic voice on the other end tells me the number I'm calling is not in range or switched off. I huff out a frustrated breath. There's no way Henrí would not have his phone on.

What is going on? Where are they?

I refuse to even contemplate that Mikhail could be dead. But considering he was already wounded, could Pavel have got the drop on him? Please let him be okay.

Footsteps moving closer to where I am pull me from my thoughts. I'm in the open and it's too late to find cover. It takes all my strength to pull one of the bodies over on top of me. Hopefully, whoever is coming doesn't look too closely.

"Burn everything." Igor's voice sends chills down my spine. "If they won't come out of the room, they'll die in it."

He's talking about Mikhail's mother. How cold can a person be to murder someone with dementia, someone who hasn't harmed anyone? I can't stand by and let this happen.

Anger causes mistakes, my instructor's words whisper inside my head. *Calm yourself*, it says. *Take a deep breath, wait, and your chance will come.*

I inhale, count to ten, then let out the breath slowly, as I've been taught. It works. If I attempted to make a move on Igor right now, I would end up dead, or worse, and be of no help to anyone.

The voices move away, and when I'm sure it's clear, I wriggle out from under the dead man and head along the hall in the opposite direction to where Igor must have gone. I must find the woman who means everything to Mikhail.

His mother.

MIKHAIL

We have him cornered. Pavel Ivanov is about to become my prisoner. He has clambered up the fire escape to the roof. His only choice now, is to surrender or throw himself off the building.

"There's nowhere to go, Pavel. Step away from the edge," Henrí calls.

I could care less if he wanted to jump and splatter his brains all over the footpath below. It does mean I wouldn't have the pleasure of killing him myself, though.

While Henrí keeps Pavel's eyes on him, I'm edging my way towards him from the opposite direction.

"I'm not surrendering to your Pakhan." Fear is obvious in Pavel's voice. "I was meant to be the one. It was *me* who had all the brilliant ideas on how to make more money for everyone. Rinaldo stole my ideas," he whines. "I was supposed to be your Pakhan. Not that snot-nosed son of his." He's digging his grave deeper with every insult.

It's a shame that you can only kill a man once.

I'm closing in on him when something gives my position away. Pavel whirls to face me, his eyes wide when he recognizes me. He throws his gun at me, as if that's going to save him. I aim a shot at his leg, and he crumples to the ground.

Henrí hastily makes his way to Pavel, checking him for any other weapons. He finds a knife in Pavel's boot, removes it and jams it in his own.

We have him.

My Avtoritets and their men drag the bleeding man down to where Tomas waits in the car, while Henrí and I follow Pavel shouts at Tomas, "Son, help me. You can't let them take me. I'm your father."

"Toss him in the trunk," Tomas mutters to the men restraining Pavel. "And gag him, will you?"

Pavel slumps, his face screwing up with a look of hatred as he curses his son and all those he believes have failed him. One of the men silently removes Pavel's shoe and sock, then proceeds to shove the sock down our prisoners throat. The trunk is opened and he's tossed unceremoniously inside.

I holster my gun before running both hands over my head and face, glad this part of my life is coming together. My father's murderer has been caught, and I will be able to avenge him. Pavel Ivanov will no longer cast an evil shadow over my family. My Otets will finally be able to rest in peace.

One of my men approaches, concern evident on his face. "We can't reach anyone at the compound. There appears to be some sort of electrical interference. There's been no communication for over an hour. The last we heard was when two of the men were ordered by Denis to take over at the front gates after you left." He runs a nervous hand through his long dark hair. "We've tried all channels. Phones aren't working either," he adds.

"Get every man available to the compound," I snap, already heading for the car. Henrí is climbing into the other side when I order Tomas to get us to the compound as fast as possible. Bringing up the GPS on his phone, Henrí directs Tomas to the fastest route.

Will this day never fucking end?

I hope Katya and Natalia are somewhere safe because right now my priority has to be my mother.

Traffic has picked up since we entered the city and even with Tomas' excellent driving, it takes longer to reach my compound.

Henrí checks the guardhouse when no one steps out to greet us. His face is serious as he comes trotting back to the car. Jumping into the back seat he slams the door while yelling orders at Tomas. "Go, go." Turning to me, he grinds his teeth, his jaw ticking with the pressure. "They're taking a run at the house. Everyone in the guardhouse is dead, including Pavel's men." Henrí pulls his gun from his holster and checks his ammunition. I do the same.

Tomas plants his foot hard on the pedal, and both of us are pushed back into our seats.

Henrí squeezes his lower lip tight between his finger and his thumb. "What aren't you saying?" I don't like the worry showing clearly on his face.

"If the women weren't with Pavel, unless they came back here, where are they?" Henrí exclaims.

22

MIKHAIL

BULLETS SLAM INTO THE FRONT OF OUR CAR BEFORE
we reach the end of the driveway.

"Give me one of your knives." Tomas reaches one
arm between the seats, and I pass him a knife. He ducks
down under the dashboard as another volley of bullets
clunk against the metal body. None of them penetrate.
We're not close enough. "Get ready to jump," Tomas
calls as removes his belt and ties it around the steering
wheel before revving the engine, speeding the car up.

Henrí opens his door at the same time as Tomas. I
slide sideways on the seat until I'm squashed up against
my friend. "Now," Tomas shouts, and we throw ourselves
from the car, rolling over the gravel drive before we get
to our feet and slip into the trees.

Pavel is still in the trunk, but we don't have time to
get him out.

We make our way to the house as fast as we can,
using the trees and bushes in the vast garden as shields.

Shouts and a hail of bullets let us know using the car as a decoy has worked for now. The ground trembles as an explosion rocks the air, and glancing back, I observe a ball of flames erupt, probably from the car.

The explosion will give us a few more minutes to gain entry into the house before they realize there's no one in the vehicle except Pavel's body. After that, his men will probably come at us in full force. There's no time to lose.

"This way." I lead Henrí and Tomas to a hidden door at the side of the house, tapping out a code on the panel. The door opens and I don't hesitate as I move as fast as I can down the steps, turning back once to make sure the others are behind me.

The smell of smoke is apparent, although the air down here is clear. Pavel's men have set the house on fire. I need to make sure Mama and Kristine made it to the panic room. Fear is a strange feeling to have, but I feel it today. Not only for my mother, but for Katya as well. My chest involuntarily tightens when I think of Katya hurt. *Where is she?* We make our way out and along a hallway through an open door. I already know what I'll find, but I check inside the room I held Igor in, anyway.

"Igor's gone," I state flatly, eyeing the empty shackles. I should've killed him when we captured him.

Heavy footsteps ahead distract us. Someone is moving down the stairs we're heading towards. Backtracking a little, we take up positions in open doorways on either side of the long hall. Two men with machine guns walk toward us and, without hesitation, I step out and shoot them. They have no cover and are easy targets. Both men fall to the ground and we continue heading to the stairs leading up to the first level of my home.

The basement doorway is closed when we reach it. I

motion to the other two to be quiet as I crack it open slightly. Not seeing or hearing any movement nearby, I open the door wider and step out. It's clear, so I motion for Henrí and Tomas to follow me.

Tomas peers at me in puzzlement when I lead us to a door beneath the stairwell. Shots can be heard from the first level and above, as well as outside.

The odor of smoke is intense here and the air is beginning to thicken with it.

We have to get to Mama's floor as fast as possible. With all this gunfire and smoke, there's no guarantee either Mama or Kristine got to the panic room. Kristine could be hurt, or dead. It's something I don't want to think about, because then I have to wonder where Mama is and what's happening to her.

Beneath the outer stairwell is a secret stairway. Over the years, Otets, then me, had the house renovated, adding new protection devices and hideaways. The secret stairs will allow us to surprise our enemy. They'll be preparing for us to come up the open stairway and will have their main concentration of weapons pointed that way.

The secret stairway is wide enough for us to walk in single file. I lead, Tomas is behind me, and Henrí brings up the rear. Our progress is hindered by the low ceiling, and we have to hunch over as we move.

It's slow going. All we have are the torches on our phones. By the time we reach the third level of the house, the smoke is thick and dark. Taking our handkerchiefs from our pockets, Henrí and I tie them around our faces. Tomas doesn't have one, so he places one hand over his mouth and nose. It's not much help, but we have few choices at the moment. None of this helps the stinging of our eyes, which blur the moment the door is cracked open.

I told Kristina to get Mama to the panic room, but I don't know if they made it before the house was overrun. The worry chokes off my air for a moment. "You okay?" Henrí mutters, his voice close behind me.

Inhaling deeply, I realize my mistake too late as smoke fills my lungs and I begin to cough. Each spasm is felt throughout my wounds. Henrí closes the door until I get the coughing fit under control in case someone outside hears. When I finally recover, I feel wet down my side, pain spreading in the same area. The coughing fit probably tore some stitches, but there's no time to worry about it. Reaching for the pain pills in my pocket, I pour some more into my palm. It's too dark to know how many fall from the bottle, but I don't care. I throw them into my mouth, chewing and swallowing them dry. "I'm fine," I lie. "Let's move."

Using the smoke as cover, we leave the safety of the stairs. Keeping close to the walls, we make our way to Mama's room. I'm sure Kristine would protect my mother with her life, but we don't know whether they're safe in the panic room or not.

The door to Mama's room is off its hinges, lying on the floor. It would have taken several men to take it down like that. The breath in my lungs, already burning from the smoke, stutters with fear.

Henrí's hand on my arm breaks me out of my thoughts. "Mére's, *mother's*, tracker just activated, drug, *brother*. She's in the panic room," he murmurs. "You know she wouldn't be there without Svetlana," he adds.

The three of us brace as the door to Mama's bathroom opens. A thickset guy steps out, too busy with his belt to notice us. He's not one of mine. We aim our guns at him, firing before he can, and in moments, he's riddled with bullets. Dead before he hits the ground.

I walk with lead-filled legs to the bathroom, step over the dead guy's body, and open the door. There's no one else in there when. The stink is overwhelming and there's the sound of water still running in the back of the toilet. The thug must have decided to take a crap. It's the last one he'll take.

"Clear," I call, exiting the room as fast as I can. I'd rather inhale smoke than the stink he left behind.

"We better get to the panic room," Henrí decides for us, leading the way from Mama's bedroom. As he steps outside the door, a few feet ahead of me and Tomas, he freezes, and I instantly know something's wrong. I signal Tomas to move up against the wall so he's not visible to the person stepping through the doorway, holding a gun to Henrí's head. Our enemies will be expecting Henrí and me, not anyone else.

Henrí raises his hands above his shoulders. The gunman must indicate for him to step back into the room. Henrí turns around slowly, locking eyes with mine as someone pushes him back inside Mama's bedroom. The first mistake the thug makes is not checking his surroundings. His concentration is solely on the two of us. He doesn't realize his mistake until Tomas steps up behind him, pushing the barrel of his gun into the thug's back.

I smile as the guy's face pales and he stops moving. "This is why you don't work for me." The thug raises his arms in the air, his gun still in his hand. Henrí spins around and takes the weapon from him. I know what he's about to do, but we need him for information.

"Where's Igor?" I demand of the man, who is now sweating profusely.

When the thug hesitates, Henrí smacks him across the face with the butt of his gun, sending him to the floor. He spits blood and a tooth out onto the floor, a bruise already starting on his cheek.

"I won't repeat myself," I snarl. Time is wasting.

Knowing I'm not fucking with him, the thug looks up, shrugging one shoulder.

He isn't going to tell us. Henrí steps forward, places the man's weapon against his forehead, and fires, before tucking the weapon into the back of his pants. The dead man slumps to the floor, his body twitching in his death throes. I step over him as if he's a piece of furniture. Tomas, however, appears to be a bit shaky. I don't particularly care how this is affecting him. Violence is a part of my life I've accepted.

"I've never seen anyone killed anyone before," he admits as he wipes sweat from his brow.

"Well, you have now," Henrí adds flatly. Like me, Henrí grew up in the Bratva. It can be a brutal world.

"I came to you and told you about Papa's plans because I'm not a violent person." Katya's brother comes across as whiny now. This isn't the time for weakness. If he can't hold his own, we'll cut him loose.

As if reading my mind, Henrí moves at speed. Fisting the front of Tomas' shirt, he pins him up against the wall, his other hand wrapping tight around Tomas' throat. "You had better grow some goddamn balls, boy. Your father and your cousin are out there killing Mikhail's men. Your sisters are missing, and Mikhail's and my mother are in this fucking house, maybe too afraid to leave the panic room," he snaps in Tomas' face. Twisting the front of his shirt tighter, he snarls, "This is the time to step up. Which is it gonna be? In or out?"

Tomas squirms under Henrí's angry gaze.

It seems like forever before Tomas answers him. "I'm in. I'll do anything to save my sisters," he gasps, fighting for air.

Releasing the hold he has on him, Henrí steps back. Tomas slumps for a moment, probably thanking God he isn't dead. Seconds pass before he straightens up, his face flushed. He holds my gaze as he commits to me, "I'm all in. Whatever you need from me, I'll do."

We have to get to the panic room. "Let's go," I nod to Tomas, accepting his allegiance. We don't sign contracts in this world. A man's word is his bond, breakable only by death. I would be disappointed if I had to kill Katya's brother, but if it has to be done, I will.

The house must be well alight now, as the smoke is so thick, our sight is close to zero. Smoke chokes us, and our eyes are red and swollen before we reach the secret stairwell again. It's hard to find the panel and I have to feel along the wall for the indent before it finally slides open.

Pavel's men must have started a blaze, trying to flush out my men. They might not have known our mothers were here, but I don't believe they care either. The smoke will eventually coax everyone out into the open. It's a matter of waiting. But Igor is not a patient man, and I'm counting on it.

If he's still alive, Pavel Ivanov has led a charmed life. He's evaded every effort to locate him since he killed my father. I won't believe he's dead until I see his body with my own eyes. Igor either doesn't know we captured

Pavel earlier, or he has his own agenda because the men haven't been called off.

A bullet soars past my ear as we exit the stairwell on the first floor, and I step back inside, pulling the door closed behind me. "Back. Move," my order is abrupt, leaving no space for anyone to disobey. I spray the now-closed panel with bullets before following.

As we move back up the stairs a few feet as fast as possible, the panel is peppered with bullets from the enemy. If we had remained in place, we'd probably all be wounded, if not dead.

"Back to the second floor. Go," I command. They know we're here now. It's probably a matter of minutes before someone comes after us. In the cramped conditions of the stairs, we're open targets. Moving upwards as fast as possible, we reach the second floor. There's yelling and movement below us. We need to find cover fast.

Bursting through the door, I slam the panel closed as the three of us scan the area for threats. The sound of gunfire echoes up the stairs we exited from moments ago, splintering the door panel and thudding harmlessly into the wall.

A door opens a fraction, and Henrí's about to shoot when I catch a glimpse of a familiar face. "He's one of ours," I call, staying Henrí's hand.

Denis appears and motions for us to come to him, which we do. As we close the door to the room, the sound of the panel door being breached reaches us. They're here. Using my torch, I find the light switch, which isn't working, before I shine it on Denis. "You're wounded," I state, seeing the rough bandages made from the sheets and the blood-soaked bed.

"I am, boss. Your woman saved my life. She dragged me in here and bandaged my wounds," he elaborates. "I must have blacked out. When I came to, she was gone. I thought it was her coming back," he adds.

My woman? "You mean Katya? Katya's here?" I swipe my hand over my face from my mustache to my beard as he nods. Keeping my face neutral, I await his answer. *Where the hell is she?*

"What about Natalia?" Tomas demands. "Is she with Katya?"

Denis sways, his face paling. He can pass out after he answers our questions. "Denis," I use his name gruffly. "Is there anyone with Katya?"

"N–No, boss. I only saw her," he stutters before crumpling to the floor.

Henrí mumbles something under his breath, but I can't make it out. "You good?" I ask him. He nods but remains quiet.

I don't have time to play nursemaid and head for the door. Tomas places a pillow under Denis' head and throws a blanket over him before he follows. I don't tell him Denis will probably be dead before this day is over. He'll learn death happens a lot in my business.

Cracking the door open a little, we wait until we can't hear any voices before leaving the room. They know about the secret stairs now and have probably set up an ambush at each level. Being out in the open is more dangerous, but we have no choice now.

"I'm getting low on bullets," Henrí stage whispers to me.

"I don't know how many I've got in here," Tomas admits.

I've got two magazines left. There are weapons

stashed in several places within the house. Sticking to the walls of the hall, I lead the others to a sitting room. The door's wide open and Henrí pushes ahead of me to check inside. "Clear," he murmurs, and we follow him, our weapons in hand, just in case, closing the door behind us. Pulling at the corner of a large painting of my grandfather, the painting moves to show a large safe behind it. Opening it, I remove the weapons stashed within.

I close it again and straighten the painting so no one knows we've been here before glancing around the room. Sitting on a bar in the corner is my bottle of Macallan, and if things weren't so dire right now, I'd take a good swig. Instead, I tuck my weapons away and grab some bottles of water from the bar fridge. My throat is parched with the smoke so I know Henri and Tomas must feel the same. I swallow down another handful of pills.

The door bursts open before we get to it and three figures burst through. Instinctively, the three of us dive behind the thick mahogany wood and leather couch, Mama, Otets and I sat on in front of the fire many times when I was a child. Bullets thud into it from the doorway, but they don't penetrate. I silently thank Mama for choosing robust furniture when she decorated the house.

Henrí crawls to one end of it and fires several shots. A grunt and a thudding noise reaches us. There's at least one man down. As I pull my pistol from its holster my shirt feels stiff and wet beneath, but I don't have time to check my wounds.

"Cover me," Tomas mutters. I'm usually the one giving orders, but I'll allow it this one time. He slips the safety catch slip off the machine gun, before licking his lips nervously. "One, two..." Both Henrí and I start firing from either end of the couch. Tomas stands up and empties his magazine towards the doorway where the shots had come from, bullets thunking into plaster and wood. And hopefully, into bodies.

"Holy shitbags." Tomas' face is wide-eyed, his excitement barely contained. "That was so fucking cool." When he squats back down, his back to the couch, we listen. There's silence.

"Stay here until I give you the all clear," Henrí takes the lead again.

He doesn't take his eyes off the doorway as, gun in hand, he strides toward it. Leaning against the bullet-ridden wall, he pokes his head out the door, checking both directions. Turning to us, he nods and we join him.

Tomas looks down at the two men he cut down with his gun with a blank face. He seems to be accepting the role he has chosen. Henrí searches the bodies for extra ammunition after confiscating their weapons. He hands me two pistols and I tuck them in the back of my pants. The extra clips go in my pocket.

23

KATYA

My throat burns, while my eyes blur constantly from the smoke. I keep wiping them on my shirt, but it doesn't help.

I continue making my way to Svetlana's suite. I'm sure Kristina will be with her, but until I make sure she's safe from Father, I won't rest. There's no telling what he might do if he finds either of them. The thought sends a shiver down my spine.

Father's men are everywhere. I'm glad I told Natalia to stay at the guardhouse. Hopefully, Mikhail will find her and protect her. I don't want her to see the death and destruction happening here.

Keeping as low as possible, I take the stairs one at a time, constantly checking below and above me. I'm open to an attack from either while I climb to the third level.

The higher I get, the thicker the smoke is, but it doesn't stop me heading to see for myself whether the two women Mikhail loves are alright.

I'm almost at the top step when Igor and another man appear from the hallway to my left. They open fire on me. The only cover is the thick wooden newel holding the banister in place. I return fire and can't help a small fist pump when Igor wobbles, letting out a yelp of pain. The other man reaches out and, grabbing Igor by the arm, drags him back into the hallway.

While they're occupied, I hightail it to the hallway on my right, away from them. Hunching low to make myself a smaller target, I creep toward Svetlana's suite. Shots sound ahead of me and I squat down behind a solid-looking wooden credenza, my heart thumping hard in my chest.

In my wildest nightmares, I never saw myself in this position. Fear in the form of sweat drips from my face and my hands are clammy, making my grip on the gun slippery.

Footsteps rapidly close in on where I am, and I curl into the smallest ball I can make. Much like when I knew Igor was coming to the house and I would purposely hide from him.

This time I'm not only hiding from him, but from Father and his cohorts as well. It's a sad world when a child fears her parent more than the Bratva.

I can't make out whether the men rushing past are friends or foes. They probably wouldn't know what side I'm on either. Thankfully, none of them look back. After waiting a few more seconds in case they're being chased, I uncurl myself and continue to the doorway to Svetlana's suite.

To my horror, the door lies on the floor. A quick scan of the room shows no sign of either woman, but I enter anyway. I check under the king-size bed, the balcony, and the walk-in robe. Nothing. Gun in hand, I enter the bathroom. No one. I hope it's a good thing.

I sit on the edge of the bed for a moment to think.

I know Igor doesn't have the two women, because there was only him and his flunky when they shot at me. There are two alternatives. Either Mikhail has taken them somewhere safe, or Father has them. Shuddering at the thought of my father capturing Svetlana, I fight the bile rising in my throat.

If, by chance, he hasn't found them yet, they would still be somewhere in the house. *Think, Katya*, I tell myself. If you were hiding in a house as large as this, where would you be?

Noises from the hallway catch my attention. Sneaking up to the doorway, I flatten myself against the wall, gun ready as the sounds repeat. There's a lot of grunting and banging. It sounds like doors are being kicked in. As they get closer, I hear them laughing and joking about how Mikhail is such a coward, and he left the door to his home unlocked for them. I clench my fists in anger, wanting to shout at them that they broke in. Nobody invited them.

The smell of smoke grows stronger, and smoke billows through the doorway. Racing to the bathroom, I grab a washcloth, wetting it under the tap. Covering my nose and mouth with it, I check the room again before I exit. The men are moving closer to me.

Stepping into the hallway, I cock my weapon, and aim in the direction of the voices, pulling the trigger until the clip is empty. Stepping back inside Svetlana's suite, I dump the empty clip onto the floor, immediately replacing it with another from my bra.

Walking over to the bed, I grab a pillow and throw it

out into the hallway. No one fires at it leading me to believe the threat is gone. Next, I poke my head out. There are no sounds now from the direction the voices had been coming from. Flames lick high in the air to my right. The acidic odor of black smoke burns my eyes, nose, and throat.

I know there are back stairs leading to the outside from this floor, but the fire has caught hold. To attempt to get past them would mean getting burned.

With the cloth over my nose and mouth, I head back in the direction I came. The smoke stings my eyes, and I don't see what's coming. Something hard connects with the side of my head. Stunned, I hit the floor, my gun falling from my hand.

"Well, hello, Katya. Your father said you might be here, somewhere. He'll be pleased to see you, I'm sure," a familiar voice sneers. I shake my head to clear it, stretching out my jaw at the same time.

"I don't have time for lessons today," I snap back at Anatole, the man who trained me in self-defense. He stands over me, hands on his hips, and a smirk on his face.

"Pavel told me I could kick your ass before I hand you over to him," the slimy asshole informs me. He rubs his hands together in anticipation before giving me the *come-on* signal.

The bastard was always too cocky. Too sure of himself. I lunge upwards from the ground, wrap my arms around his waist, and take him to the floor. While I've had the benefit of surprise, I straddle him, raining punches down on his face as hard as I can before he regroups.

We might have been sparring partners when I was in

training, but this time, Anatole's my enemy. If I don't take him out now, he'll get the better of me. He has a good fifty pounds on me, and I know if he gets up off this floor, I'm a goner.

With a roar, he rolls sideways, knocking me off him. Stumbling to his feet, he places a kick to my ribs and though I roll with it, it still knocks the breath from my lungs. He follows me as I try to roll further away from him and lands another kick. This time it lands in my stomach. I curl into a fetal position as I dry retch. He stomps on my arm, and I cry out in pain. When he tries it again, I grab his foot and twist it, causing him to flail backward.

In desperation, I crawl towards the stairs.

"Where are you going, Katya?" Anatole singsongs as he gains his feet.

Holding my arm across my stomach, I attempt to escape him by scooting backwards on my butt, before getting onto my hands and knees, crawling. I know he's behind me, but I'm trying to concentrate on getting to the stairs. His boot connects with my arm and ribs, and I tumble down the steps. Every one of them slams into me as I roll to the second landing. Tears fall silently. My mouth is bleeding from my face hitting a step, and my arm hurts like hell. I don't think it's broken, but it's badly bruised. Maybe a few ribs too. But I can't give up.

Anatole deliberately stalks me down the stairs, a wolfish smile on his face. "You know, I always thought you were the smart one. But I see now you're just another dumb blonde. Before I turn you over to your sweet, sweet daddy, I'd like to taste you, at least once." He pokes his tongue out, flicking it up and down in a licking motion. "You'd like that, wouldn't you?" An evil smile forms as he bares his teeth before gnashing them together.

I've crawled into a sitting position, gasping for breath as he closes in. The world is swimming in front of me, while my skin crawls at the thought of being at the man's mercy. But there's little I can do to defend myself right now.

Anatolé's about to grab me when a roar erupts from behind him. Two large arms wrap around his waist, and he's lifted into the air. I watch in awe as Denis tosses Anatolé over the banister as if he weighs nothing. Anatolé screams, his arms and legs reaching for something, anything to save him, but there's nothing. I twist in time to see his body thud on the marble floor below, his head cracking like an egg.

"You okay, Miss Katya?" Denis' weary voice sounds behind me. As I turn back to him, the injured man limps toward me before slumping down to the floor next to me. Tears surface again, but this time I blink them back.

I cover Denis' hand with mine. "Thank you for saving me," I whisper hoarsely, the words getting caught in my throat.

His large arm lifts to wrap around my shoulders, pulling me close to him. "No, Miss Katya, thank you for saving me."

I raise my good arm, fist closed, "So, we're even?"

Denis fist bumps me, his large meaty hand making mine look like that of a child. "Yes," he grunts. "We are even."

"I'm trying to find Mikhail's mother, Denis. Do you know where she is? I must find her before Father or Igor does." He looks down at me hesitantly. "Please, Denis," I plead. "I can't let them take her."

"They're safe, Katya," he answers, his face expressing the pain he's in. A sheen of sweat has risen above his brow and top lip and his face is once again pale. Saving me has taken a toll on what little strength he probably had. "They're in the panic room Mikhail had built after his father's murder. I'll take you," he offers.

I pat his large hand as it sits on his lap. "No. You've done enough," I try to assure him. "Point me in the right direction. I'll keep them safe until Mikhail comes."

"The Pakhan is here. Have you not seen him?" Denis glances down at my hand on his. "If he saw me touching you, I would be a dead man," he states casually. "Come, I will take you," he repeats.

Startled, I clamber to my feet, pain shooting through my body and arm. "He's here? How do you know? Where is he? Is he alright?" I toss question after question at him, as he turns to his side and rolls onto his knees before pulling himself up using the railing.

The last time I saw Mikhail was when I climbed onto his hospital bed. I flush, remembering what I did that night. The way Mikhail sounded while I sucked him off, and the power I felt when he allowed me to be in charge. My thighs involuntarily clench at the memory.

"He came into the room when I was coming to," Denis shrugs, interrupting my reminiscing. "I thought it was a hallucination, but it wasn't. He went to check on his mother. I was no good to him. I kept passing out." He grunts in annoyance at his wounds. "Come, we will go together," he commands as he takes an unsure step forward.

"Are you sure you're okay to do this?" Denis is built like a powerhouse, though he's not tall like Mikhail. He doesn't answer me, simply nods, and begins limping away. I follow without question. After all, this man saved my life, so I know I can trust him.

"When did you see Mikhail, Denis?" I ask, using his name.

"I don't know. It could have been minutes, but it could have been hours." He scratches his head as he answers me.

Denis leads me back to the landing, down a hall and into a small alcove that would not be seen by a passerby unless they knew it was there. We follow it down to where the space opens out to a larger area. As we step inside, we both freeze.

Father and Igor are standing over Svetlana and Kristina, who are kneeling at their feet. The women's faces are tear-streaked and fearful as the pair of jackals, I'm amiss to say are related to me, press gun barrels to their temples. The weapons in their other hands are trained on Mikhail and Henrí, who are standing to my right. Their guns are trained on Father and Igor. A body is slumped on the floor, unmoving. It looks like Tomas.

I gasp in shock.

"Ah, Katya." Father plasters a menacing smile on his face. "Welcome to the party." He chuckles menacingly. "Always late."

"W–What did you do to Tomas?" My voice cracks in fear and I immediately hate myself for it. I didn't want them to know I'm afraid, but it's too late now.

Waving his gun toward Denis, Igor snarls, ignoring me, "Tell your friend there to take out his weapon carefully and drop it on the floor."

"He's unarmed," I answer.

Igor points his gun at Denis and fires. I cry out in anguish as Denis grunts before crumpling to the floor.

The man saved my life. I squat down, feeling his neck for a pulse, but I can't find one. Rising unsteadily to my feet, I aim my gun at Igor, my hand trembling. "He wasn't armed, you fucking coward," I shriek, both angry and fearful, tears welling up in my eyes.

The urge to shoot them both is overwhelming. I hate them with every fiber of my being.

"Oh, stop the hysterics, Katya. This is not the time for you to throw a tantrum." Father sneers. "If you shoot Igor, I will shoot one of these delectable women," he continues as if this was a normal day and shooting unarmed people was a natural part of it.

Tomas groans from the floor. *He's alive.* My feet tell me to go to him, but I know if I move, I could be the next person shot. Blinking back the unshed tears, I try to ignore his moans. "You shot your own son?" I snap at Father, hoping to find a small hint of regret on his face.

"Son? *Son?*" he repeats, emphasizing the word the second time he spits it out. "No son of mine would commit treason on his father. You're all useless," he barks. "I should have been the Pakhan. You would have respected me then," he rants. "I'm taking what should have been mine in the first place."

Glancing around the room, I brush my hair from my face as I wonder how the hell we're going to get out of this. This time, it appears as if Pavel and Igor are holding all the aces.

24

WAVING HIS SECOND GUN AT ME, WHILE IGOR COVERS the two men to my right, Father indicates for me to come closer. When I don't move straight away, he cocks the gun he has aimed at Svetlana.

Mikhail lets out a snarl in warning, but it only serves to fuel Father's courage. He knows they won't make a move while the two women are hostages.

"You, Katya, are going to do what I sent you here to do," Father states when I'm close, his voice unemotional as always. "You are going to shoot the Pakhan. If you don't. I will kill these two whores, and your baby sister, when I find her, will be sold off to the highest bidder," he continues as if it's a normal conversation.

Mikhail's hand tightens on his gun when Father refers to Svetlana as a whore, but he stands his ground, although his growl indicates he's probably on the edge.

I'm sure, in his time as the Pakhan, he has seen, been involved in, or has ordered the death of many. However, the fear in his eyes right now is that of a son who has already lost his father and is now afraid of losing his mother. I wish I could console him. Tell him everything will be okay. But I can't.

Svetlana begins to hum, and rocks from side to side. Igor kicks her in the back, but she continues. The poor woman doesn't know how much danger she's in. Perhaps it's a good thing. Kristina reaches over, takes her friend's hand in hers, then lays them in her lap.

I move closer reluctantly, trying to remain calm. As I do, to my left, in my peripheral vision, I glimpse movement. There's a large Egyptian vase with a thick, green plant inside it in one corner of the room. I'm not sure, and perhaps I'm grabbing at straws, but there seems to be someone behind it. When I catch the glint of metal, my heart soars.

Please let it be one of Mikhail's men, I pray to any god available right now.

"Stop there," Father's voice intrudes on my silent call for help.

I obey, firmly keeping my eyes on my father and his cousin. They don't appear to know there's someone else in the room.

"Now turn around and face him, Katya. Face the man I sent you to kill. Your father's enemy," Father rants as if he's the one wronged in all of this. "The person who took from me what is rightfully mine," he continues as if he's the righteous one.

Obeying Father's orders, I turn almost in a circle to face Mikhail, trying to catch a glimpse of whoever is behind the vase. *Was it my imagination?* No, there it is again, the gun poking out from between the green plant in the large terracotta vase.

"Kill him," Father orders.

Cringing at the order, I purse my lips into a thin line. My lower lip trembles and tears blur my vision. I blink hard to keep them at bay. My mind races as it tries to find a solution other than Father's. I jump, my shoulders pulling tight as Father snaps loudly, "Do it. Remember what will happen to your sister if you don't," he grates.

Mikhail's eyes have been on his mother up until now.

Gradually the dark chocolate orbs, surrounded by long, black lashes, rise to mine. I expect his gaze to be full of hatred for me, for who I am, but there isn't any. Tears I didn't want to let fall drip to my cheeks, making a trail down my dirty face, grimy from the smoke and sweat. I try to convey to him with my eyes and tears that this isn't my choice. If it were me Father was threatening, I would let him kill me, but it isn't.

I can't allow Father to kill more innocent people. Tomas may be dead, and Natalia is all I have left. My heart breaks at the thought of what I'm about to do, but I've been given no choice.

As I point the gun at Mikhail, my hands shake. I can't do this. There's a murmur behind me and I glance behind me. Kristina tucks Svetlana's face into her shoulder, so she doesn't see her son die. It only serves to make my tears fall faster. Svetlana has had to live with the knowledge that my father murdered her husband. Now he's forcing her to watch the daughter of her husband's killer murder her son.

I rub my sleeve across my eyes to clear them.

"Stop stalling," Father shouts, startling me. I glance behind me once more when Svetlana cries out. Igor has a grip on her hair, pulling her face up and forcing her to watch what's about to happen.

Mikhail gives me a slight nod. I lick my dry lips as I shakily take aim. "Do it," he mouths. I fire on a sob and Mikhail falls to his knees, holding his chest, before sinking to the floor. Svetlana lets out a scream, and Kristine cries as she tries to soothe her friend.

Heartbroken and angry at what my father forced me to do, I break, my knees giving way beneath me.

A shot rings out behind me, and I spin around, fearing Svetlana has been shot.

Instead, my father jerks upright, dropping both his weapons. A shocked expression crosses his face as a red patch spreads across his chest. He takes a step back as another gun erupts and Igor falls back, screaming as he drops the gun he held on the hostages.

Kristina grips Svetlana by the arm and pushes her flat to the floor before leaping on top of her. I rush forward, firing at both Igor and then my father. Several other guns join in, and their bodies shudder as bullet after bullet is fired in their direction.

It all happens in a matter of moments, but it feels like hours from the time I stepped into the room to what has occurred.

My head's still spinning from the carnage around me as I rush to Svetlana and Kristina's sides. "Are you okay?" I blurt out as Kristina rolls off her friend and climbs to her feet. She has blood splattered all over her, but she assures me it's not hers. We both help Svetlana up off the floor, the poor woman's face pale as a ghost, her eyes wildly scanning the room.

"Rinaldo. Where is my Rinaldo?" Her voice shakes as badly as her hands. I turn away from them, my mind still on the man I have strong feelings for. The man I just shot.

I shot Mikhail.

MIKHAIL

When we reach the alcove where the panic room is, I can't believe my eyes. Pavel and Igor stand behind my mother and Kristina. They're using them as shields. *What the hell are they doing outside the panic room? How did he get them out?*

Pavel must read my expression and chuckles drily. "You forget, Mikhail, I was once family. Your mother's disease served me well. I told her Rinaldo said it was safe and despite Kristina trying to interfere, she opened the door," he chuckles again. I aim my gun at him, but he pulls Kristina closer.

Henrí makes a choking sound next to me. I can't allow his emotions to make him do something rash.

"Wait, brat, *brother*. You know he won't hesitate to kill your mother or mine if he thinks there's no other way out," I murmur.

"Let the women go, Father," Tomas urges. "They've done nothing to you."

Pavel fires a shot, snarling as he does, and Tomas cries out as he falls to the ground. If he's willing to shoot his own son, then I know he's desperate enough to shoot his hostages.

I wasn't able to save Otets, but I'll willingly give up my life if it means saving Mama.

Denis, the injured man in the bedroom earlier, limps into the alcove. I'm shocked that he's still alive, but even more shocked to see Katya with him. Her beautiful blonde hair is unkempt, her clothes are disheveled, and she appears to have been beaten. If whoever put those bruises on her is still alive, they won't be for long.

Even bruised and bleeding, Katya is still the most beautiful woman I've ever seen.

Pavel fires the pistol he isn't holding on Kristina and Denis drops to the floor with a grunt. He motions Katya forward and after he threatens to shoot the two women, one who means everything to me, she obeys.

When her father orders her to shoot me, the indecision on her face is obvious. I know she doesn't want to obey him.

Katya hesitates and Pavel cocks the gun he has aimed at Mama. Rage rises from my core and if it were a weapon, Pavel and Igor would be disintegrated right now. Mama is an innocent party. She's already had to deal with Otets' death, and now this maniac is going to put her through more trauma. I snarl at them like an animal, unable to control my hatred for both men.

Katya's eyes widen more than before, her fear unmistakable. She jumps, hunching her shoulders as her father shouts orders and threats at her. I stare into her eyes as they fill with tears. Her hesitation is obvious, her indecision clear. The gun in her hand is unsteady as she trembles with fear.

I don't want to die today, especially in front of my mama, but both she and Katya have lost enough. She has watched her father shoot her brother and heard him brag about killing her mother. All she has left is her little sister.

"Do it, Katya," I murmur. Tears drip from her eyes onto her cheeks as she pulls the trigger. The bullet hits me in the chest, pain explodes throughout my body and the world goes black.

KATYA

As soon as I know Svetlana and Kristina are okay, I move as fast as I can to Mikhail's side. He's crumpled on the floor next to Tomas. I skid to a halt, sinking to my knees, momentarily forgetting my own injuries. Mikhail's lying on his side and as I roll him over onto his back, he groans.

He's alive. Mikhail's alive.

"You're okay," I whisper, more to myself than him. "You're okay." *I didn't kill him.*

"I'm sorry, I'm sorry," I whimper repeatedly. In my attempt to find his wound, I tear his shirt open, buttons flying in all directions. It takes a few moments to register Mikhail's wearing a Kevlar vest. The bullet I fired didn't pierce his chest. I release a whoosh of breath in relief as he opens his eyes, blinking and groaning.

I lay his head on my lap as Mikhail continues to groan and cough. "Oh, fuck, that hurts." A teardrop leaks from my eyes and lands on his face. He looks up at me and I wait for the rejection and hate he must have for me to expel from his mouth. "Thank you, malen'kiy olen'," he murmurs. "Thank you for saving everyone."

Shaking my head in confusion, I blurt, "But I shot you."

"Don't I know it." he groans again as he rises to a sitting position. "Help me up," he grunts to Henrí. "I want to check on Mama," he commands.

With his shirt open and hanging loose from his pants, Mikhail is all business, as he makes sure his mother is okay.

Henrí and Mikhail help the women from the floor. Svetlana steps forward. Reaching out, she grips Mikhail's shoulders. Her voice is full of apprehension when she asks, "Are you alright, Mikhail? Are you hurt?" She's looking directly into her son's eyes as she asks her questions. The shock of everything that's happened in this room must have brought her into the present.

"I'm fine, Mama," Mikhail's voice breaks with what I'm guessing is the sheer joy that his mother has momentarily remembered her son. He wraps his arms around her, enveloping her, and she does the same. I watch on, my heart swelling with love as the hard, emotionless man most people know hugs his mother tightly. "I'm fine," he repeats, a smile he probably reserves only for his mother appears on his face, and it's breathtaking.

Tears brim in my eyes again. A tingle of jealousy runs down my spine. I wish that smile was for me. At the same time, I love how, at this moment, Mikhail has his mother back. Watching the two of them also reminds me my own mother is gone. She wasn't the best mom in the world, but she was mine.

More of Mikhail's men arrive with medics. He probably has them all on speed dial. The first person they're directed to is Tomas. He hasn't moved throughout the whole ordeal. Guilt wracks my body as I realize I've been more worried about Mikhail than my own flesh and blood. I move to where the doctor and others are kneeling on the floor next to my brother.

"Is he…" My voice trails off. I don't want to know the answer.

"He has a pulse," the doctor states. "It's weak, but it's there." I blow out a breath of relief. *Tomas is alive.*

While others finish attending to my brother, the doctor rises and moves to where Denis lies, where he fell when Father shot him.

Denis had already received extensive wounds. I don't expect him to be alive, but according to the doctor, he is.

More men arrive with stretchers and medical equipment. They load up Tomas and Denis; the doctor ordering the less wounded to be taken to a room on the first level of the house. "Shouldn't they be taken to the hospital?" I inquire.

"That's not how things work in my world, Katya." Mikhail's voice behind me startles me. I didn't hear him step up behind me and I spin around to face him, almost losing my footing. Mikhail stops me from falling, pulling me to his side, his hand firmly on my hip. He peers down at me as I glance up at him. "They'll be fine," he murmurs. "There are people here who are medically trained. The doctor will do everything he can to stabilize the worst wounded. Once he's done, ambulances will be called for those who need to go to the hospital."

As he fills me in my eyes scan the room. "Where's Natalia?" I don't see her anywhere and no one has mentioned her. Mikhail should have found her when they arrived at the gate. "Is she safe?"

Mikhail frowns at me. He appears confused. "What makes you think I know where your sister is?" His lips dip down at the corners.

"I left her at the guardhouse," I whisper. My eyes widen as I cover my mouth with my hand. "I left her there to warn you when you arrived. I left her there so you would keep her safe." My voice breaks.

"Henrí inspected the guardhouse when we got to the gate. It was wide open," Mikhail states, his brows drawn together as he continues to watch me closely. "The bodies in the guardhouse when we got there were all men, Katya. Natalia wasn't there, or Henrí would've found her," he adds softly.

What have I done? Where's Natalia?

A noise from behind the large terracotta vase draws our attention at that moment, and every gun available is drawn and pointed at it. Henrí signals everyone to wait as he warily steps closer to it.

I'm surprised when Henrí returns his gun to its holster and reaches around the vase. When he steps back, he has Natalia in his arms. Henri gently eases the gun she's holding out of her hand. Sobs rack her small body, as she clenches the front of Henrí's shirt.

I squirm loose from Mikhail's hold and run to my sister. "I killed him," she sobs loudly, her eyes filled with horror. "I k–k–killed Father, Kat. I'm a monster," she wails.

"You did good, malysh, *baby*," Henrí croons in her ear, still holding her tightly. "You saved your sister," he assures her. He nods at me. "You saved us all."

"You did good, Nat," I tell her as well. "How did you get here?"

Through hiccups and the occasional sob, Natalia informs me she followed me to the house but lost me once she got inside. Her naivety causes Henrí to huff. She found the hall by accident and was already in the alcove when Father and Igor arrived.

At the time, she didn't know what they were doing,

so she hid behind the vase. She listened as Pavel and Igor discussed what they were about to do and was disgusted. They had planned to kill everyone once they succeeded in convincing the two women in the panic room to come out. Natalia was afraid. She knew she couldn't show herself, not after what Father had tried to do to her earlier. She was terrified he would still try to marry her off to Igor. Or worse.

She watched the events unfold and Father's cruelty was too much for her Hearing his threats and feeling helpless as I was forced to gun down Mikhail, she closed her eyes and pulled the trigger. It was pure luck the bullet hit Father in his chest.

When she's finished telling her side of the story, she breaks down again. Henrí mutters something about taking her downstairs to the doctor and giving her a sedative.

He and Mikhail discuss the fire, and what damage it might have done. They agree the safest place for the moment is the first floor for the time being.

"Go with them, malen'kiy olen', get the doctor to check you over," murmurs Mikhail, who is standing behind me. He gives me a gentle tap on my behind. "We need to clean up here. I'll find you when we're done."

Luckily, the fire has been extinguished, according to one of the men. Everything from the second floor up needs to be inspected due to the damage.

He orders Kristine to take Svetlana to get checked over as well, and everyone heads down the hall. I turn to follow them, then hesitate. I feel I should apologize again for my actions. Hopefully, over time, Mikhail will forgive me.

Turning to Mikhail, I'm shocked to find him still

standing so close behind me. My hands land on his hard chest as I stumble. He catches me, his hands landing on my hips as he does. The words I wanted to say are momentarily stuck as I stare into the deep wells of darkness his eyes have become. Several seconds tick by as we stare at each other in silence.

"You know I never wanted to hurt you," I blurt out, my voice shaky. "I couldn't…"

"I know, malen'kiy olen'. I know," Mikhail cuts me off, brushing loose hair from my face as he does. "Thank you," he murmurs.

Cocking my head in confusion, I repeat his words. "Thank you?" *Is he thanking me for shooting him?* I tip my head back, confused, my eyebrows knitting together, as I try to decipher what he means.

"You shooting me, saved Mama's life, Katya. No one has ever granted me with such an honor." His words stun me, but not as much as what he does next. He leans down, his lips crashing into mine. At first, I'm shocked, but then my reflexes take over and I kiss him back. My mouth opens as I take the oxygen from his mouth and his tongue enters mine. It flicks and licks my tongue in a dance.

My legs weaken and Mikhail moves his hands to my ass, lifting me as if I weigh nothing. Wrapping my legs around his waist, his erection rubs against the seam of my pants, and my core clenches at the same time as my panties dampen with need.

When we finally part, we're both gasping for air. Mikhail rests his forehead against mine. "I'll come for you tonight, malen'kiy olen' as soon as I finish with this mess." It's a statement, not an invitation.

It's not the most romantic thing a man has ever said

to me, but from this man, it's the world. I smile wide and toothy.

"Yes, sir," I purr. "Any other orders, sir?" I cheekily tease him as he slides me down his body until my feet are planted firmly on the floor. My hand moves on its own to grip the hard-on I know he has. It jumps under my hand through his pants and Mikhail's quick intake of breath gives me courage.

"You're looking to be punished, malen'kiy olen'?" he teases back.

One of his men calls to him, breaking the moment.

Mikhail replies he'll be there in a moment. He strokes my cheek with the back of his hand, and I lean into it like a purring cat. "Go with the others," he murmurs, nodding his head in the direction Henrí and the others went. "I need to check what damage has been done."

I know he'll want to inspect the fire damage. And though he doesn't say it, I know he'll also have to deal with the dead and wounded.

His and Father's.

25

MIKHAIL

MY EYES ARE GLUED TO KATYA AS SHE WALKS AWAY from me. The natural way her hips sway is hypnotizing. She's a special woman, this one. I've known it since I first caught sight of her at the charity banquet.

I've never tried to picture a woman in my life before her. I've fucked women, but I've never had a relationship. Most women can't deal with the world I live in. A world that can be volatile at the best of times. Dangerous at the worst.

Like today.

It's the first time I haven't been one step ahead of someone plotting damage to me and my family. I'm startled when I conclude I already consider Katya as part of that family. Cuffing my neck, I stare down at the ground as I allow it to sink in. It doesn't worry me as much as I thought it might.

I have strong feelings for her.

"Boss, this one's still alive." A voice brings me out of my head.

Turning to Dimitri, the man who spoke, I frown at him. He points to the floor where the bodies of Igor and Pavel lie.

I don't understand who he's talking about until I notice Pavel's finger twitch. *The bastard's still alive? How?*

"Get Henrí and a medic back here, now," I demand. Dimitri nods, and as he moves past me, I wrap my hand around his forearm. "You tell no one else," I inform him, my grip tight, my eyes locked on his. "Understand?"

Dimitri nods and I release him.

Stalking over to where Pavel lies on the floor, I stare down at him. In my head, I go over everything the man has done. He killed my father. He murdered Katya's mother, and attacked my home, the one place everyone should have felt safe. The prick even threatened to kill my mama.

I pull my gun and aim it down at the unconscious man on the floor. My hatred for him overwhelms me. Darkness clouds my mind as I click off the safety. I should finish him off here and be done with it.

He's probably drawing his last breaths, but I don't want Katya to know this piece of shit is still in her world. She thinks he's dead. I'm determined to leave it that way.

"Don't do it, brat, *brother*," Henrí's softspoken words penetrate the darkness surrounding my mind. "He deserves a slow death, not a quick one. Do you honestly want to show him mercy?"

I contemplate his words before returning my gun to its holster. Sighing tiredly, I rub my hand over my face. "What do you suggest we do with him?"

"I know you want Katya to feel safe. Her and her

sister." I glance at him when he mentions Natalia, but I say nothing. "But he deserves to pay for the hell he put you and everyone else through."

I nod. *Henri's right.*

Turning to the doctor standing nearby, I nod toward Pavel. "Find out how badly he's wounded. If you can, keep him alive, and if you tell anyone, you and everyone you love will regret you running off at the mouth." I stare him down as he visibly gulps. "Am I understood?"

The doctor gulps again as if he has lumps in his throat before squeaking, "I understand."

Leaving him to work, I order two of my men to stay with him. If he stabilizes Pavel, they can place him in the basement until it's safe to move him.

My men and my staff are experts at cleanup duties, and those who are able, set to work. Igor will be dumped in the back storage shed, in a large cool room, with the rest of his and Pavel's men. They'll be dealt with later.

Until the fire authorities have been through and inspected the damage to the house, I'll keep them on ice.

Even the Pakhan has to follow some rules. Once I know what the damage is and how long it'll take to repair, I can organize it. If it's not stable, I'll have to move everyone to somewhere safer. It's the first time I'll have had to do this, as no one has ever dared to attack me on my home ground before. It took guts to do what Pavel did today. Or stupidity. I'll give him credit for the former in this instant because he almost succeeded.

He's grown balls since the cowardly fuck killed my father by shooting him from behind. The fact he already knew the house well added to his advantage.

For now, though, I must find Katya and her sister. They need to be kept busy while Pavel is taken to the basement. Hopefully, they'll be too worried about Tomas to be wandering around.

My men, the ones who sacrificed their lives trying to defend my home and my family, will be buried properly as soon as this is done. Their families will be taken care of. Loyalty deserves to be rewarded.

Payments will be organized for the right authorities to keep this all under wraps. Most of them aren't interested in Bratva killing Bratva. It means less work for them.

KATYA

Following Henrí's lead, I follow them to the room Natalia has been sleeping in. Thankfully, there's little fire or smoke damage in this area.

Henrí lies Natalia gently down on her bed. He whispers something to her I can't hear and brushes his lips across the top of her head before he moves away. *Does he have feelings for my baby sister?*

Henrí's older than Natalia. I'm not sure of his exact age, but this life isn't what I pictured for her future. It's the one reason I agreed to do Father's dirty work for him. It's also why I protected her from Igor's lecherous hands by putting myself at his mercy.

Natalia's still young enough to go out into the world and explore. She deserves to enjoy her life. I wish a better life for her. I hope she might go to college. My baby sister deserves a wonderful life. Getting herself tangled up with a Sovietnik, second to the Pakhan, isn't where I hope to see her life going.

I know I sound like a hypocrite. Mikhail and I undoubtably have sexual chemistry. But it's like everything else in my life. It won't last. He'll tire of me soon enough and move on.

It hurts to think about it, but it's true.

Before I can summon up the courage to ask Henrí what his intentions are where Natalia's concerned, there's a knock at the door. Henrí opens it, his hand on his pistol, ready to use it if it's one of Father's men. He exchanges words with someone we can't see for a few moments before Henrí glances over at Natalia, then me, his face blank.

"Stay here and take care of your sister," Henrí's voice is stern when he looks at me. I nod silently before he turns and leaves. *Did he think I wouldn't?* I've spent my life looking out for her.

My thoughts turn back to my situation. I came here to kill Mikhail. There's no way he would fall for someone like me. He deserves someone like his mother. Beautiful, loyal, and classy. Not a failed assassin.

Not the daughter of his father's murderer.

The sexual tension between us is just that. It's pheromones. Once we finally do the deed, I'm sure he'll come to the same conclusion and kick me to the curb. Mikhail can have anyone he wants.

Natalia's weeping brings me back to the present. Moving to the bed, I lie behind her, wrapping her in my arms, and spooning her. Just as I did back at our mother's house whenever she was upset and needed consoling.

Holding Natalia tight, I wait for her to fall asleep. The sedative the doctor gave her doesn't take long. Slowly, not wanting to wake her, I peel myself away, slide off the bed, and slip out the door.

Tomas required medical assistance, and I head that way to check if he's okay. I can't lose anyone else.

As I stand at the top of the first landing, Mikhail appears down below me with Henrí and several other men. Several men are carrying a stretcher. I can't see who's on it. A blanket covers the body and face. It's probably someone killed in the attack.

A cough escapes me, alerting Mikhail to my presence. He freezes, locking eyes with mine while muttering something inaudible. Henrí and the men with the stretcher continue walking.

Leaning on the staircase banister, he keeps his dark eyes on mine, his face schooled. My heart flutters at the sight of him.

I break the stare-down to rake my eyes over this man who has my hormones in a twist. Mikhail's a muscular man, with broad shoulders. He must have removed the Kevlar vest and is now wearing a white shirt which is unbuttoned and hanging loose from his pants, revealing a dusting of dark hair on his chest. My fingers twitch, longing to run them through it. I brush my eyes over him imagining the hard six-pack leading to the V disappearing into the top of his pants.

The bandages from his previous wounds have blood seeping through them. "You're hurt." I state the obvious as he climbs the steps toward me. He watches me constantly, silently, until he arrives in front of me.

I'm standing on the top step and Mikhail halts a step below, bringing us almost eye to eye. Lowering my gaze, I pause on a large bruise darkening on his chest in the spot where his heart is. Shakily, I reach out to trace the outline of it. "It's where you shot me, malen'kiy olen'," Mikhail murmurs, wrapping his large hand around my finger as I freeze in shock.

"I could have killed you." I gasp as electricity runs through me at his touch. He must hate me.

Instead of hate, his dark eyes soften as he drops my hand to cup my cheek. "You did what you had to, to save your family," he says softly. "Besides, if you had meant to kill me, you would have shot me in the head," he adds with a smirk as if trying to lighten the situation.

"I was aiming for your head," I state, schooling my face.

His eyes widen in shock until he sees my lips twitching. I can't keep a straight face and burst into laughter.

Mikhail huffs before bending and shoving his shoulder into my stomach. He stands tall, tossing me over his shoulder like a sack of potatoes. I smack his backside and he smacks mine in return, the sting a surprise, wrenches a squeal from me, as he begins to stride back the way the wounded were taken.

I tense as a thought hits me.

"Wait. Stop. Mikhail, where's Tomas? Please? Is he okay?" I beg.

Immediately, he stops and lowers my feet to the floor. Disappointment is evident on his face, but his voice is gentle. "Of course. Let's go find your brother." His hand lowers to my back as he ushers me down the stairwell to the room where the wounded are being taken care of.

When we enter, Tomas is sitting in an armchair, a beautiful brunette tending to him. He has already been bandaged. I'm surprised to see him looking so well. The doctor informs me the bullet Father fired had been a through and through, luckily missing Tomas' vital organs. He must have passed out from the pain, which probably saved him as Father might have shot him again if he'd known he was still alive.

I'm beyond relieved my father is dead. He can't hurt anyone anymore.

26

KATYA

Mikhail leaves to deal with the fire department and police officials.

After being assured Tomas is receiving the treatment he needs, I wander over to where Denis lies. He's still unconscious. The doctor informs me it's touch and go whether he'll survive his wounds. It brings tears to my eyes that the huge man before me, the man who saved my life, might lose his. I lean down and kiss him on the cheek before whispering in his ear, "Thank you for saving me."

The doctor promises me he'll do his best and I wander around the room checking on the other wounded, helping where I can. I'm not a medic, but I can hand out water bottles and sandwiches along with the kitchen staff. My waiting skills finally finding a purpose. When the seriously wounded are carted out to ambulances, and the rest are bandaged and medicated, I return to Tomas.

I remain by Tomas' side, knowing Natalia will still be sleeping. The sedative the doctor gave her should ensure she's out until at least the morning. I wish I could have one too. I'm exhausted, but each time I close my eyes, visions of me shooting Mikhail and him falling to the floor replay on a loop inside my head.

My brother, pale from the pain of being shot, yawns beside me, and I do the same. His painkillers are probably kicking in. We're both beat.

Tomas bids me goodnight and I walk beside the wheelchair he's in as the brunette who tended to him earlier, wheels him to a room that's been made up especially for him. He refused to go to the hospital. As I walk away, Tomas calls to me. "Where are you sleeping?" I shrug. I don't know.

"I'll find somewhere." I wave to him over my shoulder without turning back. "I'll be fine," I call. I always am. I've been looking after Natalia and myself for most of my life.

The threat is gone. Father and Igor are dead. I am… No, *we* are free.

A strange feeling runs through me.

Everything blurs around me as tears begin to fall. Not understanding what's happening, I open the first unlocked door I find. It's a large guest bathroom. Stepping inside, I begin to pull at my clothes. I'm not sure what I'm doing, or why, but I feel dirty, mad, and sad, all at the same time.

Huge sobs break free from me as I turn on the shower and step inside the stall. I slap the walls and stomp my foot. I growl and I curse as the steaming hot water pours down on me. My body begins to shake uncontrollably, and I wrap my arms around myself tight.

I'm barely aware of sliding down the tiles to the floor, sobbing. I stay there, curled up even when the water turns cold. The vision of Mikhail's body falling to the ground from my bullet running through my head on constant replay.

MIKHAIL

I've been dealing with the fallout from Pavel's failed coup for hours now.

I've paid off those who can be bribed and answered the questions of those who cannot. I give them my version of the truth. The law isn't interested in the violent world I live in unless they're looking for a promotion, a payoff, or have a death wish. Or all three.

They don't want to dirty their hands in the world of the Bratva. Especially when we're killing each other.

The only time they try to mess with us is when they think they have enough evidence for an arrest or promotion time comes around. When they think it will put their names in the spotlight. Most times, they don't bother. It's not worth losing their lives for.

What happened here today involved the need for aggression in the form of self-defense. My mother was attacked. My home was attacked. My woman could have died.

The fire department has done their inspections and suggested we move to a more stable residence until this place can be fixed. Henrí is already out looking. I own many residences, but none in the immediate area. I've told him to find us somewhere close by, no matter the cost.

I heave a sigh. It's been a long fucking day. Running my hand down my face, I review the last few days leading up to Pavel's attack inside my head. I need a strong drink. Heading to one of the many stocked liquor cabinets in the house, I pass by one of the guest bathrooms. Water seeps out from under the door and I almost slip in it.

Steadying myself against the wall, I open the door thinking perhaps the fire has damaged the water pipes. Something might have burst, causing the flood.

What I find when I step inside freezes me in my tracks momentarily.

Katya, her beautiful blonde hair wet and matted around her face, is lying on the floor of the shower. She's shivering and her naked skin has a blue tinge to it.

Willing myself to move, I lunge forward, turning off the water, which is ice cold. My heart beats so hard it feels like it's going to jump out of my chest as my mind races. Scouring the room, I make a plan. There are large fluffy guest towels on a rack, and I pull them all down, sitting them on the sink bench so they don't get wet. I don't know what's happened or how long she's been here, but she has definite signs of hypothermia. "Hold on, milyaya, *darling*. I got you."

I bend down and pick Katya's tiny, frame up, not caring about getting soaked myself. She's frozen. Her normally warm, soft skin feels like ice. I have to get her warm. Grabbing from the pile I made, I wrap as many of the towels around her as I can. Lifting her from the floor and holding her close to my chest, I walk as fast as possible down the hall to where the medics are tending to the wounded.

The door's ajar, and poking my head through, I yell for a doctor. Katya doesn't even flinch. One looks up and I yell again. "Follow me. Now." There's no room for argument in my order. Katya is my priority. I couldn't care less if anyone else needs him, I need him more.

There's a sitting room next to the room the wounded are in. With the doctor now in tow, I wrench the door handle, slamming the door open so hard it slams against the wall.

Striding to a leather couch placed near a fireplace, I take a seat, Katya still in my arms.

"I–I need to examine her," the doctor stammers.

"Then do it," I command, glaring at him.

"Y–You'll have to unwrap her, sir," he stutters again.

I don't want to unwrap her. She's naked and I don't want anyone else to see what is mine. But I must put my ego aside for the moment. Katya's life is on the line. "Fine, but you better keep your hands and eyes where I can see them," I snarl.

I unwrap Katya to the top of her breasts. The doctor, his hand shaky, checks her temperature, then her pulse, before listening to her heart. As he steps back, I cover her up again.

"Do you have a thermal blanket available?" he asks thoughtfully, a frown settling on his face. I can see he's worried. So am I.

"Thermal blanket?" I scratch my head. "No. What if I place her in a hot bath?"

The doctor shakes his head quickly. "No, it's the worst thing you can do." I glance up at him in surprise as he continues, "If you don't have a thermal blanket, the next best thing you can do for her is to strip down to your boxers." My eyes shoot wide at this comment. "Skin-on-skin heat transfer works best. Hold her close and wrap yourselves in a thick comforter. There's one next door. I'll go and get it," he offers.

I nod silently and the doctor dashes for the door. Lying Katya gently on the couch, I begin to strip. I don't give a damn if the doctor sees me naked.

By the time he returns, I've removed all my clothes. He hesitates at the door for a moment before clearing his throat and entering the room. "You're bleeding," he murmurs.

"I don't give a fuck at the moment, doc. Leave us." I snatch the comforter from him, not giving a shit if I offend him.

As soon as he closes the door behind him, I strip the towels from Katya's body, tossing them onto the floor in a damp pile. I take her in from head to toe. She appears even tinier now she's naked, her perky breasts rising and falling with her faint breaths. My eyes can't help but lower to her shaved pussy. I've had my fingers in there, but this is the first time I've seen it. Her leg moves slightly, as if she's opening herself up for me to see more, and I ogle the fuck out of the pretty pink flesh between her legs.

"Fucking perfect," I murmur to myself as I adjust my cock. This isn't the time to be getting a boner. Tucking the comforter in under her unconscious body, I climb onto the couch behind her, spooning her, before covering us both with the rest of the comforter. Wrapping my arms and legs around Katya's body, I pull her as close to me as I can.

She fits within my large frame perfectly. Swiping stray, damp hair from her face, I nuzzle my face into her neck. Her unique perfume is still there, despite her being in the shower for God knows how long, and somehow it calms me. "Fucking perfect," I repeat as my eyelids become heavy and I drift off.

KATYA

Opening my eyes is hard, and I groan with the effort. When I attempt to lift my hand to brush my hair from my face, I realize I can't. Something is pinning it down.

Am I tied up? My mind feels like sludge as my blood pumps in fear. I suck in oxygen as my heart rate picks up in panic and I begin to struggle. *Was it all a dream? Did my father win? Is Mikhail dead?* I kick out frantically.

"Whoa," Mikhail's deep voice murmurs in my ear, his hot breath sending goosebumps across my skin as I freeze in place. "It's okay, Katya. I've got you. You're safe," he assures me. My heart slows at his soft words, the panic subsiding as I discover I'm not trussed up in ropes. Instead, I'm being held in his strong arms. I wriggle a little, trying to look over my shoulder at him.

"Hold still, woman," he mutters again as I recognize what the large, hard, *weapon* settled between my ass cheeks is. *Is Mikhail naked?*

"I–I… bathroom," I manage to get out.

With his large, tattooed arms still around me, he rises to a seated position, settling me in his lap. He picks up a large fluffy towel from the floor and gently wraps me in it. Once he's done that, Mikhail carries me to the bathroom, depositing me in front of the toilet before stepping outside. Once I've relieved myself, I wash my shaky hands, vying for time as I try to recall how I ended up naked, wrapped in a comforter with him.

"You can't stay in there, Katya. Sooner or later, you'll have to come out," Mikhail calls as if he's reading my mind. "And if you don't, I'll come in after you," he adds.

Well then, I guess I better go back out there.

I wrap the towel back around myself before exiting, not fighting Mikhail when he again picks me up and walks back to the room. The whole time he's naked except for a pair of boxers, yet doesn't seem to care. I'm embarrassed enough for the both of us, purposefully keeping my eyes on his face, although it's tough.

Wordlessly, he slides me down his body until my feet touch the carpet and strips the towel from me, while still holding me close. He straightens the comforter on the lounge with one hand, places me on the couch gently before climbing in behind me again and wrapping us both back up.

Wide awake now, I glance around the room again. *I don't remember coming in here. I was having a shower, then everything went black.* "How did I get here?" I ask, confused.

Mikhail loosens his grip on me, and I turn to face him. His dark eyes are still dull from sleep, his hair is loose, hanging in waves, and his face has a slight scruff on it. He probably hasn't had time to shave properly over the last few days. I continue running my gaze over him. He's normally impeccably groomed. I think I like sleepy Mikhail.

"I found you in the shower," he begins, his voice appearing deeper than usual. It awakens my lower parts even more than the erection now poking me in my stomach. My abdomen moves forward on its own mission, rubbing against his cock, clenching with need as it does.

Mikhail lets out a low growl. "You were frozen and unconscious, malen'kiy olen'." His hand brushes my cheek. "I had to warm you up, and the doctor thought this was the best way," he continues softly, not taking his eyes off mine. "For the third time in my life, I was scared."

"The third time?" I don't know what else to say. He strikes me as a man who doesn't frighten easily.

"The first time was after Otets was murdered and I took his place as the Pakhan. The second was when Pavel put a gun to Mama's head," Mikhail pauses, brushing his lips across mine. "The third was when I found you in the shower, blue and unconscious," he continues, his voice cracking a little as if he's fighting to control himself.

I flinch, licking my lower lip before sucking it into my mouth. Mikhail's eyes follow the movement. "Malen'kiy olen', I don't ever want there to be a fourth time." He raises his dark chocolate eyes back to mine, his voice stern.

"I–I don't understand," I croak, my voice tightening in my throat. "Do you want me to leave?" My eyes blur as I attempt to unravel the comforter so I can escape. No one wants to stay where they aren't wanted, including me.

"Where are you going?" There's confusion in his voice.

"I don't want to be a burden to you," I mumble, embarrassed at my nudity, but unable to do anything about it momentarily. "I'll find Natalia and Tomas, and we'll go." I force my voice to remain neutral, not wanting him to know how hurt I am.

Before I can stumble to my feet, my body is whipped around, and my back is slapped down on the couch. Mikhail's large body is over me, caging me in. His large hands have mine pinned above my head; his thick thighs are on either side of my legs. I scrunch my eyes closed. The tenderness he had shown to me moments ago is now gone.

"Open your eyes, Katya," he demands. "Look at me." I obey instantly, knowing he's serious because he's using my name.

A pissed-off Mikhail is a sight to behold. His hair falls in waves on either side of my face like a curtain of darkness, and his eyes are alight with anger. The colorful tattoos on his large, veiny biceps leading up to his huge shoulders are bunched, the muscles bulging as if they are trying to contain his rage.

"What do you want from me, Mikhail? You want me to go, I'll go," I hiss through gritted teeth. I'm as angry as he is now. I've been pushed around most of my life and been made to feel unwanted and worthless. I don't need another man treating me the same. Most of all, I hate the way my body reacts to the mountain of a man above me.

For the first time in my life, I was allowing myself to hope. Hope I might have found something real to hang on to. As usual, I was wrong.

27

———

KATYA

MIKHAIL'S FACE LOWERS UNTIL HIS HARSH BREATH whispers across my lips. "When did I say I wanted you to leave, Katya? What part of what I just admitted to you said I want you to go?" The words exit his perfect lips slowly, deliberately, and his eyes, like deep, black pits, gaze deep into my soul.

I frown, my eyes narrowing. "So… you want me to… stay?" I ask slowly, totally confused, unwilling to hope, but daring to at the same time. This man is going to give me whiplash.

"It has to be your decision, Katya," he states quietly, his eyes burning into mine. "My life is not for the squeamish, malen'kiy olen'." He's using his pet name for me again. It's a good sign, I guess. "I understand if you don't want to live this life. It's hard. Especially on women. You would be living with a target on your back, as I do." Mikhail's voice has lowered, and his eyes have softened. "If you decide to leave, I will make sure you and your sister never go without. I'll set you both up in a way that you won't have to work a day in your lives," he promises, his eyes now darting all over my face.

I twist my head a little trying to get a read on him. The sadness in his voice as he speaks of his life as the Pakhan belies the strong, confident man I've seen.

"And if I decide I want to stay?" The question scares me. I'm not sure I want to know the answer. "What will happen?"

"You will be at my side always. I will be your protector, malen'kiy olen'. You'll never feel alone."

"What exactly does that mean?" I hold his gaze with bated breath, hoping against all odds that he means what I think he does.

His lips brush mine so lightly, I wonder if I imagined it. "It means you will be in my life and my bed. You will be the other half of me if you want to be. If you stay." The vulnerability on his face as he watches me carefully, is visible. My heart swells, because I don't imagine anyone outside of a few people, if any, gets to see this side of him.

"I want to," I whisper back, my eyes filling with the tears I refused to let surface when I thought he didn't want me. They're warm as they trickle down the sides of my face. "I want to stay, Mikhail. Here. With you," I state softly.

Mikhail wipes the tears away with his thumbs before gently kissing each of my eyelids, my nose, and then my lips.

It doesn't take much for things to get out of hand. Our kiss becomes desperate. Mikhail's hand slides down my side to my thigh. He lifts my leg to wrap around his hip before palming my ass, pushing his erection into my pussy harder. His other hand tangles in my hair, holding my head in place as he draws the oxygen from my mouth. I run my hands over his shoulders, feeling his muscles twitch and bunch.

If he wanted to crush me with his strength, he could easily do it. Yet, the gentleness in his touch is over-whelming. I rake my nails lightly down his sides, careful of his wounds. They remind me that not so long ago, he was hooked up to machines because he took a bullet for me and I hesitate momentarily.

Mikhail must feel it. "What's wrong?" he murmurs.

"You're hurt," I answer as if he doesn't know. "Are you sure we should be doing this?"

"I'm fine," he huffs, as if offended I should even ask. "I am about to show you how fine I am." He winks. Damn. This man is *fine*, in more ways than I can count. Leaning on one arm, his large hand glides over my skin to my breasts, his hooded eyes following the movement. He runs his finger tantalizingly around my nipple before pinching it, hard. I gasp with the pain as he ducks his head, enveloping the stinging skin with his mouth. Pain turns to pleasure and my body arches up to meet him.

Mikhail pulls his mouth from me before blowing gently, watching as my nipple swells to a peak, harden-ing. He does the same with my other breast as I gasp and squirm from the pain and pleasure of his attention. Through all of this, I continue to run my nails a little harder each time, up and down his abs, feeling him twitch beneath me.

I whimper with the loss as Mikhail moves away from me, sitting back on his haunches. He gazes down at my body, his eyes raking over me from my head to my breasts, then down to my sex. I don't attempt to cover myself as I'm hypnotized by the large cock, erect and angry looking, poking its purplish head toward me, pre-cum dripping from its slit, as he slides his boxers down. Fisting himself, he pumps it twice before smearing his pre-cum over the head with his thumb.

I don't believe I've ever seen anything so erotic that it caused my pussy to weep, but I have now. I've had Mikhail's cock in my mouth, but I'm unsure how it's going to fit inside me.

"Are you okay, malysh, *baby*?" Mikhail surely knows what's running through my mind by the smirk on his thick lips.

"I–I'm fine," I squeak, unable to look him in the eye.

"Katya, eyes on me," Mikhail commands, and I obey him instantly.

"Yes sir," I practically purr at him. Commanding Mikhail is a turn on. I think I like a bossy man in this situation, even if it does aggravate me at other times.

He picks up my hands, covering them with his. I watch on in fascination, wondering what he's going to do. Placing our joined hands over my breasts lightly, he runs them over my skin to my waist, stopping at my hips. "Touch yourself, malysh. Show me the pretty pink pussy I finger fucked under the table the night we met."

Oh, wow. Mikhail is a sexy hunk of a brooding male at any time, but dirty-talking Mikhail is even hotter. My juices dampen the comforter under me at his words. I obey slowly, still a little embarrassed. I haven't had many encounters with sex, and those I've had were often forced.

As if reading my mind, Mikhail's hooded eyes rise to meet mine, lust darkening his eyes until I can't tell the difference between his iris's and his pupils. "Are you sure you want this?"

Without hesitation, I nod. "Yes, I want this. I want you, Mikhail." It makes me feel in control that this monster of a man is asking my permission to take me. He could so easily overpower me and take what he wants, but he's asking my permission instead.

He nods, before gently taking one of my hands and placing it over my opening. "Then touch yourself," he urges. "Open up your beautiful cunt for me to see."

His words tip me over the edge, and I spread my opening wide with my fingers, my clit pulsing beneath my palm as I do. I let out a moan. Urged on by Mikhail's gaze, I slip a finger inside me, needing something to relieve the pressure. My legs squirm, trying to close, but Mikhail's body between them doesn't allow it. I whimper when he growls, "I didn't say finger yourself, did I? That's my cunt to play with, Katya, not yours. Understood?"

"Then fucking play with it, Mikhail. Stop torturing me," I groan, feeling emboldened.

With a feral sound, Mikhail slips his arm under my legs and lifts my body to his mouth. I yelp with shock, not because it's now only my head and shoulders on the couch, but because his hot mouth lands on my pussy and he feeds on it like he's a starving man. I've never had oral sex, even if I had been forced to give it. His mouth sucks, then his tongue plunges inside me before returning to suck on my clit. My body convulses each time he sucks on my little bundle of nerves.

I whimper and I moan, my hands gripping the comforter while my head thrashes from side to side. My body feels like a spring being wound tighter and tighter.

Without warning, Mikhail slips one of his large digits inside me before gripping my swollen clit between his teeth and flicking it hard with his tongue.

I explode with a scream, Mikhail's name rolling off my tongue along with several expletives. I can't help myself. It's an out-of-body experience I want to have over and over. My body convulses, as electrical charges explode inside me, my toes curling while my hands clench the comforter as if to keep me grounded. The room spins, so I close my eyes, sparks flashing behind my eyelids.

Mikhail continues to lick me clean before laying me gently down and sliding up my body. He kisses me and I taste myself on his lips. It's such an erotic thing to do, but it feels natural at the same time. I tangle my hands in his hair, which is now damp at the hairline from his hard work.

Pulling back from me, he swipes stray hairs from my face before staring down at me. "Fucking perfect," he whispers.

MIKHAIL

Katya's reaction to my mouth on her is music to my ears, and when she cums, I almost do too. I haven't even fucked her yet, so I'm concentrating hard on keeping my cock contained while I lick her clean then crawl up her body. I know she can taste herself on my lips, but she doesn't hesitate. Pre-cum weeps down my cock as it grows impatient.

It'll have to wait, though. I'll need to prepare her.

She's so tiny, I'm worried I might hurt her if I don't slow things down a little. I move my lips from hers, sucking and licking at the places on her neck I've found she reacts to. Katya squirms and moans beneath me, arching up when I begin licking and biting her little pink nipples until they stand as erect as my engorged cock.

Sliding one hand down her body, Kaya jumps as I reach her clit. It's still tender from my mouth, but I need to bring her close to orgasm again. It will help in lubricating her before I enter her. My cock twitches with joy at the thought. I swipe some of the precum from my cock, using it to swirl my thumb around her clit.

Katya's nails rake down my back and I hiss with the sting, before sliding a finger into her opening. It's silky and soft and wet and hot inside her all at once. I continue to play with her clit as her insides grip my finger like a vise, sucking me in. Katya hisses a little as I add another finger. "It's okay malen'kiy olen', I need to open you up a little, so your tight little cunt doesn't strangle my cock when I fuck you," I whisper in her ear, before adding a third. Her sweet pussy sucks my thick fingers into her warm chamber, her wetness squelching as I slide them in and out, stretching her. My thumb rubs and presses her clit over and over, bringing her close to orgasm again.

"Mikhail," Katya moans. "I want you to fuck me. Please," she begs. "I need…" She moans again, unable to finish her sentence.

"I know, malysh, but I want to be sure I don't hurt you," I answer. I know her experiences with men up to now haven't been great, and this should be as good for her as it will be for me. To wipe away the bad memories; to show her how consensual sex feels.

I know I sound full of myself, but I also know my capabilities. I was introduced to sex when I was fifteen. My father took me to a place where I learned how to draw from and give pleasure to women while receiving the same. Even at that age, I was built like a man, always towering over others. I made sure Henrí had the same when he was of an age where he was interested in women, also.

Over the years, I've indulged in sex in many forms, but Katya isn't a paid partner. It will be exciting to show her all the pleasures of consensual sex. For now, all she needs is to be shown sex is something she doesn't need to fear. The monster who visited her and her mother is not going to take away the pleasure she should know in being made love to.

I want to show her the difference.

I want to be her first. In everything.

Katya moans again, her velvet muscles tightening around my fingers, while her cream drips onto my hand. She tenses before crying out, her hands firmly gripping my shoulders as she orgasms again. Her teeth sink into my shoulder as she moans my name, while I suckle her nipple hard, prolonging it as long as I can. Katya gasps and then huffs in protest at the loss of my fingers as I remove them, unable to hold myself back a moment longer. Bending her legs until her knees practically sit on her chest, almost folding her in half, I spread her as wide as I can.

I line the head of my cock at her entrance and push inside her walls slowly. My toes curl and my balls pull excitedly as her tight cunt tries to suck me into its vise-like grip. If I enter her too fast, I'm going to lose the fine edge of control I'm hanging onto, and I could hurt her. I edge in further, and Katya's fingernails scrape my sides, hard. There's no turning back now.

"Give me all of you, Mikhail, please," she moans. And I do, pushing forward until I've sheathed myself to the hilt inside her pretty pink pussy. I stop, savoring the moment. She feels like nothing I've ever known before, but what I do know is, there will never be another woman for me like my little deer.

Katya whimpers a little, as I do. "That's my good girl," I murmur before kissing her, pushing her legs harder into her body. "You've taken all of me, malysh," I add proudly. Not all women have been able to deal with my size, least of all someone as small as Katya. I pull out slowly before pushing back in, allowing her time to adjust to me. I feel every ripple inside her and it takes everything I have to stave off my orgasm.

Imagine what a disappointment it would be if she thought I was a two-pump ejaculator. "What are you smirking at?" Her voice cuts into my concentration, and I open my eyes as I push back inside her body. Katya's eyes roll back inside her head, sexy little whimpers escaping each time I move. I wish I could keep that look there forever. This little pixie of a woman has captured my heart and I think I'm okay with it.

She moans my name, and I pick up the pace a little. Katya grunts and cries out in pleasure as I slide in and out of her tight little cunt. She's practically purring as my cock starts to swell with the need to orgasm.

"Harder, Mikhail, please. Give it to me," she wails, and I lose control. I thrust my hips, driving into her harder. I shift to a kneeling position, lifting her legs over my arms as I piston into her. My hands grip her hips tightly, slamming her onto my rock-hard cock. I'm sure she'll have bruises tomorrow, but I've lost all control.

My orgasm hits me like a freight train, and I roar with ecstasy as Katya writhes and clenches around me. It's like nothing I've felt with any other woman. The heavy thudding of my heart, my chest heaving, I need a moment to gain control of myself. I slide my arms from beneath Katya's legs, staring down to where my cock glistens with the mixture of our juices. I feel like shouting *mine* from the top of the tallest mountain. I continue to slide in and out of Katya's drenched cunt slowly, feeling the after spasms of our orgasms until I start to soften.

When my cock finally softens, I pull out, immediately missing our connection. Rolling to my side, I lean up on one elbow, brushing her hair back so I can see her face. Her lips turn up in a lazy smile as she glances at me. Her cheeks are flushed, and her breasts still rise and fall rapidly from our lovemaking. She licks her lower lip, and I lean down to catch it in my teeth, tugging gently on it. Reaching down between Katya's legs, I swirl my fingers through our entwined juices, painting her abdomen, stomach, and perky tits with it. "What are you doing?" she asks, her voice still breathy from our exertions.

"I'm marking you, malen'kiy olen'," I reply, watching my hand trace her belly button before gliding up to her nipple.

"Marking me?" She turns to face me, her crystal blue eyes shimmering, her swollen lips tipped at the edges in a smirk.

"Yes, marking you. You're mine now." I lean over and kiss her languidly before pulling back a little to gaze at her. "You are mine for as long as you want me," I add. Hopefully, it will be forever, but I don't say it out loud.

28

"You are mine, and I am yours, for as long as you want me." Mikhail's words run on repeat in my head as I watch his fingers dip between my legs before drawing imaginary patterns on my body with our combined orgasms. He leans down, kissing me languidly before going back to what he was doing.

The smell of our lovemaking surrounds us, and the endorphins released from it permeate my mind. I've never had anyone make love to me before. It was always someone taking what they needed or wanted from my body without worrying whether it hurt me or not. "I love you," I blurt, slapping my hand over my mouth straight after.

Great, Katya. One good fuck and you're head over heels? Great way to scare someone off. A-grade clinger much? I screw my eyes shut, hoping Mikhail wasn't listening.

"What did you say?" Mikhail's mouth is so close to my ear that I can feel the warmth of his breath. It sends shivers down my spine, goosebumps rising on my skin. *Shit.* "Open your eyes, Katya. Look at me," His voice is a little sterner now. And he's using my name. *Shit, shit, shit.*

I open my eyes so they're barely slits. My muscles tense, waiting for the inevitable shutdown I'm expecting. Instead, Mikhail is wearing the breathtaking two-dimple smile I've rarely seen since I've been here, and it takes my breath away.

Mikhail slides his arm under me and rolls to his back, taking me with him, so I'm lying on his stomach. His cock is hard again. I know this because it's wedged in between us. "Say it again." The words are softly spoken, but there's a demand in there also.

Huffing out a loud sigh, I avert his gaze as I repeat the words. "I love you. But you don't have to say it back, Mikhail. I under—"

Mikhail's large hand wraps his fingers in my hair and pulls my face down to his, cutting me off. He kisses me hard, his hands moving to grip my face in both his hands. I don't miss that he didn't tell me he loved me too. For now, though, this is enough.

MIKHAIL

We make love again before a knock sounds at the door. The real world filters back in when Henrí enters, a smile pulling at his lips as he spies us wrapped in the comforter. I'm still lying on top of Mikhail, lightly dozing.

"I hate to spoil your fun, brat, *brother*, but there's still work to be done. I've found suitable quarters, and the fire department wants us out of here as soon as possible," Henrí states. "The men are packing up whatever is salvageable —"

"Leave it all," Mikhail interrupts him. "We take Mama's keepsakes, and whatever we need for our business," he stipulates. Tipping his head back to see his friend, he adds, "Bring me some clothes. I best be dressed to deal with everything."

It's then I realize I don't have any clothing either.

"Um, Henrí, would you mind bringing me some clothes too, please?" I can feel my face flush with my question. Mikhail's body shudders beneath me as he attempts to stifle a chuckle and I slap his chest lightly.

MIKHAIL

Business takes over for the next few days and I don't see much of Katya. I'm not happy about it, but there is stuff to be dealt with regarding the attack. People to track down and punish for helping Pavel. Funerals to arrange. Payments have to be made to take care of the dead and the injured's families.

Katya's busy caring for everyone around her. It's one of the many things I love about her. When I climb into bed at night, she's already asleep. I don't wake her if possible as I know she's been run off her feet.

Pavel was wrong when he thought he could make her into a killer. Katya is a nurturer. She may have shot people during the attack on the house, but she was trying to protect herself and the people she loves.

Katya and one of my men, Denis are forming a

strong bond. He came to her rescue during the failed coup, despite being badly wounded himself. Thankfully, he's out of the woods and will make a full recovery over time, the doctor informs me. He'll be thanked for saving her life, monetarily, and he'll take on the role of head of Katya's bodyguards when he's fully recovered. They'll be men I know and who will be willing to die for her, protecting what is mine.

Tomas is enjoying the attention he's getting from the young nurses who not only attend to his wounds, but I believe to his other needs as well. I'm beginning to believe he isn't hurt as badly as he makes out.

Natalia has Katya worried. I see it in her eyes every time she looks in her little sister's direction.

Katya has shielded Natalia all her life from the truth regarding Pavel and Igor, and the hell she's seen and been through herself. The young woman is still finding it hard to deal with the fact she shot her father. Even though it meant saving her sister.

During the little time Katya and I've had to spend together, she has relayed her thoughts that perhaps she needs to take Natalia away from here. It's not a satisfactory conclusion for me.

I need Katya here. With me.

I've been working on a compromise. Hopefully, it will solve the problem.

Katya once mentioned how talented and smart Natalia is. I'm going to offer to pay her way through college if it's something Natalia wants to do. I'll set her up in an apartment, where she can learn to become independent. She'll have her own security detail. This way, Katya won't have to worry about her too much.

Henrí doesn't appear to be happy about it, but he

agrees Natalia deserves to be able to experience life; to perhaps grow up a little. He has stipulated he wants to choose her security himself. If I didn't know better, I'd think he has a soft spot for the young woman. He assures me it's not the case. He says he's simply looking out for her.

***

It's hard to relax in this strange place we find ourselves living in while the compound is repaired. I've only ever known one home, and this isn't it.

While I know there's no threat at the moment, perhaps having Katya has made me feel more vulnerable. I've doubled my security forces. It's late in the evening, and I've poured myself several fingers of Macallans before slouching down in a large armchair in one of the sitting rooms. I've thrown my jacket off, unbuttoned and rolled up my shirt sleeves, and undone the buttons at the top of my white silk shirt. I'm tired. The past few weeks have taken a toll on me.

Between my men being killed and injured, my injuries, and Katya almost being killed, then being forced to shoot me, I'm second-guessing everything. Perhaps I should step down as the Pakhan and let Henrí take over.

Am I going to be able to keep Katya safe in my world? Is she going to willingly stay if she learns the dark side of the Bratva? We're known for blurring the lines of the law.

If I were a good man, I'd probably let her go, but I'm not a good man.

"There you are." Katya's voice breaks into my thoughts.

Placing my drink on the table beside my armchair, I

motion for her to come to me. She does so without hesitation, her hips swaying sexily as she moves. I can't see her expression because I'm sitting in the dark. It suits my mood tonight.

Her hand cups my cheek as I settle her small form on my lap. "What's wrong?" she murmurs.

"What makes you think something's wrong?" I tease.

"Hmmm, let's see," she teases back. "You're sitting in the dark sipping alcohol, all by yourself." Her finger draws a light line along my skin from my chin to my chest as she leans into me, nuzzling the hollow of my neck. This isn't the time, but my cock twitches in eagerness.

"There are things we need to discuss." I may as well get this over with.

Katya's body tenses as she straightens up a little, putting some distance between us. "Like what?"

"Natalia, for one. She's unhappy here," I begin slowly. "I thought perhaps she might be happier somewhere else."

"Like where? Are you saying Natalia can't stay here?" Katya's voice rises a few octaves, worry in her tone.

"I'm not saying that at all, malen'kiy olen'. What I'm suggesting is perhaps she needs to be with people her own age. She needs to experience life. Go to school. Meet people." I'm rolling with it while I can. "I can organize for her to go to a college nearby. Set up in her an apartment. Whatever she needs, she'll have," I continue, feeling emboldened when she doesn't interject.

When Katya doesn't say anything, I prompt her. "What do you think?"

"But how? I don't have the means to set her up like

that. Neither does Tomas. Father made sure we couldn't access his money. If he had any left," Katya concludes sadly.

"Ah, but *I* did. I employ people with many talents, Katya. Finding and accessing your father's money wasn't as hard as he thought it would be." Pavel wasn't as smart as he thought in hiding his money away. It took my hackers a day to find and access his accounts. "There's enough for Natalia's education, and an apartment, with plenty left over for you and Tomas."

Katya grows quiet. I'm not sure I like it. I can hear the wheels spinning in her head. All of this is new to her.

Pavel kept his children on a string. One he could pull and jerk to manipulate them into doing what he wanted. Now she has her freedom, Katya is unsure of everything.

Unsure of us.

I don't like it.

"What are you thinking, malen'kiy olen'? Talk to me," I murmur, wrapping her in my arms and pulling her close. Her body gradually relaxes against me as she fills me in on her thoughts.

"I want all those things for Natalia too, Mikhail." Her head tips up as she continues to speak. "Thank you for finding Fath… Pavel's money. And thank you for being so generous." I don't miss how she's trying to distance herself from her father by using his name. "I–I don't know what Tomas and I are going to do now—"

"Tomas has accepted a job as my driver," I interrupt her. "Now, what do *you* want, Katya?" If she chooses to go with her sister, I'll survive, but I won't like it.

Henrí and I discussed my feelings for Katya over drinks one night recently. My wish is for her to remain here with me. But Katya has been manipulated her entire life by men and forced to do unthinkable things. If she chooses to stay, and it must be her choice, I'll be the happiest man on earth. If she chooses the other path, I won't like it, but I'll let her go. I'd never force a woman to stay if she didn't want to, even though I could.

She will still have my protection for as long as she needs it, no matter what her choice is.

"Mikhail?" Katya's voice breaks into my thoughts. She's struggling to move. As my thoughts darken, my arms squeeze her tighter to my body, unconsciously trying to keep her here with me. I release her before reaching for my glass. If this is bad news, I'm going to need it.

"Where did you go?" The soft lilt in her voice is followed by her lips touching mine. I'm glad it's dark, so she can't read my face as I prepare myself for the worst. "Don't you want me to stay?" Her voice quakes with her words.

"What I want doesn't matter, malen'kiy olen'," I reply hoarsely around the lump forming in my throat. "This has to be your decision." I stroke her back gently, assuring her I'm okay with this, even though I'm not. If I thought locking her away would keep her here, I'd do it. Allowing her a choice is undermining everything I am.

The man who controls everything around him with an iron fist. The Pakhan.

"Even if I decide to go with Natalia? She'll need guidance, Mikhail. It's a nasty world out there. I'd never forgive myself if she was hurt." My head falls at her decision as I feel Katya's body tremble on my lap. *Is she afraid of my reaction? Does she believe I'll hurt her in some way because she doesn't want to stay with me? Or does she think I'll keep her here against her will?*

I sigh deeply before swallowing down the entire contents of my glass.

Katya takes the glass from my hand, setting it down on the table beside us. "If you guarantee me Natalia will be safe at all times, I'd like to stay here. With you." Her words are little more than a whisper and I'm unsure whether I've heard her correctly.

Gripping her chin between my thumb and pointer finger, I turn her face to mine. "Say it again," I demand, needing to be sure I heard her right.

"I said, I'd like to stay with you. If you want me to." Her voice is childlike, as if she's not sure of what I'm asking of her.

I sigh in relief at her words. "I want you always, malen'kiy olen'. I want everything with you. Everything. With. You." Each word is committed with a kiss. First on her forehead, before moving to place my lips on her eyelids one by one, the tip of her nose before giving her the gift I hope she's been waiting for. "I love you, Katya." My mouth meets hers in a long, languorous kiss as I commit everything I am to the woman on my lap.

29

KATYA

Natalia has settled into the life of a student well. She protested the security detail at first, but Henrí insisted.

She was a little worried about leaving Tomas and me until I explained to her, we all thought she needed the opportunity to spread her wings. She has a keen mind, which she uses to cruise through her classes. I'm so proud of her.

On her first break, Tomas, Mikhail, Henrí, and I accompanied her back to our mother's country to say farewell to her. Mikhail's people found her body somehow, after Pavel—I refuse to think of him as my father— killed her. Mikhail had her cremated, and we're going to spread her ashes in the sea today. This way, she'll finally be free. She deserves that, at least.

Natalia and I stand barefoot in the sand, the others sitting close by, watching. Opening the lid of the urn, I pour some ashes, first into hers, then some into mine.

"Fly high, Mother," I murmur before throwing her ashes into the air.

"Love you, Mama," Natalia's voice wobbles as she copies my movement.

We repeat tossing her ashes to the wind, watching them blow out to sea, until there are none left. Afterward we stand side by side, our arms around each other's waists, heads leaning on each other while watching the waves roll in and out. Although the urn is empty now, we remain there watching, both of us lost in our thoughts. I believe she did the best she could under the circumstances. She was as controlled by Pavel as we were and for much longer.

"Can I tell you a secret?" I keep my voice low, so the others don't overhear.

"Of course you can," Natalia replies.

"I think I'm pregnant," I blurt out, before slapping my hand over my mouth. I've been stressing about it all week. With everything that's happened in the time leading up to now, I had forgotten to have my implant renewed. I couldn't keep it to myself any longer. I had to tell someone.

Natalia turns to me in surprise, her hands gripping both of mine, her eyes dancing with joy. "Is it what you want, Kat? What did Mikhail say? Oh my gosh, I'm going to be an aunt," she giggles unable to contain herself.

Her enthusiasm is contagious, and I smile so wide my mouth hurts. "Yes," I answer her the best I can as she wriggles with excitement. "But I haven't told Mikhail yet," Her smile falters as does mine.

My mother was manipulated and controlled by my father after I was born. Although I don't believe Mikhail would do that, we haven't known each other long. He did say he wanted to be with me, but we haven't spoken about anything like marriage or children. "Besides, I don't know for sure yet. I haven't done a test yet, but I'm normally as regular as clockwork, so..."

"Well, we'll start with that," Natalia takes control of the situation. "Once we know, either way, we'll deal with it." I'm filled with pride at the newfound confidence. My baby sister has grown so much. She's changing from the shy, repressed young woman she was, to a happy, fun-filled, confident young woman. "No matter what you decide, I'm here for you, Kat."

I hug her tight. "Thank you."

<hr>

Kristine must have picked up on how edgy I've been lately and cornered me in the kitchen this morning. I broke down and told her what was bothering me. Instead of judging me, she took my hand, leading me to a room where medical supplies are kept. Fussing around in a cupboard full of women's products, she locates two pregnancy tests. I cock my head at her when she hands them to me, my brows arched in question.

The older woman shrugs. "You never know what a situation calls for. Come on, let's go find out. No point worrying until you're sure."

Should I be worried? Her words make me even more tense than before, but I follow her anyway. Natalia follows behind, close on my heels. She had entered the kitchen as I was telling Kristine my worries.

I take the two tests with me to a bathroom and do what's necessary, before washing my hands and returning to where my sister and Kristine are waiting for me.

It doesn't take long for the results.

I sigh, long and loud. "Well, there it is." Handing Natalia the stick with a shaky hand, I can't stop staring at the two pink lines on it.

I'm pregnant.

"Shall I get Mikhail for you?" Kristine's soft French accent pulls my eyes from the stick to hers, as they widen in alarm. "You have to tell him, Katya. He has a right to know," she adds, her voice sharpening a little at my reaction.

MIKHAIL

"Mikhail has a right to know what?" I came looking for Katya. She's been different since before we went to spread her mother's ashes in the sea. Our lovemaking is as passionate as ever, yet she's putting up walls between us in our everyday life. She hasn't been sleeping well either, often thrashing around our bed, mumbling and whimpering.

I had thought it was the aftermath of everything she's been through, added to worrying about Natalia. But I fear it's more than that.

What if she has decided a life with me isn't what she wants after all?

All eyes swing to me, and I don't think it's my imagination when Katya pales a little. Her eyes are wide and frightened, just as they were the night our eyes first locked on each other. She reminds me of a deer caught in the headlights.

There's something going on with her. I want answers, and I'm going to get them. Now.

"Leave us," I command.

Kristine obeys immediately, laying her hand lightly on Katya's forearm before she does. Natalia is a little more hesitant, obviously feeling the need to protect her sister. *Who from? Me?*

Katya nods, telling Natalia it's okay. She hesitates next to me for a moment. "Be gentle, she's scared enough," Natalia murmurs, hesitating in front of me. She lays her hand on my arm while locking eyes with me, as if in silent warning, before I move for her to exit the room.

Glancing back over, I find Katya nudging the edge of the carpet mat with her foot, her eyes on her nervous movement, her lower lip sucked into her mouth. "Katya? What do I deserve to know?" The words sound a little harsher than I mean them to.

"Please don't be angry," she finally answers while squeezing her eyes shut. She doesn't open them as I walk toward her. Instead, she folds in on herself, wrapping her arms around her waist, as if she's afraid. *What could be so bad it would make her think I'll be angry with her?*

I stop in front of the woman I love, my heart thudding like sludge in my chest. Lifting her chin with my hand, I'm surprised to find tears shimmering in her sea-blue orbs. "Malysh, what's wrong?" I frown down at her, confused. "I can't help you if you don't talk to me." My tone softens, silently pleading with her. I swore Katya would never be sad again, but here she is before me, obviously hurting over something.

Something I might have caused.

"I'm pregnant," she mumbles, her face screwing up as a tear escapes. "I'm sorry, Mikhail. I know you aren't ready for this kind of commitment," she apologizes as she moves away from me, sniffing loudly.

"What did you say?" I need her to say it again, so I can be sure that's what I heard. The sludge in my veins has thinned and my heartbeat picks up.

I step toward Katya, and she steps back.

"What did you say, Katya?" I ask a little more sternly, cocking my head to the side while forcing myself to stay where I am.

Katya bites her lip before taking a deep breath, blurting out louder than before. "I'm pregnant, Mikhail."

"Are you sure?" We haven't been together long, but we have been fucking like rabbits. We haven't used a condom, either. I kick myself for being chauvinistic in assuming she would have been on the pill or something. It takes two to make a baby. I should have asked.

Katya picks up two white stick things off the coffee table, shoving them toward me. "Here, see for yourself," she snaps. When I take them from her hands, she moves away again. I frown at her avoidance, but I say nothing.

Both sticks have two pink lines on them. I guess that means positive. A tingling sensation slithers up my spine and my vision blurs momentarily. Blinking hard, I try to focus on Katya, who now has her back to me as she pretends to look out the window, her arms still wrapped around herself. Cuffing the back of my neck, I state the obvious like an idiot, "You're pregnant?"

"Yes, Mikhail. For the third time, I'm pregnant," she snaps without looking at me. *Is she angry at me because of it?*

"Are you unhappy about it?" I inquire tentatively, frown marks creasing between my brows.

"Are *you* unhappy about it?" she echoes.

That's what she's afraid of. She thinks I won't want her if she's pregnant.

"Why wouldn't I be happy about it, malysh? Of course I want to have babies with you. I told you I want everything with you" I remind Katya as I advance slowly to where she remains staring out the window. My hands brush her arms, and she startles, yet still refuses to look at me. Moving forward until my arms wrap around her, I notice she's trembling. "Katya? Are you afraid of me?" I'm puzzled at her reactions as her body stiffens more in my arms.

When she doesn't answer, I turn her body until she's facing me. Her cheeks are wet with tears, and I run my thumbs over her pale cheeks to wipe them away. "Talk to me, malen'kiy olen'," I urge her gently. "What's going on in that beautiful head?"

Unwrapping her arms from her waist, Katya places her hands on my chest. She inhales deeply, as if needing to steady herself. Cupping her chin in my hand, I raise her face to mine so I can gauge her emotions.

Rubbing her lips together, she begins. "Mikhail, I love you. Please don't doubt it." I nod but remain silent. Her gaze flickers from mine for a moment and I dread there's a *but* coming. "I watched my father use us against my mother for years. He manipulated her from the time he discovered she was pregnant. He would withhold money until we were starving, or the electricity was turned off. Pavel mentally abused her, but he did it in a way that she didn't realize what he was doing. He broke her."

Katya must feel my body tensing as she pours out her feelings to me. Her hands grip my shirt as if to hold me to her. "She wasn't a great mother, Mikhail, but she tried. She was caught up with the wrong man. Pavel wore her down until she was his puppet, with no mind of her own. I was old enough to know what was happening, and I shielded Natalia from it as much as possible. I believe Mother loved him right up until he killed her." The last few words, Katya whispers, as another tear rolls down her flushed cheeks.

"And when Igor began *visiting*." She spits the word out as if it tastes bitter. "Mother fought him at first. I'd hear her asking him to leave her alone, begging him not to hurt her. He probably threatened her, or maybe he threatened to hurt me, until she gave in. Igor was worse than Pavel." Katya's eyes still won't meet mine. I hate this, but she needs to get it off her chest. She sucks her lips into her mouth before continuing. "Then Igor came around one day. Mother hid. I didn't think she was home. I answered the door. He—He forced me to—to have sex with him." Her eyes rise to mine again, a frown knitting her brows together. "I was fourteen. He hurt me. I thought I was going to die." She hiccups a sob, and I pull her tight to my chest.

"It's alright, Katya. I've got you. It's okay." I rub her back as she sobs into my chest. Right now, I wish I could bring Igor back to life so I can kill him again.

Although she's mentioned the assaults Igor rained down on her and her mother, this is the first time she's gone into detail. I can't imagine how Katya's life has affected her, but I know she needs me to listen to her if I'm going to keep her with me.

"No, you don't understand," she cries as she tries to

pull away, but I sweep her off her feet and stomp over to a large armchair, plonking us both down in it.

"What don't I understand, malysh? Tell me, please." I kiss the top of her head, forcibly keeping my tone level, so she'll keep talking. I hope she can't detect how angry I feel right now. My anger isn't aimed at her.

"M–Mother was home the day it happened. She was hiding in the wardrobe in our room the whole time Igor did... was... while he..." Katya hesitates as if she can't find the right words.

"While he raped you?" Although my voice is quiet, it's dripping with anger. My fists clench and unclench as I try not to picture the scene Katya just painted.

"Uhuh." She nods quickly, pushing her body hard into me as if trying to hide from the memories. "Mother was there the whole time, watching him do those things to me." She wails as if she's hurting, and I guess she is.

Anger rises against her mother, despite the fact she's dead. I can see how much this is hurting the woman cradled tight on my lap. The woman I love. I'd give anything to be able to wind the clock back and save her from all of this, but I can't.

"A–After Igor left, Mother climbed out of the wardrobe. She took my clothes and the sheets from the bed outside and burned them. Then she ran me a bath and told me to get in and scrub myself. I did as she said, crying the whole time. I scrubbed and scrubbed, but I still felt dirty." She hiccups again, her voice hoarse from her crying.

Katya tips her head back, looking up at me. Her eyes are red and swollen, yet she still looks beautiful to me. The horror of her memories dulls the light in her eyes. "Mother never even told me she was sorry for not protecting me, Mikhail. Not once did we ever speak about it. She pretended it didn't happen. And every time after, when Igor touched me, she did the same. Pretended it never happened."

I don't understand why someone didn't protect her. Her mother should have at least tried. Yes, Pavel was a manipulating monster, but this was his daughter. I've killed men for much less.

30

MIKHAIL

"I LET HIM DO THOSE THINGS TO ME." KATYA'S VOICE is shaky as she continues. "I need you to understand. Please, Mikhail," she begs, reaching up, placing her hands on the sides of my face, bringing my gaze down to hers. "I let him do those things to me. I stopped fighting him after my father told me it was my fault. I had to protect my sister. Do you understand? Please understand, Mikhail. I couldn't live with myself if Igor took Natalia's innocence like he took mine." Her eyes plead with mine along with her words.

"This is why I was afraid to tell you about the baby. I don't want to end up like my mother. I don't want to resent my children or allow someone to hurt them. I can't live like that. I won't bring a child into this world if it's not wanted, Mikhail." Her words are coming from years of degradation and manipulation. I know this. Still, it hurts that Katya would consider there were any similarities between me, Pavel, or Igor Popov. "If you can't be with me now you know what I've done, I understand," she whispers, her eyes skittering away from mine again.

Mikhail needs to understand what I'm feeling and why I feel this way. It means going into detail about my life, but if we're going to make it, he needs to know.

I've explained myself the best I can. It's up to him to decide whether he wants in or out. I know he won't let me leave now I'm pregnant, but if that's all we have, then I'll find a way to deal with it. I can't live a life like my mother.

He tells me he loves me, and I love him with everything I am, but will it be enough?

Did Pavel ever tell my mother he loved her? Did he love Tomas' mother?

Mikhail's been silent for a while and while I understand he needs to let everything sink in, the tension in his body is obvious. He's wound up as tight as a spring.

His silence unnerves me.

After minutes of silence, I decide it's time to leave. He can't answer my question, which I consider an answer in itself. I pull at his arms, trying to release them so I can climb off his knee.

MIKHAIL

"Where are you going, malen'kiy olen'?" Katya is pulling at my arms, which brings my thoughts back to her.

That's right, she asked me a question. One I didn't

answer because I was repeatedly killing Igor Popov and her mother, over and over again in my mind.

Instead of releasing her, I manipulate her body until she's straddling mine. Her eyes are red and raw from the tears she has shed. I hate that she feels this way.

"Okay. Now I need to tell you something, Katya, and you need to listen. Can you do that for me?" I ask, before running my hand down my mustache and goatee.

Katya nods, her chin still lowered to her chest. Placing a finger beneath it I lift her face to mine. "Eyes on me, milyaya, *sweetheart*," I command softly.

Again, she complies. My beautiful, frightened deer gazes up at me, her swollen eyes shimmering in the light.

"You are not to blame for your parents' behavior, Katya. They were adults. They chose the lives they led." I kiss her forehead softly, before continuing. "Your mother chose to stay. When she had you, she could have run. Maybe she tried, I don't know," I add as Katya shakes her head. "You are also not to blame for the things Igor did to you. Your mother failed to protect you. She failed you, Katya. Not the other way around. She. Failed. You. Pavel. Failed. You." I pronounce my words one by one, trying to penetrate the thick wall of guilt she's carrying.

"I love you, Katya Ivanov. I want you and our baby." I lean down to kiss her nose. "You are not your mother, and I am not your father." I lean closer to her lips, brushing mine lightly across them, as my cock hardens under Katya's sexy ass. It's not the time, but he has a mind of his own. "You will never be treated in the same way your mother was. I will keep things regarding the business away from you." It's best to be honest with her now. "I've told you before, I am not a good man. Some of my businesses are outside the law. When I keep things from you, it will be to keep you, and our family, safe. But I promise you will always be safe with me, Katya."

"You promise?" Her fingers pick at imaginary lint on my shirt, her eyes following the movement.

"I promise." My hand tangles in her hair as I repeat my words, gently tugging her head back so I can lean in and kiss her properly. As soon as our lips connect, she reaches up, pulling me down harder. I kiss her until we have to part for oxygen, our chests heaving. It never ceases to amaze me how swiftly a simple kiss escalates with her. I'm rock hard under her, which I'm sure she can feel.

The urge to be inside her is almost desperate. Lacing my hands together under her tight little ass, I pick her up and head toward our room.

As I exit the sitting room where I'd discovered I'm going to be a father, a noise to my left alerts me. Glancing sideways, I recognize Katya's sister seated on the floor, her hands around her knees, her head between them. She doesn't look up.

Did she overhear our conversation?

With Katya held tight to my chest, I pass her by without stopping. Natalia should know the sacrifices her sister made for her. She deserves to know how much Katya loves her and what she was willing to put herself through, to keep her safe.

Natalia will also learn the lengths *I* will go to for my *malen'kiy olen'*. Katya will never be hurt again as long as I live.

Averting her attention, because I know Katya has had all she can deal with for now, I kiss her again. When our lips part, Katya's lips tip up in a small smile. "I can walk you know," she teases.

"Ah, yes, I know this. But I'm doing this to get in some practice for our wedding," I tease back.

When she giggles, it's like music to my ears. My heart swells hearing it. "If that's a proposal Mr. Korbicov, it's a pretty lame one." She slaps my chest in mock indignance.

"Oh, so you want a big proposal now?" I join in, smiling down at her. "I'll have to give it some thought then. I suppose you want a big rock and all."

Her smile dims and I worry her insecurities are going to ruin the joy she showed moments before. I stop walking. "What is it, malen'kiy olen'? Did I say something wrong?"

"No, Mikhail, you said nothing wrong. Matter of fact, you said everything right," she murmurs. I frown in confusion when tears appear in her eyes again. "It must be these damn pregnancy hormones," she curses. Katya brushes her hand down my face before playing with the whiskers in my goatee. "I'm so happy right now. I love you."

Katya and I make love before she falls asleep. After the emotional rollercoaster she's been on, I'm not surprised. But I find myself wide awake afterward.

Leaving my woman in our bed, I wander through the house we've moved into. It's not as old as the one Otets and his father built, but it's enough for all of us, for now.

Mama has been a little unsettled, but Kristine assured me it's normal. I head upstairs to say goodnight, hoping it might help Kristine to calm her.

As usual, I knock on her door and wait for Kristine to call me in. Mama is seated in a white wooden chair in front of a dresser the same color, with a large mirror attached to it. Her furniture from the old house was unsalvageable, unfortunately.

She smiles at my reflection as I step up behind her. "Brush my hair for me. I love it when you brush my hair," Mama urges as she picks up her brush and hands it to me. Her long hair, now completely gray, hangs down past her shoulders.

I run the brush through her long, silky locks several times, the same as I had seen my Otets do. "What's wrong, son?" Mama asks, tilting her head while watching me in the mirror. I halt mid-stroke.

"I'm in love, Mama." The words tumble from my mouth. "And we're having a baby," I add quickly, ecstatic she's with me at this moment.

Mama smiles and nods. "I know, son. I met her. She's a good girl, Mikhail. Nothing like her father." Mama's words hit me in my chest like a sledgehammer. I'll ask Kristine later how she knows all of this, but I dare not take my eyes off Mama's reflection. "You make sure you make an honest woman of her, Mikhail. Your Otets would be proud of you."

Tears blur my vision as I return the brush to the dresser before leaning down to kiss the top of Mama's head. "I love you, Mama," I whisper in her ear before I straighten.

She pats my hand where it rests on her shoulder. "I love you too, my beautiful boy." She turns and beams at me. "Now go, look after your family." Turning away from me, she calls out. "Come, Kristine, I need to prepare for my husband. We're going dancing tonight."

The small window of her being in my world has passed. But the joy of her calling me her beautiful boy swells my heart to where I feel it could burst. It's what she would call me when I was younger, when I would run to her with my little boy problems. She would say, "Come, my beautiful boy, tell Mama what's troubling you." I would climb up on her knee and she would solve all my problems for me before sending me off with the nanny to play.

I'm almost to the door when Mama calls out, "You make sure Pavel can't hurt another person, Mikhail. Do that for me and your Otets."

The words shock me, and I glance back at her but Mama's chatting with Kristine as if she didn't say anything. Perhaps I imagined it. Kristine winks at me, then shrugs. *Who knows how the mind of someone with dementia works.*

"Your prisoner is conscious, sir," the voice on the phone informs me.

"I'm on my way," I advise him.

Henrí's phone rings for a while before he answers. "Where are you?" I ask.

He clears his throat before informing me he's driving Natalia back to her apartment. "Where's her detail?" I inquire. She has bodyguards for that.

"They're following," he replies. "She's upset," he continues. "I'll take her home and come straight back, okay?"

I know why she's upset. What I don't know is why Henrí felt the need to drive her home. He has been a little distant lately. I feel bad for neglecting my friend. When he arrives home, we'll have a couple of drinks, and I'll ask him what's wrong. Hopefully, he's not upset that I've found someone.

"Mikhail? You there?" His voice sounds panicky. "What's wrong?"

"I'm here," I assure him. "Our friend is awake. We need to deal with him. See you when you get back." I end the call before he can say anything else.

It's past midnight when Henrí finally arrives back at the house. He immediately locates me in my office. Strutting in and seating himself on the deep brown leather lounger against the wall of my office. "What's going on?" His tone is all business.

Running my gaze over him, I notice his normally neat clothing is disheveled. Also, his hair is sticking up in places as if he's been running his hands through it constantly. Totally out of character for him.

"You tell me, brat, *brother*," I answer as I hand him a glass of Macallan.

He takes the offered drink before leaning back into the leather. Bringing his right ankle up to rest on his left knee, he stares into the amber liquid in his glass for a moment.

"Is it me and Katya? Do you have a problem with our relationship?" I hope he doesn't. Henrí and I have been friends since childhood. We've been through a lot together.

"No, of course not." Henrí shakes his head. "It's

Natalia," he admits before running a hand through his hair. "The girl frustrates me no end," he continues.

I can't help the smirk pulling at my lips as I ask, "What do you mean?"

My best friend takes a sip of his drink before answering. "She wants to go out to nightclubs. She wants to date," he exclaims. "It's a fucking nightmare. How the hell am I supposed to keep her safe when she's out and about?" His hands fling in all directions. "And the guys are all too fucking handsy with her," he exclaims, before running his hand through his blond locks again.

I rub my lips together to stop myself from laughing at him before answering. "Why don't you take her out, then? Then you'll know who she's with, and can be on hand if anything bad happens?"

"Because she's too young for me," Henrí replies too quickly. "She needs to find someone her age. Guys her age are all sex fiends, though. I mean, who wouldn't want to get into her pants? She's gorgeous and has a body to die for. And she's smart, you know?" He glances up at me as I lean against my desk, enjoying his discomfort.

His hand grips his whiskey glass so tightly, I'm sure if it weren't hardened glass it would shatter.

"Would you be one of those who wants to get in her pants, my friend?" I tease, still trying hard not to laugh. My best friend is a ladies' man. He has a different girl each week. To think the young, naïve Natalie has unnerved him is hilarious. He's as much a control freak as I am. Probably more. "If I wasn't in love with Katya, Natalia would have been on my radar," I joke. It's not true. Yes, Natalia is pretty, but Katya outshines her like a megawatt star in the sky.

I chuckle when a growl erupts from Henrí.

Placing my hands up in front of me in a surrender sign, I finally give in to the laughter bubbling inside me. "I'm pulling your chain, brat, *brother.* Look at your face. You were ready to punch me." I chuckle as Henrí glares at me. Picking up the bottle, I walk over and pour him another finger, which he swallows down in one gulp.

It's time to be serious.

"Pavel's awake. I wanted you here with me for this," I inform him, my tone full of emotion. This man has so much to pay for. I've imagined this day, the day I would be able to avenge my father's murder, for years.

At my words, Henrí's stands from the lounge, placing his glass on my desk.

He runs his eyes over me before nodding. "Let's do this."

Pavel is being held in the basement. Henrí and I make our way down the stairs silently, our moods somber. Pavel Ivanov has been a pain in our asses since the day he murdered my Otets. Chasing him down took far too long. He was either smarter at hiding than we thought, or someone was helping him. Not even Igor had the connections to keep Pavel safe, I'm sure of it.

On reaching the basement room Pavel's in, I pay the doctor in cash and order him from the room. He will no longer be needed. Tonight, I end this. But first I require a few answers. I had been going to get them from Igor when I held him prisoner, but the attack happened, and he escaped. Now Igor's dead, which leaves only one man.

The fact he didn't die from his wounds amazes me.

The doctor informs me he was wearing a new style of Kevlar under his clothing, which took most of the bullets.

As we step up to the bed Pavel's chained to, he opens his eyes. He probably thought we were the medics because when he realizes it's me, his eyes widen in panic. He struggles against his restraints, but they aren't going to budge.

"What do you want?" he sneers, attempting to school his face. But his fear is obvious, and it makes me feel good.

"Seems you have the lives of a cat, Pavel Ivanov. It's a shame you've used up all those lives, though," I fake smile at him from one side of the bed. Henrí moves around to the other side. "A new type of Kevlar, huh? Good work." I clap my hands a couple of times. "It's a shame your cousin wasn't wearing it."

"Where am I?" Pavel inquires, ignoring my comments.

"Oh, no." Henrí waggles his finger in front of the restrained man's face. "You don't get to ask the questions here. We do." He points at me, then himself.

"Who bankrolled you?" We know someone was paying him. The money he had in his accounts when working for Otets would not have kept him in the lap of luxury for long.

Pavel remains silent.

"Who helped you hide from us all this time?" Henrí asks the next question.

Nothing.

I rip off one of his bandages before poking my finger into the wound. The man chained to the bed screams. Henrí works on the other side as we torture him to gain the information we need. Pavel tried to lead us in the wrong direction, but I already had my suspicions, which he quickly and painfully discovers.

Before the night is over, we have all the information we need. Pavel is writhing in pain, which doesn't bother me in the least.

As Henrí cleans his hands, Pavel croaks out, "Did you know it was me who organized the car bomb that killed your father, Henri?"

We both freeze in place, our eyes glued to the sweating, bloodied form.

Pavel begins to chuckle, low at first, then growing louder. "Kristine and your fucking parents were all supposed to be in the car. My intel was good," he continues rambling. "But you," a trembling finger points at Henrí, "came down with a cold, and your mother chose to stay home with you."

"Your parents," he snarls at me. "Had unexpected visitors, so they stayed home as well." His eyes are wild now as he pulls and fights with the chains holding him in place. "It was a good plan!" he exclaims loudly. "They should've all died that night. I should've been the Pakhan—"

He doesn't get to make another sound as Henrí and I put our guns to his head and pull the triggers.

Pavel Ivanov will not hurt my friends or family ever again.

31

KATYA

MIKHAIL HAS BEEN DIFFERENT THE PAST FEW DAYS. He's been extra sensitive to my needs, and particularly secretive. It's driving me crazy. He's up to something but won't tell me what. He simply tells me I'll know soon when I try to press him.

We're staying in a swish hotel tonight. Mikhail's booked out the entire top floor. He has guaranteed me we're safe here, as our bodyguards are everywhere.

All he's told me is we're going on a real date tonight. I'm beyond excited. Yes, I've been on a few dates with men, but they always ended up a disaster. I know it won't be the case with Mikhail, but it doesn't make me any less nervous.

This morning, I had a massage, before having a whole pamper package performed. I've been waxed and shaved in my most intimate places before being dressed in a white fluffy robe and returned to my room.

Mikhail had Denis, who is recovering well from his

wounds, deliver to our room a spectacular white, fitted, strapless silk dress, overlayed with fine lace with fine silver thread woven through it. This is paired with a gorgeous pair of matching pearl-white heels with fine silver patterns reflecting when the light catches them.

The finishing piece is a gorgeous necklace he's bought for me to wear. It's out of this world. It consists of the same fine lace on my dress, held together with fine white gold chains, with white gold strings hanging down, in an uneven fringe-like pattern. The fringe chains each have three pearls attached at the ends.

My hair is being styled, while another young woman does my makeup. I've never been pampered like this before, and I love it.

I wish Natalia was here with me. She would undoubtedly enjoy all the attention. Unfortunately, she has some overdue essays and decided to stay at her apartment to finish them.

Having overheard Henrí and Mikhail talking one time, it seems Natalia could be partying a little too much. I'll have a chat with her when I see her next. I don't want her wasting the opportunity she's been granted. There was a time when I would've loved to be able to go to college.

Mikhail is probably trying to wrangle my little sister on his own. Poor thing. I doubt he has any idea how to handle her. He has never had siblings. He'll be trying to keep any issues away from me. Lately, he's been handling me with kid gloves. Anyone would think I was some frail, high-maintenance woman.

I admit, my mood swings are unpredictable. Kristine assures me it's natural. I hope Mikhail understands too.

Finally, my hair, nails, and makeup are done, and Kristine shoos everyone from the room. "It's time for you to dress," she tells me, picking up the hanger draped over the back of the white leather couch. "Mikhail will be here soon. You don't want to keep him waiting."

I already have on the white silk bra and G-string that were laid out on the bed this morning when I returned from the pamper session.

Mikhail is going all out for this date.

"Do you know where we're going?"

"Don't be so impatient, child," Kristine replies as she indicates for me to put my arms up so she can slip the dress over my head. Once it's in place, she does up the zip. I was worried it would make my stomach protrude, but I'm barely showing yet.

I smile as I place my hand on my stomach. Tears threaten to spill as my heart swells with the love I already have for my unborn baby. "No tears now, child. We don't want to spoil our makeup, do we?" Kristine chides as she breaks into my thoughts, and I blink them away quickly. I don't want to go on a date with Mikhail with red, swollen eyes and running mascara.

Next, Kristine places the necklace around my neck, fixing the catch at the back. She straightens out all the fine chains and pearls until they sit perfectly in place. After that's done, I put on my footwear. Thankfully, the heels aren't too high. It wouldn't do for me to be wobbling around on my date.

Moving around to the front of me, she peruses me from head to toe. Kristine frowns, placing her finger on her lower lip before cocking her head at me.

"What? Is there something wrong?" Please don't let her tell me I look like a whale in the dress. Butterflies flutter in my stomach while Kristine draws her brows together in thought.

"Something is missing," she murmurs, tapping her lower lip a few times before her eyes widen and she gasps. "I've got it. Wait here, I'll be right back." Before I can answer, Kristine heads for the door.

"Okay, then," I say to myself, widening my eyes momentarily as I shrug. I've no idea what she was talking about.

With nothing else to do, I stroll over to the three-piece, full-length mirror. "Wow," I exclaim, finding it hard to believe what I see. I run my hands over the necklace. It looks even more exquisite on than it did in the box it arrived in. The dress clings to my curves perfectly. Turning sideways, I softly rub my tiny bump with the palm of my hand.

When I glance into the third mirror, which reflects my back, I notice the lace is see-through. My tattoo is visible from the top of my spine to my lower back. Mikhail loves my tattoo. I often wake to find him trailing his fingers up and down it, tracing the pattern. After the baby's born, I'll have Mikhail and the baby's name intertwined the same as I have Natalia, Tomas, and my mother's.

Perhaps Mikhail's tattooist will do it. That is, if he'll forgive me for choking him out when Tomas and I escaped.

The opening of the door takes my attention from the past when Kristine re-enters the room. She's holding a box similar to the one my necklace came in, except it's smaller. "This is what it needs to finish everything off perfectly," she singsongs as she approaches me. Her face appears to be flushed, as if she's been hurrying.

Before I can ask what's inside, she opens the box to show me a smaller version of my necklace. Removing it, she wraps it around my wrist before latching the clip. From her pocket, she removes a dainty pair of pearl and silver gold earrings. "These are mine, Katya. I noticed you don't have your ears pierced. Neither are mine." She clips the earrings on my lobes as she remarks, "These will match everything beautifully."

Kristine turns me to the mirror again, and I scan myself from head to toe. Even admit I look like a princess. I can't believe everyone has gone to all this trouble for a simple date.

Mikhail, though, is not a simple man. He's a complex being, with many sides to him. His employees and the people he deals with see only the hard side of him. The Pakhan, the head of his section of the Bratva; their boss and associate.

His mother, Svetlana, sees him as her beautiful boy, her son. At times she believes him to be a young Rinaldo, which I know pains Mikhail, but he understands. The disease gradually taking his mother from him is incurable, and it frustrates him no end that he can do nothing for her.

His friend, Henrí, sees a man who is as close as a brother to him; someone who he trusts with everything he is.

I see him as my everything. Mikhail is everything I never knew I wanted. From the moment I laid eyes on him, I think I began falling in love with him. Even when I thought he was being purposely cruel, I know now it's because he feels responsible for protecting his family and those close to him. He needs to be a hard man at times. The Bratva world is not a place where the weak last long. It doesn't have the rigid rules of the mafia.

A phone buzzes. Kristine reaches into her pocket, pulls out her cell phone, checking the screen. "It's time, Katya. Mikhail is waiting. Come," she commands gently.

"He's not coming to pick me up?" I ask, disappointment obvious in my tone.

Kristine moves forward, taking my hand and patting it. "It's all part of your surprise, Katya. Now we have to go. We don't want him to think you're not coming, do we?"

MIKHAIL

I've been pacing up and down for what seems like hours now. Henrí tried to get me to sit down, but I'm too wound up. He hands me a glass, half full of Macallans. "Here, I think you need this, brat, *brother*." He chuckles as I take a large gulp. He laughs even harder when I glare at him.

"This isn't funny, asshole," I snap, my nerves pulled tighter than guitar strings. The feeling of uncertainty is alien to me. I hate not being in control. Everything I've done up to this moment has gone perfectly. Katya is the unknown entity. She's the one part of my elaborate plan I can't be certain of.

The phone in my pocket buzzes and as I read the text, my heart rate picks up. "She's here," I inform Henrí. "You can go now," I nod at Henrí. He grips my shoulder, giving it a light shake before leaving.

"It'll be fine, Mikhail, you'll see. Katya loves you." I glance up, his positivity relaxing me minutely.

I promised Katya the best date of her life after she admitted to me the dismal few she's had and how they mostly ended up. Henrí thought it was hilarious that Katya refused to name and shame them in case I went looking for them. He knows me well. It appears Katya is learning too.

After our late-night chat about her life before me, I began hatching a plan. Tonight is the execution of that plan. All I can do is hope everything goes smoothly.

Katya thinks I've only booked out the top floor, but I've booked out the hotel restaurant also. The chef is at our disposal to cook whatever Katya wishes to dine on, and I've selected several songs to be played in the background as we eat. Cuffing the back of my neck, I concentrate on my shoes as I reflect on everything leading up to this night.

"Hey, are you okay?" Katya's lilting voice pulls me from my thoughts.

The breath leaves my body as my gaze falls on the most beautiful creature I've ever seen. A current surges through my body that feels like electricity, my heart races, and a small bead of sweat appears on my forehead. I run a finger around the collar of my tux, which momentarily feels too tight, before pulling at the bowtie.

Say something, Mikhail, I shout inside my head. Stop behaving like a hormonal teenager.

I'm glad my suit pants are a little looser in the crotch area as my cock has sprung to attention at the sight of the woman I love. This night needs to be over with so I can strip the dress she's wearing from her body. She can keep the necklace on. It will look damn sexy dangling from her neck as I slam inside her from behind. Not caring if she sees how much she affects me, I reach down and adjust myself. That part of my anatomy will have to wait.

First, I want to taste her.

Stepping up to her I gaze down, stripping her down with my eyes. Her chest rises and falls quickly. *Was she fantasizing too?* "You are exquisite, milyy, *beloved*. I hope you like what I chose for you?"

She flushes a beautiful shade of pink as she touches the necklace. "I love it all, Mikhail," Katya smiles shyly. "But you didn't have to go to all this trouble for me." Her eyes lowered to the floor. *Is she embarrassed because I believe she's worth treating like a queen?*

"Hey," I call softly, bending my knees until my face is level with hers. Cupping both her cheeks, I let her know, "You deserve the best, milyy. Don't ever doubt it." I gaze into the large blue orbs that sucked me in the night I first saw her. It kills me how little worth she puts on herself. Katya is always thinking of others. It's time she had someone show her how much she's loved.

My lips brush hers lightly before I straighten up. "Come, Katya, let's sit." With my arm around her shoulders, I direct her to the only table set up in the dining room. Pulling out a chair for her, I wait until she's seated, before moving to the opposite side and seating myself.

I cough, clearing my throat. This has to be the most nervous I've ever felt. If my plan goes wrong tonight, there's no coming back from it.

A waiter appears with a bottle of non-alcoholic champagne. If Katya wasn't pregnant, we'd have the real thing. He pours us both a glass before leaving the table. "Where are our menus?" Katya frowns as she looks around. "And why are we the only ones here?"

I squeeze my lower lip between my thumb and pointer fingers. "So, we could enjoy our date, in peace," I make an attempt at a part truth while nervously scratching the side of my face.

What if it all goes wrong? Kristine helped me arrange everything. After all, what do I know about romance?

The song *All Of Me* by *John Legend* begins to play in the background, and I stand before offering my hand to the beautiful woman sitting opposite me. Tugging Katya up, I begin to slow dance with her. She gazes up at me, her eyes shining in the low light before resting her head on my chest. We move around the dance floor, not speaking.

The song ends and I kiss the top of Katya's head before whispering, "We aren't here to eat, Katya. There's something important I want to ask you." The song has ended, and the room is still and silent as I get down on bended knee. For a man who has been in control of his destiny for so long, I feel humble and vulnerable right now.

She gazes down at me, a slight frown of confusion on her beautiful face. Brushing my hand over my mustache and goatee, I decide it's now or never. "I am not a romantic man, as you know. But from the night I laid eyes on you, I knew I had to have you in my life. You are going to be the mother of my child, but I hope you will also be my wife."

I produce the *Tiffany* box I've been toting around the last few days, opening it for her to see the ring inside. It has a large diamond in the center and two smaller blue sapphires on either side, set in white gold.

It feels as if time has slowed down as I watch Katya's face, trying to gauge her answer. The thrumming of my nerves, along with my thudding heartbeat, becomes even more erratic as she continues staring at me silently.

Is she going to say no?

32

KATYA

I SHOULD'VE KNOWN SOMETHING WAS UP WHEN Kristine delivered me to the hotel dining room door. She hugged me tight before telling me to go in, as I was expected.

The sight before me was like something from a movie when I entered the room. I found a path of red rose petals leading to a table in the center. It was set with a white tablecloth and a centerpiece consisting of a vase of white lilies, my favorite, and nothing else.

Candles flickered from all around the room, bathing it in a romantic light. Standing at the table is Mikhail, dressed in a tux, the material clinging to all the right places on his large body perfectly, and his hair is braided. It reminds me of the first time I saw him. The man is sexy anytime, but when he's dressed like he is now, it takes all my strength not to jump him. My libido goes into meltdown at the sight of him.

The way his eyes roam over me, as I approach him, I

can tell he feels the same. He leans down to kiss both my cheeks before asking if I'm happy with his choice of clothes and jewelry. I assure him I am, as his scent wafts over me.

Mikhail pulls out a chair for me, and once I'm seated, he takes the chair opposite. As soon as we're seated, the waiter brings us our drinks. I'm so enamored with Mikhail I hadn't noticed until now that there's only the two of us here. Is it because he wants to be alone with me, or is he afraid someone could be in the restaurant to hurt us?

He appears as nervous as I am, as he leans an elbow on the table, his fingers fidgeting with his lips. Cocking my head at him slightly, I'm trying to figure out why, when he abruptly stands and walks around the table to me. Tugging me up into his arms, a love song begins to play and we sway to the music.

There are many things I don't know about Mikhail Korbicov, but I hope I get the chance to find them all out. I smile before laying my head on his broad, hard chest as he leads us around the area he's chosen as our dance floor.

When the song ends, Mikhail drops to one knee in front of me. For a moment I'm confused as he fumbles through his pockets for something.

He pulls a Tiffany box from his pocket, opening it up to show me a gorgeous ring inside. My hands slap over my mouth as I dare to hope this is what it appears to be.

Mikhail is on one knee with a ring in his hand. For me. He's asking me to be his wife. Goosebumps rise all over my body, while my throat constricts. I hope I'm not dreaming.

"Katya?" Mikhail's voice sounds hoarse, bringing me back to the present.

Damn, he asked me a question, didn't he? "Yes," I squeak, as it's all the air in my lungs will allow me. For the umpteenth time today, tears threaten to fall. My legs fail me, and I fall to the floor in front of him. Cupping his cheeks, I kiss him as hard as I can. "Yes," I repeat louder when we finally separate for air.

Mikhail wastes no time placing the ring on my finger before he rises to his feet. He helps me up, then pulls me into him as he shouts, "She said yes."

Applause erupts from a doorway, and I glance around Mikhail's large body to find Kristine, Henrí, Tomas, and Natalia entering the empty restaurant. Both women are crying, while the men wear toothy grins stretching their mouths wide. Natalia hugs me, then Kristine. Tomas chuckles as he spins me to face him before hugging me tight. "Congratulation. sis," he whispers in my ear, his voice raspy.

Henrí grips my shoulders as he places kisses on both my cheeks before stepping back. He slaps Mikhail on the shoulder. "For a second there I thought the answer was going to be no, brat, *brother*," he chuckles.

I glance at Mikhail at the same time he glances at me, a slight frown on his face. Did he think I'd say no? Surely the confident man I'm coming to know wouldn't believe that. Smiling, I lean into him as his arm curls around me, his hand on my hip, his fingers digging in slightly.

The waiter who served Mikhail and I appears with a tray of drinks. He hands each glass out individually. When he hands me my glass, he assures me there's no alcohol in it. Henrí raises his glass. "To Mikhail and

Katya. Congratulations." Everyone clinks their glasses together, drinking to Mikhail's and my engagement.

We've no sooner finished our beverage when Henrí checks his watch. Please don't let Mikhail have to leave for a meeting or something. I want him here with me.

"The cars are here. We have to go," Henrí taps Mikhail on the shoulder.

"Where are you going?" I know I sound clingy, but I was hoping Mikhail and I would be celebrating our engagement longer than ten minutes.

Mikhail smiles at me despite my whining. "I am not going anywhere, but we are." His finger waggles between the two of us. "There are more surprises in store today, malen'kiy olen'." He swipes a piece of loose hair from my face, gently tucking it behind my ear. "Come. It's time to go." He tangles his fingers in mine. We place our glasses on the table, walking in pairs out of the restaurant. Staff at the front desk look up as we stroll through the hotel foyer, out of the front doors, and down the steps.

Denis is waiting beside a white, stretched limousine, with blacked-out windows, holding the rear door open. In front and behind the limo are black sedans, filled with bodyguards. These are things I'll have to get used to if I'm going to be Mikhail's wife.

Everyone climbs into the limousine, and I'm surprised to find Svetlana already seated inside. Kristine sits next to her, patting her hand. Svetlana's face is blank, as if she isn't aware we're all here. Henrí and Tomas climb in next, then Mikhail and me.

It's the first time I've ever been in a stretched limousine before, and I glance around the interior wide-eyed. "It's so roomy in here," I gasp, and everyone laughs.

Night is falling outside, as we all sip drinks, laugh, and chat in the back of the limo. Even Svetlana joins in. It's lovely to see everyone relaxed and happy. It's still sinking in that I'm engaged. I'm not just engaged though, I'm engaged to Mikhail Korbicov, Bratva Pakhan. The most beautiful man I've ever met. He hasn't let go of me since we left the hotel. His fingers are tangled with mine as if he needs to touch me, to make sure it's real. I understand. I feel the same.

We've been driving for a while when the limousine slows to a halt. Denis cracks the front passenger window open slightly, muttering something I can't hear. He nods before sliding the window closed again, and the car moves off. We're out of the city now, but we're not headed back to the house we've been staying at.

It's not until we're almost at our destination that I realize where we're going. The trees lining the driveway give it away. "We're going home?" I glance up at Mikhail. The smile he gifts me with is broad and toothy, both his dimples flashing. He squeezes my fingers and I flush as he continues to stare at me. "What?" I ask, feeling the crimson spreading across my cheeks.

"I love that you called it home, malen'kiy olen', because that's exactly what it is." He tightens his grip on my hand a little more. "Our home."

"But the fire." I frown a little at the memories rushing through my mind.

Our cheerful little group quiets down as Mikhail and I discuss the house his grandfather built for his grandmother. The same house his mother and father lived in and made their own. The place where Mikhail was born.

It saddens me that all the love it had held was

destroyed when Pavel and Igor decided to attack its occupants, killing and maiming so many.

"This is another part of your surprise tonight, milyy, *darling*." Mikhail kisses me gently on my forehead. He's probably having flashbacks himself. A lot of things have happened in this house, some good, some bad. But I understand his draw to it. It's the last place he spent time with his father, and the only place his mother remembers, even though her memories are becoming more sporadic as each day passes. "The entire house has been refurbished from the ground up. Thankfully, my grandfather had the forethought to frame it with steel beams. The fire did some damage, but because of its strong bones, everything was fixable," he assures me.

I'm surprised when we don't pull up at the front of the house. Instead, the car drives around the side and carries on past it. Mikhail glances down, noticing my confused look. "Patience, malysh, *baby*," he leans in and whispers.

It's a short drive before the limousine pulls to a full stop. Two men dressed as valets step up, opening both doors. Mikhail pulls me to him as everyone exits the car, kissing me hard. His lips trace my skin to my neck, where he nuzzles the place he discovered drives me wild. I melt into him, letting out a slight moan, holding him there, wishing we were at home in bed right now.

Someone knocks on the window, breaking our moment. "It's time, Katya." Mikhail raises his face to mine, his face serious again. He watches me warily as I gather myself before he exits the car. He steps around to my side, offering his hand to me. I take it and step out of the limo.

There are fairy lights as far as I can see. An arch

nearby is covered in white lilies and more fairy lights. People are milling around chairs which have been set in neat rows, their backs to us. A path has been left void of anything between the chairs. Above the path, fine wisps of white silk cover the archway path from the back forward.

I've never had a party before, for any reason. I'm grateful to Mikhail for having organized all of this for our engagement. I turn, pull him down to me, lace my hands around his neck, and kiss him hard. Whistles and clapping reach my ears and I separate from him blushing. "Thank you," I breathe.

Mikhail's brows draw together for a moment. "What for?" He appears puzzled.

"For everything you've done tonight." I kiss him again. "For asking me to marry you. For organizing this party to celebrate." I swing my arm indicating in the direction of the party, my gaze locked on his. "But most of all, thank you for loving me and our baby."

He breaks our gaze, his face dipping to the ground for a moment, before blowing out a breath and glancing back up. He sucks his lips inside his mouth, and at the same time, his thumbs rub back and forth on my shoulders. His eyes bounce away from mine, making me believe he's not telling me something. "Mikhail? What is it? Did I get it wrong? Is this party not for us?" I'll be disappointed if it isn't, but it won't change my opinion of him.

"Hey," Henrí calls from the archway. Times like this I'd like to tell him to go away. My fiancé and I are talking, but I don't. "Are you ready?"

I glance at Mikhail, pursing my lips and narrowing my eyes. "What's Henrí talking about? Are we ready for what? What's going on here?" I'm becoming more than frustrated with his silence.

Mikhail averts my gaze, his eyes on his shoes, before cuffing his neck with one hand. He kicks the ground with the toe of his shoe, reminding me of a young boy caught doing wrong by the teacher. The silence between us is a matter of a few seconds, yet seeming like minutes before he looks up again. He bites his lower lip momentarily before speaking. "This isn't an engagement party, Katya. It's a wedding."

"A wedding," I repeat. "Whose wed…"

He continues watching me as it sinks in. I can't say anything more. I'm speechless. Suddenly, the world spins. Mikhail becomes a blur in front of me, as my head grows light and my knees give way.

33

____

KATYA

"Shit," Mikhail curses, catching me before I hit the ground. "Katya. Malyshka, *baby*, can you hear me? You're okay." Mikhail is speaking to me, but I can't answer. People are fussing around me, but it's all white noise. Someone places a cool cloth on my forehead while Mikhail continues to assure me I'm okay.

When I open my eyes, I'm lying across one of the seats in the limousine. Mikhail's lap is my pillow, and the doctor who tended to the wounded after Pavel's attack is checking my pulse. Glancing up, I find the sunroof wide open and Nat and Tomas peering in, worry evident on both their faces. I redirect my eyes to Mikhail. His face is drawn with worry. I reach up with one hand, touching his cheek, reassuring him I'm okay. When he locks eyes with mine, I see turmoil in his dark chocolate pools.

"Ah, you're back with us, Miss." The doctor's voice brings my gaze to him.

"What happened?" I remember arriving here and

getting out of the car. I also remember Henry calling out to Mikhail. It all comes flooding back in a rush. "Oh my gosh, our wedding." My gaze returns to Mikhail as my voice rises a few octaves. "I've spoiled our wedding," I whine as tears drip down the side of my face.

"You're okay, Miss," the doctor assures me. "I've been told you've had quite an exciting day. It's not uncommon to have dizzy spells when you're pregnant." He hands me a bottle of water. "You've probably not kept yourself hydrated properly. Your blood pressure is a little higher than it should be, but as long as you take it easy, you should be fine," he informs me.

I accept the bottle, uncap it, and take several sips.

"I'll take her straight home to bed," Mikhail rumbles.

"No," I blurt out, attempting to sit up. "We're here to get married." Turning to Mikhail, I frown, confused. "I didn't dream all this, did I?" I grip my left hand with my right, bringing my hand up to my face to double-check. Nope, the ring is still there. I let out the breath I was holding in a rush.

Mikhail chuckles beside me. "No, you didn't dream it, malen'kiy olen'." His face becomes more serious as he adds, "But we can do this tomorrow. You should rest—"

I don't allow him to finish. With a growl I push past the doctor, almost knocking him over as I scramble from the car. "I'm here for a wedding." I turn back dipping down to look back at Mikhail, who is still seated in the car. "Do you want to marry me or not?" I snip.

Feeling ridiculous, I step back and shout at the top of my lungs, "All those in favor of sticking around for a wedding, say yes." Yes," erupts from everyone. "I'll be waiting for you at the arch, baby." I poke my head back in the car, catching Mikhail's amused look. Winking at him, I add, "I'll be the one in white."

I hand off the water bottle to the doctor, before walking over to the archway. Before I reach it, Mikhail is beside me.

"Are you positive you want to do this right now?" He wraps his arms around me from behind, his large hands splayed on my stomach.

I nod. "You?" Mikhail smirks as he nods. "Well, let's do this. We mustn't keep our guests waiting."

"There's one last thing, malysh. This decision, I leave up to you." My soon-to-be husband grips both my hands in his. "I didn't know who to choose to walk you down the aisle."

Looking around at the spectators, I realize there are very few people I know here. But then, I don't know anyone outside my family.

Family.

"Tomas?" I call watching as he slides off the trunk of the limo. Natalia attempts to do the same thing, but Henrí is there in front of her. He lifts her down before gently setting her on her feet. Something passes between them before my sister tears her eyes away, a blush creeping across her cheeks. She straightens herself up before strolling over to us.

"What's up, sis?" Tomas steps up next to us.

"Would you consider... Will you..." I blow out a breath, shaking my hands out in an attempt to collect myself. "Tomas, will you walk me down the aisle? Please?".

"Yes," he shouts, fisting the air. He looks around at our audience, wide-eyed, his smile wide as he puffs out his chest. "I'm walking my sister down the aisle," he shouts, as if no one knew what's happening.

"Well then..." I glance at Mikhail coquettishly. "If there's nothing else?" Raising one eyebrow at my fiancé, I wait for a moment, just in case there's something else needing done. "I guess we're getting married."

Mikhail nods before kissing me gently on the cheek. He and Henrí take their places at the other end of the aisle. We're about to step forward onto the red carpet when Natalia sidles up to me. She hands me a bouquet of white, scarlet, and black lilies with stems of baby breath between them, before checking my makeup.

Placing her fingers either side of her lips, she lets out a most unladylike, loud whistle, and *Perfect* by *Ed Sheeran* begins playing. Then, holding a basket of petals, she walks ahead of Tomas and I walk arm in arm down the aisle.

Glancing around me, I realize every white chair has someone seated on it. There's no point looking for anyone I know because they're all within my sight. Silk strips of material on the arch flutter in the breeze, while the thousands of fairy lights give off a romantic glow.

As my brother and I follow my baby sister down the aisle, I go over the day's events. The white dress Mikhail had delivered, along with the sexy lingerie. Then having my hair and makeup done before Kristine arrived with the necklace. Something new. Were the earrings really forgotten, or was that Kristine's way of gifting me with something borrowed? I hesitate for a moment, then remember my engagement ring. Glancing down to where my hand is hooked through Tomas' I spot the two blue stones on either side of the diamond. Something blue. Tomas pats my hand and I smile up at him.

Mikhail waits for me at the other end of the archway, Henrí beside him, as always. I step up the pace, wanting to reach my husband-to-be as quickly as possible. It's as if someone placed large magnets around us, the pull toward him overpowering. "Whoa, sis," Tomas places his hand over mine. "You'll get there fast enough. Let yourself soak in the atmosphere. You deserve this," he croons quietly.

For the first time in a while, I allow myself to relax. I slow my pace, lock eyes on Mikhail. Mikhail returns my look, his smile as wide as mine.

How is this my life?

<hr>

MIKHAIL

The music begins, and Natalia steps into sight, dropping flower petals on the red carpet. Following her down the aisle is Katya on the arm of her stepbrother.

The song playing is what Mama says is the most romantic thing she's ever heard. Kristine has found playing soothing music for Mama when she works herself up into a state, helps to calm her. I glance over to where they both sit in the front row, holding hands.

Being in a strange house has taken a toll on my mother. Dark shadows are visible under her eyes. Dementia is a bitch, stripping people of not only their cherished memories but their pride as well. I paid the builders triple the money to restore the house as swiftly as possible. They've been working around the clock. Admittedly, I've had them modernize most of it while ensuring Mama's rooms are kept exactly as she remembers them.

Katya's eyes are locked on mine as she sashays down the aisle to me. I'm pretty sure there's a little more sway in her hips than normal. I smile broadly at her as she beams back at me. She's different from the young woman sent by her father to kill me. I'm disappointed for Katya that her mother was part of Pavel's collateral damage and will never know how beautiful her daughter looked on her wedding day. Then I remember what she allowed to happen to Katya, and I'm glad she isn't here, because I would have to punish her for the shit Katya lived through.

Katya will never have to worry about her father ever again. Pavel Ivanov, the man who killed my father, will forever lie buried in an unmarked grave, in a location known only to myself and Henrí. I hope his soul is tormented in hell.

But she will have a family now, and forever. I'll spend the rest of my life keeping her and our baby safe and making her happy.

KATYA

It feels like it takes forever to reach the makeshift altar, a smaller arch than the one I walked under to reach Mikhail. It's a mass of white ribbons, roses, and more lilies. He must have bought every white rose and lily from every florist in town.

The minister asks who gives me to Mikhail, to which Tomas replies with a simple, "I do."

Tomas smiles down at me, and kisses my forehead, before releasing me into Mikhail's hands. It's not until my husband-to-be takes my hands in his that I realize I'm shaking. Not with fear, but excitement. Mikhail raises both my hands, kissing my knuckles. "Are you okay, malen'kiy olen'?" he asks gently.

"I'm better than okay," I breathe, my smile hurting my face.

Mikhail cups my cheek as he leans down to kiss me. It starts gentle enough, but I reach up, grasp his suit front, and pull him to me. Our tongues delve inside each other's mouths, fighting for domination as our kiss becomes feral. If it weren't for the minister, we probably wouldn't have stopped.

"Ahem." He clears his throat loud enough that we both stop what we're doing and turn to him. "You're supposed to kiss the bride at the end," he reminds us.

Mikhail presents him with a dirty look while I giggle nervously. We end our private little tête-à-tête, anyway.

It's as if I'm having an out-of-body experience as the minister asks us to repeat the vows he reads out. Mikhail produces a ring matching my engagement ring when it comes time to exchange rings. A blush creeps across my cheeks. I don't have a ring for him.

Does a Bratva Pakhan even wear a wedding ring? I'm still speculating about it when Natalia steps forward. She taps me on the shoulder and hands me a small box containing a gorgeous white-gold ring with a small deer engraved on it. Its eyes are two small blue sapphires.

It represents the pet name he calls me: malen'kiy olen', *little deer.*

I repeat the minister's words as I fit the ring to Mikhail's finger. It takes me a moment to pull myself together. It's so surreal. I am marrying the most handsome, sexiest man alive. Tears fall again, one plopping heavily on our joined hands. "Damn hormones," I blurt out, causing a ripple of laughter among those people close enough to us to hear me. Mikhail chuckles, beaming his megawatt, dimpled smile at me, causing my legs to buckle a little and my panties to dampen.

When it comes to the question of whether anyone thinks we shouldn't be married to step forward now, I don't look away from Mikhail. I'm certain if anyone objects, he or Henrí, or both will dispose of them. If they don't, I will.

Finally, the minister declares us man and wife. Mikhail wraps his arms around me, leans down, and kisses me hard. I kiss him back, tears of joy streaming down my cheeks.

MIKHAIL

Cheers go up as I kiss my wife for the first time. We're lost in each other until my best man taps me on the shoulder reminding me we aren't alone. Katya's giddy smile is on par with mine, as we steady ourselves.

Henrí gives the signal, and a bunch of fireworks go off nearby as part of the celebrations.

I wish I could take her home and spend the rest of the night worshipping her body, but I can't yet. Instead, I pick my wife up bridal style and kiss her again and again, my heart swelling with the knowledge Katya Korbicov is mine, forever.

Katya is asleep on my lap as the car pulls into the garage. Before Denis opens the car door, my phone pings with a text.

It's done.

"Is everything okay?" Katya's sleepy voice asks as I return my phone to my pocket.

"Everything is perfect, malen'kiy olen'," I assure her as the car door opens.

I carry my new wife up the front stairs to our house, knowing for now, my family is safe. Those who stood with Pavel have been found and punished. Even so, I will not let my guard down. There will always be someone who believes they can take my place. One day, one of them might succeed.

Or not.

The End!

ABOUT THE AUTHOR

B.A. Childs is an Australian author, married, with two adult children, one cat, and four grand-fur-babies. I began writing the type of books I want to read. Now I consider it to be an addiction. I enjoy immersing myself in a story, whether I'm writing, or reading it. I also enjoy interacting with readers and other authors.

Remember, there's nothing more authors love than to read a reader's review of their books.

MORE FROM B.A. CHILDS

www.bachilds.com
amzn.to/3Fyn7Wd

Broken Halos MC:
Jezebel Found
Jezebel Undone
Daughter Of The Devil

Second Chance Romance:
Kasey's Volley